RICHARD STERRY

THE

BLIZZARD

OF '32

A NOVEL

RIVERBEND
PUBLISHING

Also by Richard Sterry

Over The Fence, a novel
Far Out: My Life on the Edge, a memoir
At Large: Whimsical Travel Tales
The Cloudbuster and Other Stories
Native, a novel.

The Blizzard of '32
Copyright © 2018 by Richard Sterry
Published by Riverbend Publishing, Helena, Montana

ISBN 13: 978-1-60639-116-7

Printed in the United States of America.

1 2 3 4 5 6 7 8 9 0 LS 25 24 23 22 21 20 19 18

Design by Sarah Cauble, www.sarahcauble.com

Riverbend Publishing
P.O. Box 5833
Helena, MT 59604
1-866-787-2363
www.riverbendpublishing.com

For Nedra

DECEMBER 22

I

Will Anderson got to the Lutheran Church before dawn, walking over the frozen ground by starlight, every step of the way hating the whole idea of the Christmas tree expedition to the Sweetgrass Hills. But Mama had insisted, saying that his dislike of Pastor Bakke and Chopper Martinson was the very reason he should go, that he should see it as an opportunity to develop more acceptance and understanding.

It wasn't fair. He'd been longing for Christmas vacation, for a chance to get away from the Sage Prairie School and its stupid kids, even if it were only for a few days. Needing to get away. And now this, three days with Wacky Bakke and Chopper, riding in a grain wagon and camping in below-freezing weather. Cecil had a truck that could make it to the Hills in a fraction of the time, but the Christmas tree trip had always been done by wagon, and it would be done that way again this year. It was a tradition. And if you were invited, you went. Why Pastor Bakke had invited him instead of any other boy in the Lutheran League who'd lived in Sage Prairie all his life was beyond Will.

Cecil Halstead arrived at the church with his big grain wagon and horses, Stubb and Jubal, at about the same time as Will. Cecil was wrapped in an old buffalo robe.

"Morning, Will," he nodded slowly. Cecil did everything slowly, but he was a good man, and the only friend Will had made since Mama had dragged him to Sage Prairie. Cecil was on the school board, and when Mama and her family arrived, he saw their situation and hired Will to work on his thresh-ing crew and Mama to cook for them. He'd treated and paid Will like all the other men, though he was only seventeen, and Will deeply appreciated it.

Inside the parsonage, Pastor Bakke's tall, pinch-faced wife had oatmeal and toast for them. She set the table brusquely, clattering the bowls and spoons. She clearly did not like the idea of this trip, but then Will had never seen any evidence that she liked anything at all.

"Will, would you like to maybe think about going through the rigging and checking the tie-down on the runners?" Cecil said when they had finished eating oatmeal. "Give Stubb and Jubal a little rubdown?"

Will went, eager to get away from Mrs. Bakke.

It was still and cold, the sky sprayed with crisp stars. Will had spent a week's worth of summer wages on a new canvas coat from Montgomery Ward, so he didn't throw his arms around the horses' necks as he did during threshing season. The coat had sheepskin on the inside and a sheepskin collar that turned up and buttoned across the face. It was the first new coat he'd ever had.

The horses were steaming from their pull to the church but

they weren't sweated up. Will took off his gloves and patted down the animals and murmured to them the same way Cecil did. It had been part of his summer work to care for them.

"That you, Cottonwood?"

It was Chopper.

"Yeah. It's me."

"See what I got?" Chopper held something. There was just enough light that if Will put his face close, he could see it was a single-shot .22 caliber, almost certainly the Remington in Montgomery Wards that he'd been looking at. Will knew exactly what it cost. When he ordered his coat he tried to talk Mama into letting him order this same rifle with more of his summer earnings, but she had said no.

"My Christmas present," Chopper said. "They gave it to me early so I could shoot jacks on the way."

"Nice," Will said, hating Chopper Linfield.

Chopper was fond of telling the story about how he'd gotten his name. Once at age four, after being locked in the woodshed as a punishment, he took the ax and chopped his way out. He was punished, but he'd been Chopper from then on, though Will had learned that his baptized name was Rolph.

Cecil and Pastor Bakke came out of the parsonage and climbed on the wagon's bench. The driver's bench was really the top of a storage box with all of their tree-cutting tools. Food for two suppers was also in there.

Will and Chopper stood in the wagon box, holding onto the sideboards. The box was new wood. Will knew that Cecil's hands, though slow, were never empty of a task. The old wheeled wagon was almost an antique and would never again haul grain, but Cecil had replaced all of its wood, stove-bolting the new sideboards as if the wagon needed to last another fifty years. Will knew that Cecil only kept up the wagon for the annual Christmas tree trip.

"What are you going to get for Christmas, Cottonwood?"

"I haven't thought about that much," Will said.

Will once made the mistake of talking about his friends in Cottonwood, where he'd lived the last three years, and saw that in Sage Prairie you had to be careful about what you said and did because it quickly got exaggerated and made the rounds, and nobody forgot anything. Kids in Sage Prairie were like chickens that'd been shut in too long, pecking each other constantly, or if someone new came along, pecking them.

"Is your dad coming home for Christmas, Cottonwood?" Chopper asked, holding his new rifle across his lap and sitting on his thick bedroll.

"I don't think he can make it."

"Why not?"

"He's a salesman. He's on the road a lot."

"What's he sell?"

"Baskin's Products."

"What's that?"

"You're full of questions, Rolph. Do you really care?"

"Don't call me Rolph, or I'll peel your face."

"Why not, Rolph? Isn't Rolph your name, Rolph?"

"Boys!" Pastor Bakke said.

Though Pastor Bakke was skinny, his layers of clothes made him look like a large man except for his narrow face framed by a scarf wrapped around his head. He'd started the tradition of the Christmas tree trip to the Sweetgrass Hills when he first came to live in the parsonage at Sage Prairie many years ago, and he had made the trip every year since. It was known to be a grueling journey always undertaken on nearly the shortest day of the year. It was sixteen hours of bumping along in the wagon on the first day, from well before dawn to well after dark, pressing all the way across many miles of prairie to the trees at the base of the Sweetgrass Hills. The second morning they would take the wagon into the hills to find a good stand of young trees, cut the required number, and immediately start for home. They would camp on the plains the second night, about halfway back to Sage Prairie, and if all went well they would arrive home before noon of the third day.

This year they intended to spend extra time looking for more filled-out trees than had been brought back in previous years. The plan was to start very early again the second morning, so they could go higher up and find a better stand. Will knew that both Cecil and the pastor were looking for some measure of redemption. The Sage Prairie Catholic Church also sent out its tree wagon every year, and everyone knew the Catholic tree cutters brought back superior trees. Will had only lived in Sage Prairie six months, but he had heard about the quality of the Catholic trees several times.

Will stood up and gripped the top of the box. The sky behind the Bear Paws was beginning to brighten with a faint glow. In front of them the Hills still looked very distant. This was going to be three long days.

Chopper began eating his food before the sun was barely over the Bear Paws. Except for the two suppers, each person was responsible for bringing his own food, and Will wondered how much Chopper had brought, considering that he ate two beef sandwiches with a pickle by late morning and several carrots and a piece of cake before mid-day, shooting at jack rabbits one after the other with his new .22. Will ate nothing. He was used to hunger.

"That your bedroll there?"

Chopper sat on his own bedroll, twice as big as Will's.

"Does it look like my bedroll? Mind your own business, Rolph."

"Don't tell me what to do, you little shit," Chopper said casually, "Or you'll be spitting out teeth like shelled corn." Chopper blew out a puff of air disdainfully. He was strong for seventeen and used to having his way with other boys.

Will leaned close. "You come at me, Rolph, and you'll bleed." He'd been wanting to say that to Chopper ever since school started.

"Boys!" Pastor Bakke said sharply.

Will knew he could make Chopper bleed. He'd battled bullies before. He was quick, and he had learned that one hard blow to the nose stopped almost everyone. It had taken him a long time to establish his place in Cottonwood, and more than one fight. And then, just when he was finally somebody, there came another of their endless series of family emergencies, and another move.

"This is God's work we're doing here, boys," Pastor Bakke said sternly. "I don't want to hear any more of that."

The jacks were completely white for the winter and easy to see against the brown stubble of the wheat fields and the gray/lavender winter prairie. They mostly hopped only a few steps and then stood up and waited to be killed by Chopper, who jumped off the wagon to make his shot and then ran to catch up, laughing.

"Have a shot, Cottonwood," Chopper said finally, and

handed the .22 to Will. Will sighted down the barrel and held the cold stock briefly to his cheek. Then he handed it back.

"No thanks," he said.

"Jesus, you're really something, Cottonwood," Chopper said, and Will could tell that Chopper was deeply disappointed. It made him feel good.

Wacky Bakke turned and glared at Chopper. "If you blaspheme the Lord's name again on this trip I will have to talk to your parents. Is that understood?"

"Yes," Chopper said, his head down. He'd grown up knowing Pastor Bakke.

Cecil stopped the team. "Why don't you maybe come up here and hold the reins for a while, there, Will," he said, one word at a time. "I think I'd like to try shooting a jack with Chopper's new .22 there."

As soon as Will had shaken the reins and clucked Stubb and Jubal to life, Pastor Bakke said, "So what are your plans for the future, William?" For the first time Will saw that Pastor Bakke wore cocoa-colored dress wool pants with a fine crease. He thought they must already be fatally stained or ripped in some way since they were sure to get ruined on the trip, handling pitchy Christmas trees. "I'm going to go back to Cottonwood," Will said. He hadn't talked to anyone about this, and it felt good to say it out loud.

"Hmmm. Interesting." Bakke began to frown even harder. "And what will you be doing there?"

"I'm going to finish school there."

"You mean instead of at Sage Prairie? Why would you want to do that?"

"It's where I want to be. I have friends there."

"But won't your mother need you?"

"No. We've talked about it."

This was a lie. He was sure, in fact, that the idea of his leaving had never crossed Mama's mind, and he'd worried what she would do when she learned about it.

"After school is out, then what?"

"I haven't thought about it," Will said, but he had. Get away from Montana. Join the Marines.

"Have you thought about the ministry?" Bakke said.

Will couldn't help chuckling out loud, thinking for a moment that Pastor Bakke was making a joke.

"Why was that humorous?" The pastor's narrow face pinched in even more.

"I'm sorry. No. I don't think I have. Not seriously."

"Perhaps you should."

"Why?"

This question seemed to take Bakke by surprise. He looked at Will sharply. "Well, it's God's work."

Will wanted to say that God did plenty of damage on his own without help from preachers, at least that's what he had heard many times from Papa Swan. Instead he replied, "I'm probably not patient enough." Or unimaginative enough or stupid enough, he thought.

"What a wonderful way to learn patience," Bakke said, and smiled his gloomy smile, as though he had some special knowledge of this. "The reason I mention it is that I've heard you are interested in attending college. Is that right?"

"Yeah," Will said cautiously. He'd agreed with Mama that it would be a good thing if he could manage to go, but he never really thought it would happen. That's why he was making other plans.

"I know of a Lutheran scholarship fund for…to help boys like yourself who might consider studying for the ministry."

"A scholarship, Pastor? Why would you nominate me and not Chopper or one of the other guys?"

Pastor Bakke cleared his throat and turned to look back at Chopper and Cecil walking behind the wagon. Will could see he was considering answering that question but decided not to.

"Mind you I'm not saying you *would* get it, but I can nominate someone. It's for Concordia College in Moorhead, Minnesota. It's where I studied. You would need to work for your room and board, but Mr. Halstead says you are a good worker."

The words of praise made Will feel warm under his sheepskin. He thought for something to say, but nothing occurred to him.

"As part of the application you would have to write an essay about yourself, about why you feel called to the ministry. Principal Albertson has shown me some of the things you've written in your English class, and I see you write very well. Your mother has done a remarkable job raising you children."

You mean without a husband? Will wondered, but he said nothing.

"And after graduation you would be required to work for the Lutheran Brotherhood in some capacity for two years. At a salary of course. Very minimal."

"Some capacity?"

"Not necessarily in the ministry. Perhaps as a missionary."

"A missionary? Boy. I don't know," Will said. It was all he could do not to laugh out loud, and Bakke's perpetual frown deepened.

"Or a teacher," Pastor Bakke said.

"My mother's a teacher," Will said. "I don't think that's what I want to do."

"Well. You let me know, William. Just think about it as an opportunity," he said. He pulled a New Testament out of his pocket and began to read.

Cecil and Chopper caught up with the wagon and sat on the tailgate. There were no more rabbits.

By mid-afternoon the Sweetgrass Hills were close enough to fill the horizon and look like mountains for the first time. Will realized they were much farther from Sage Prairie than he'd imagined. He'd been eating bulgur grains, softening them in his mouth and then chewing them up. Mama had sent two apples, two egg-salad sandwiches, and a lump of cheese. He was going to make them last as long as possible.

Will was driving the team when Cecil leaned in from the box and tapped him on the shoulder. Will pulled Stubb and Jubal to a stop.

"We might want to think about maybe turning back," Cecil said.

"Turning back?" Bakke asked.

"Take a look," Cecil said, and nodded toward the direction they'd come from.

Will stepped down from the wagon and saw a thick wide bank of dark clouds crowding over the Bear Paws, far away across the flat horizon.

"That's a storm coming," Cecil said, pointing with his chin. "A guy turns around now he could maybe beat it."

Predicting the weather was an art cultivated by all prairie farmers, and Will knew Cecil was especially good at it. He said if they turned back now and kept going after dark, they might be able to get back to Sage Prairie before the storm hit them.

Will watched with close interest. A chill wind had started

the minute the sun came up and had grown stronger as the day went on, blowing against their backs. Please let's go back, Will prayed to himself. He didn't care if he had a Christmas tree, since there really wasn't going to be much of a Christmas anyway. Not at his house.

Pastor Bakke nodded as if he agreed with Cecil, but then said they should confirm which direction the storm was moving before they committed to turning back. It may be that the clouds weren't moving their way at all, Pastor Bakke said. He took out a round, worn, hard-leather case from his duffle bag and removed a brass telescope. He peered through it at the line of dark clouds over the Bear Paws.

Cecil removed his gloves and scratched the palm of one hand with the nails of the other. Will had seen the palm-scratching many times. Cecil did it when agitated. Slow as he was about most things, he wasn't good at waiting when decisions had to be made.

After a time of watching through the spyglass, Bakke said he could see no movement in the clouds at all. Cecil said that could mean the storm was coming straight at them. Bakke agreed but said it also probably meant that it was coming very slowly, or perhaps even stalled over the mountains.

Chopper stood on the driver's bench with the spyglass. Nobody had offered it yet to Will.

"A guy turns around right now he might still have a chance to get back," Cecil said again, speaking in his deliberate cadence.

"I'm sure most people would understand," Pastor Bakke said. "Though they would certainly be disappointed."

Just then Chopper said he saw another wagon far behind them, coming their way. The more they adjusted the long telescope, passing it back and forth between them, standing on the driver's bench, the more Cecil and Pastor Bakke agreed that it had to be the wagon from the Catholic Church, and they were pretty sure they knew who was in that wagon: the Bohunk Tuma twins and Father Pilletti. They were famous for coming back with perfect trees for the Catholics.

"Those are the Tuma piebalds, all right," Cecil allowed.

"Do they know something we don't know?" Pastor Bakke wondered mildly.

"Bohunks," Cecil said, "never could read weather."

"Now that would be embarrassing," Pastor Bakke pointed out, and Will knew he meant if the Catholics got trees and they didn't.

Cecil was tearing at his palm with his fingernails as if there were a deep itch he couldn't quite reach.

"Well," Pastor Bakke said. "It's in God's hands."

Cecil glanced at Will and then put his gloves back on. Will knew it was really in Cecil's hands.

"Well, we'll have to go all the way to the hills tonight, then, and not stop for supper till real late," Cecil said. "And we'll have to load and leave first thing in the morning and travel all day tomorrow. Maybe in a storm."

"Oh, man!" Chopper said. "This is going to be fun."

I hate this, Will said to himself.

Cecil climbed onto the driver's bench, covered his shoulders with the buffalo robe, and clucked Stubb and Jubal. Chopper sat in the wagon box with his .22. Will walked behind the wagon rather than ride in the back with Chopper, thinking, I can do this. It's just a few more days. After Christmas I'll be back home in Cottonwood.

2

It was the first day of winter vacation, and Adelia Anderson slept late, till eight o'clock, something she almost never let herself do. She lay for a time with her eyes closed and listened to the ringing silence. Complete and utter. No prairie wind gnawing at the house for the first time in...how long? She rose and looked out the single frost-edged window at a blur of snow falling straight down, thick flaked and fluffy, such as she'd rarely seen on the Montana plains where snow was more likely to blow in sideways. So they would have snow for Christmas.

Curled back into her warm place in the narrow bed, Adelia considered the novelty of a gentle snow with no mean wind. She and Will and Viola would make fudge, play cribbage, set up a tumbleweed tree.

Then she remembered and was suddenly cold despite her blankets. Will was out there! Out on the prairie! Her Will! What if this was the beginning of a blizzard? Surely, she thought, Cecil Halstead would have turned around at the first indication of a bad snowstorm. He knew the dangers. She wondered when the snow began. If they'd turned around last night, they might be home soon.

And what about the Christmas dance? If a blizzard blew up, the dance would be cancelled. Adelia sighed deeply. She knew she had come to depend too much on her sandwich sales at the dance's midnight supper for enough money to carry her till her next pay. She closed her eyes and prayed earnestly for God to hold back the blizzard. Then up. Time to get up. For her sake. For Will's sake. For everyone's sake.

Viola still slept as Adelia rolled quietly and slowly out of the bed. She wore long underwear, two pairs of socks, and a nightgown. Over these she put her overcoat. Her breath came out in small, pale wisps.

A lovely thin light lit up the two-room cabin. It had been, she had seen when they moved into it, a granary at one time, into which someone had fixed windows, one on each wall, and added a door. Later a small lean-to bedroom had been added on one side. When Adelia first saw the massive coal-fired range in the center of the main room, she'd thought it an inefficient location, but since it was the only warm place in the cabin, it turned out to be a blessing when cold weather came.

Adelia dotted a piece of dry cow dung with lamp oil and lit it in the stove's fire box, careful to do it with only one match. She let down the lid gently to avoid waking Viola. She quietly put the tea kettle and the milk bucket on the stove top. When the dung oozed its blue flame she added some slivers of kindling and adjusted the chimney draft.

She was eager to get back to her letter to Edward. It would have to be dropped off in the post office this morning if it were to reach him by Christmas day. She'd already written about the Christmas dance and her hopes for it. She'd told him the funny story about Rachel Swingen's hair, and about William's Christmas tree trip to the Sweetgrass. She'd meant to write something about Viola. What was it?

Adelia checked the progress of the fire and sat at the table to write.

> *Viola has started to make friends here in Sage Prairie finally. She's becoming a woman in front of my eyes, all at once, just the way Ruby did. I wish I had a picture to send. She is as tall as me, though slender, and has such a glow about her. I've made her a dress to wear to the Christmas dance, and I can hardly wait to see her in it. She is still a sweet child.*

> *We are having a lovely snowfall, our first. Very time-ly. We're planning a rather modest Christmas, but all of us have been looking forward to the vacation from school.*

> *I hope that you are well, dear Edward, and that you will write to me again soon. I will be thinking of you and praying for you on Christmas day and on every day as usual.*

> *Mama*

When the letter was finished, Adelia found the ice in the bucket on the range had loosened, and she emptied it on her way to the pump house. The light snow was accumulating straight up on the well house roof, and the fence posts around the chicken yard looked like they wore little white top hats. Surely Cecil would have turned back this morning, she thought, as she pumped the bucket full.

After she filled the pan and basin on the range and set the teapot to the side, she rekindled the fire with a couple of good lumps of coal. Then, bundled up, she set out from the teacherage on the flat mile of road to Sage Prairie, leaving Viola sleeping in. The snow fell straight and thick like tiny white feathers, forming a glowing bowl around her. The road was untracked, and the snow was light and easy to plow through in her galoshes. Better snow than mud, she thought, since the galoshes leaked.

The silhouette of Sage Prairie began to appear through the white haze, a faint, jagged line of rooftops with chimneys leaking dark coal smoke. There was the flat roof of George's General Store, and the spindly, shingled spire of the Lutheran Church behind it. Adelia made out the dark square of the Sage Prairie School, and there, finally, loomed the community's two grain elevators, side by side next to the railroad tracks, like brooding sentinels standing guard. There were almost no irregularities on the landscape around Sage Prairie. The surface was as flat as a cookie sheet, except for a barely noticeable low rise where the Sage Prairie Cemetery was surrounded by a tumbleweed-filled barbed-wire fence. Adelia thought it beautiful. She stopped and stood in the snow, her face tipped up and her eyes closed. Thank God vacation was finally here. There had been times when she thought she might not make it.

The floor of the Sage Prairie Post Office was wet with melted snow brought in by earlier galoshes and boots, but when Adelia entered nobody was there except Boneless Austin, the postmaster, and his tiny, birdlike mother, Nadine, the human crocheting machine. They lived in two rooms behind the post office.

"Hello, Mrs. Anderson. Still think we'll be havin' the Christmas dance?" Boneless peered at Adelia through the grated window above the counter.

"If it doesn't blow," Adelia said.

"You think it won't blow?" Boneless asked, surprised.

"I didn't say that."

"It'll blow. It always blows," Boneless pronounced. "Isn't Will out with Pastor Bakke and Cecil?" He was so short that he didn't have to bend over to look at Adelia through the grate.

"He is, and I don't like it." Adelia replied. "Cecil would have turned back, though, don't you think?"

"You never know," Nadine piped up from her rocking chair behind the counter. "Men."

"Hello, Nadine," Adelia said.

Nadine seemed always to be crocheting. She turned out full-sized tablecloths in the time others turned out doilies and antimacassars. She crocheted during Ladies Aide meetings and school programs, her lips pressed together and her eyes narrowed, bent tensely over her work as though under a critical deadline.

Through the small glass window of her mailbox Adelia saw there was something inside and her heart quickened. Sometimes there was a Christmas letter from Swan. Once there had even been a few dollars. *Swan.* He'd been popping up in her mind lately, as he always did around Christmas, and she cautioned herself against bitter thoughts. When she was angry her heart pounded too hard and she heard herself giving scolding speeches in her head. If she allowed herself to be angry at Swan, it was like a fire she could not stop feeding, taking a kind of sinful warmth from it.

"Letter from your son in Deer Lodge," Boneless said, and before she could turn the combination numbers on the box he brought the letter to the grate and slid it though. Both Boneless and Nadine knew—everyone knew—that Deer Lodge was where the state prison was, and little else.

"Maybe your son will be home for Christmas?" Adelia heard Nadine sing with her lilting Norwegian accent.

"Wouldn't that be nice?" Adelia sang back. A letter from Edward always brought her joy.

"Well, Merry Christmas," Adelia called. She dropped her letter to Edward into the mail slot and went outside.

Adelia often made herself delay the small pleasures that came into her life so that they could be enriched and expanded by anticipation, but she was unable to do that with personal letters, especially ones from Edward. They were always clever and funny, as though prison was some kind of extended summer camp that he found endlessly fascinating. Of all her bright children, Edward, her first, was the brightest.

This envelope felt disappointingly slim. Standing there in the falling snow, the air glowing with an early blue light, she shook out a single page with a single line on it, written large.

"I'll be home for Christmas!"

Adelia squeezed her eyes shut and folded her hands around the letter. "Thank you, Lord," she said. She turned around and stuck her head in the post office door.

"You were right, Nadine. He *is* coming home," she said.

"Then we'll see him at church?"

"You will if it doesn't start to blow."

"It always blows," Boneless said with great satisfaction. "It's going to blow like hell. A real Alaskan Express."

Adelia turned the envelope in her hands to look at the post-mark. He'd already been released. Was already on his way.

So this is what the Lord has planned, Adelia thought, shut-ting the post office door behind her. Edward would come home as her Christmas gift. Oh, God, she could hardly wait to see him again. Of course she knew he couldn't stay, would surely not even want to stay with her in Sage Prairie. She hoped he had a bedroll to bring.

Adelia walked to the empty school and into her cold class-room to write her report cards, thinking carefully about what she listed under "remarks." *Benjamin must work on paying at-tention. Lyle has been making good improvement on his deport-ment. Lydia must learn to participate more in class discussions.* She knew the wrong word could cause a child to suffer a beat-ing or bring parents boiling mad and threatening to withhold their school taxes.

When she had finished, she went to the furnace room. She always carried a small cloth bag in her large purse, and when the opportunity presented itself, as now, she would put a few good-sized lumps of coal in the bag to carry home. She knew she was stealing, but she also knew that the school board's allotment of coal for her teacherage had been woefully inad-equate.

The tiny basement furnace room felt faintly warm, though the furnace had been turned off since yesterday, the last day of school before vacation. The room was meticulously swept and neat. Adelia went to the coal bin and searched for the right-sized pieces that would fit easily into the cloth bag.

"Hello, Mrs. Anderson."

Adelia spun around, her heart pounding.

"Oh, Dort! You gave me a start!" Adelia said, putting a hand on her chest. "I was working in my classroom and came down to see...to see...." Dort Shultz was janitor of the school, a deacon in the Lutheran Church, and the father of several of the more vacant-eyed children in the school. "To see if the fire had gone out."

"Yup," Dort said. "I let it go out to save coal." Dort had bristling gray eyebrows and a thatch of chalk-white hairs sprouting from his nostrils. He always wore a greasy, bill-less mechanic's hat. "But we've got this weather now," he said, shaking his head gravely.

"I'm glad to know the school building is in good hands, Mr. Shultz," Adelia said, discretely wiping coal dust from her fingers. There was an uncomfortable silence as she closed her purse.

"Well," Dort finally said. "Do you suppose the dance will be called off?"

"I hope not," Adelia said.

"Maybe the Fulps won't be able to get here, then, with the weather," Dort said, pressing his eyebrows together as if this issue was something he had been worrying about at some length.

"Well, if it isn't blizzarding, the Fulps will find a way to get here," Adelia said. "If it is, they won't." She was still blushing for being so nearly caught. She turned to go.

"They might have to shovel their way down," Dort observed, following her.

"If it blows, it blows, and we'll just make the best of it," Adelia said.

"Someone will offer to shovel for them, maybe," Dort said at the door, his hands jammed deep into his pockets. "Everybody on the Hi-Line is looking forward to the dance."

On her walk home along Main Grade, the strange snow still coming straight down, Adelia was glad to see a set of vehicle tracks. Perhaps Cecil had brought William home. She hurried on. Yes, there was a dark shape in front of the teacherage, but coming closer, she saw it was not Cecil's truck. This one had fancy lettering on the side.

BASKIN'S KITCHEN PRODUCTS.

My God, it was Swan!

3

Wayne Snodgrass unlocked Eddie's cell. He took one of Eddie's elbows and the new guard, Mitchelson, took the other. The new guy gave Eddie a hard, narrow-eyed look. Hadn't been broken in yet. Still thought he had an important and dangerous job to do.

"When do I get my stuff?" Eddie asked. They walked across the empty, late-morning yard, leaving footprints in the fresh snow. Eddie knew other prisoners were watching his release from all the windows. He had watched too, many times.

"Don't worry about your stuff," Snodgrass said. He was a fanatic Roosevelt Democrat and was nice to inmates who would talk politics, but Eddie had never obliged him. Only two kinds of people talked politics, Papa Swan used to say. Rich people and fools. Snodgrass qualified. Eddie didn't.

"Hold on tight, boys," Eddie said, "or I might run back and slam myself into my cage."

"Shuddup." Snodgrass said. "I'll be damn glad to hear the last of your lip."

"I'll bet he'll be back," Mitchelson said.

"Chances of that are infinitesimal," Eddie said.

"I don't know why the Chaplain likes you, Anderson."

"My peerless conduct," Eddie said.

"Everybody else thinks you're a prick," Snodgrass observed. "Except for that Stanley character."

"And thus I have succeeded in being left alone," Eddie said. Except from Stanley.

"You think they'll leave you alone in the army, smartass?"

They passed under a sign warning "No Inmates Beyond This Point" and entered a narrow hall with a windowless, closed door at the other end. Caged light bulbs on the stone ceiling cast a dim yellow light, and the air smelled of rats and mold.

"Stanley's the kind who'll be back here real soon," Snodgrass spoke to Mitchelson as if giving him a lesson. "And you're right, so is Anderson here."

"No, Mr. Snodgrass, you're dead wrong about that," Eddie said. "I'm going to Officer Training School and serve my county. I'm going to make Chaplain Pierson, Warden Notting, and the entire state of Montana proud and pleased that they offered me this munificent opportunity."

The door at the end of the hall opened into a small room that stank of rancid, stale air. The room was empty except for a plank table with a low stack of folded clothes next to a cardboard suitcase.

"Is that my new suit?" Eddie stepped toward the table. He'd imagined a new suit on a hanger.

Out of the corner of his eye Eddie saw Snodgrass tip his head at Mitchelson, who went out, shutting them in.

"Take off your shoes," Snodgrass said.

"What?"

"Take 'em off, Anderson," Snodgrass said. "Those are pris-on shoes. They're mine."

"You're going to send me into the snow without any shoes?"

"Take 'em off." Snodgrass had a confident look on his face, and Eddie knew what was going to happen.

Eddie handed his shoes to Snodgrass. He immediately pulled out the inner sole of the first shoe.

"Well, well," Snodgrass said. "Contraband. Ignoring the rules to the very end, I see."

"Please let me keep my money," Eddie said. "Please, Mr. Snodgrass. It took me a long time to save that money."

Snodgrass removed another layer of bills from the second shoe.

"I've watched you, Anderson. I watched you the whole time. What kills me is that you think you're so smart. No. You're going out of here the same way everybody else does."

"Go ahead, take half," Eddie said.

Snodgrass laughed and counted the money. "Hey! This ain't right," he said. He picked up the shoes and felt deep inside each one. "Where's the rest of it?" he hissed.

"That's all there is. Please don't take it all, Mr. Snodgrass," Eddie said.

Snodgrass dropped the shoes as he looked at Eddie. "Same as everybody else, smart guy. A new suit and twenty-five bucks. Same as everybody else." He put the bills in his pock-et. "Hurry up and change," he said.

"Where's my new suit?" Eddie asked. "Don't I at least get the new suit?"

Snodgrass nodded at the stack of clothes. "Nobody said 'brand' new." He smiled his most satisfied smile at Eddie before he shut the door quietly behind himself.

Eddie opened the suitcase. It contained the personal items from his cell. His slouch cap. His shaving works. The thick bundle of Mama's letters. His chess pieces and his folding chessboard. In the dim light he looked at the chessboard carefully and ran his fingers along its edges. It felt the same as he'd left it, and he slowly exhaled. At least he still had his two hundred dollars. A few minutes ago he had two hundred and thirty-eight.

In the pile of clothes were a pair of wool pants and a threadbare black jacket, a white shirt and a new undershirt. There was a worn brown belt that looked too long. Deeply disappointed, Eddie stripped off his prison uniform and put on the clothes. They kind of fit. Finally there was a heavy wool coat, calf length. When Eddie shook it open it gave off a faint petroleum odor; it must have been soaked in stove oil to kill lice.

Inside the jacket pocket was a crisp white envelope containing twenty-five worn dollars and a bus ticket from Deer Lodge to Great Falls.

Eddie knocked on the door and it opened.

Eddie and the guards started down another hall.

"Well, boys," Eddie said. "Tomorrow night you'll be here manning your posts, sentinels at the gates of justice. I'll be having my willy worked on by a professional at the Honky Tonk in Havre."

"On twenty-five bucks?"

"Oh, that's right. You've got all my other money. Hey Mitchelson, you know Snodgrass here just took fifty-eight dollars off me?"

"Listen, Anderson...."

"Since it's contraband I'm sure he's going to turn it in to the warden," Eddie said. "It's in his pocket right there. See that bulge? You're working with a corrupt man, kid. Don't let him corrupt you."

Snodgrass slammed Eddie against the wall. "How'd you like to pick up your teeth with stomped fingers?"

Mitchelson was looking at the bulge.

"Next he'll offer you a cut if you'll keep quiet about it," Eddie said.

For a moment Eddie thought Snodgrass was going to swing at him and he tensed, but the moment passed, and Snodgrass let him go.

"It's the proceeds from illegal activity," Snodgrass said to Mitchelson. "And of course I'm going to turn it in. And it's not fifty-eight, it's thirty-eight."

"It's fifty-eight," Eddie said. "I know how much money I had. I may write the warden and file a complaint, make sure my fifty-eight dollars got turned in."

"You're a miserable, lying, son-of-a-bitch," Snodgrass was flushed with rage, and it made Eddie smile.

Mitchelson used a large key to open a metal door in the stone wall. He pushed Eddie outside. Before the door was even closed Eddie heard Snodgrass trying to explain about the money, so the first thing Eddie did on the outside was laugh. He dropped the suitcase, leaned back against the metal door, and laughed harder and longer than he had laughed in two years. Then he turned around and pounded on the door.

"Hey! I've changed my mind," Eddie shouted, laughing. "I want to come back. Please!"

Smiling, Eddie picked up his suitcase. Across the road through the falling snow was a blinking light that said "Flats

Fixed." Eddie remembered the service station now. It was where the Greyhound had let him off when he was brought here. Through the station's window Eddie saw a person sitting at a desk in front of a wall of fan belts.

Eddie walked across the street. Free. Tomorrow he would do his business at the Mercantile and tomorrow night—the Honky Tonk and a wet willy. He'd imagined that somehow Stanley might be here to greet him, and he was glad he wasn't. If he never saw Stanley again, it would be fine with Eddie.

The suit was a grave disappointment. He'd grown attached to the idea that Mama would see him in a new suit. Now he wondered how much one would cost. He wouldn't buy it at the Mercantile, though. He wasn't going to go in there and let old Meyer see him in prison cast-offs. He wanted Meyer to see him in a new suit. Good thing he'd have some time to shop in Great Falls before he got on the Galloping Goose to Cottonwood.

The man behind the littered desk in the service station worked on a row of figures. He did not glance up. "Be late causa the snow," he said.

The room smelled of engine oil and cigarette smoke. Eddie's eyes were drawn to a dusty glass case of candy bars and tobacco products.

"Pack of cigarettes. Luckys," Eddie said. "And a candy bar. Butterfinger. And a box of your matches there."

It was like seeing money for sale. Over his time inside Eddie had never smoked a cigarette or eaten a candy bar, though he had owned and brokered hundreds and hundreds of each.

The man rose gingerly out of his chair, slid aside the case window and reached inside. His fingernails were black and the tip of his little finger twisted off at a surprising angle. Eddie brought out his envelope and withdrew a dollar. A wallet, he thought, and added it to the list he kept in his head of the things he needed to buy before he went home to Mama and the kids. Eddie sat on a wooden bench, lit a Lucky, and took out his letter of introduction.

Captain Lawrence Reynolds
Recruiting Officer
United States Army
Great Falls, Montana

Dear Captain Reynolds:

I have little doubt that Edward Anderson, whom this letter introduces, has the capacity to qualify for Officer Candidate School. In spite of his unfortunate background, which I have described to you in previous communication, he is possessed of the kind of rare intelligence, character and determination which I feel the military can put to excellent use. I have, as I indicated, arranged for his felony record to be expunged if he enters the service. Please contact me when he has done so.

Sincerely,
Millard Pierson
Chaplain
Deer Lodge Penitentiary
Deer Lodge, Montana

Eddie laid his chess board on the bench next to him, spilled the pieces from their leather bag, and began to play a game with himself.

The man with the crooked finger suddenly sat back from his ciphering and looked up.

"Yer just a kid," he said, as if angry about it. "What you in for?"

"Assault," Eddie said at once. "With a deadly weapon. Crowbar. Had the unlawful urge to defend myself against a man with a club."

"Hmm." The gaunt man attended to his row of ciphers.

"Did you kill the guy then?" he asked after a time.

"No. He just got a bump on the head. But he was a cop."

"Oh," the man said. "Well, here she comes."

The bus heaved through the falling snow and stopped just long enough for Eddie to board before it pulled back onto the road. The nicotine had started a slight ringing in his ears, but other than that he felt wonderfully calm and alert.

"We're gonna be too late to make the Goose connection at Great Falls," the driver said when Eddie boarded and handed him his ticket. "Causa the snow."

"Thanks," Eddie said. He'd already figured he'd miss the train. He'd have to spend the night and part of a day in Great Falls. Fine. He had a suit to shop for. He'd still get home to Mama and the kids in time for Christmas.

4

Viola got up as soon as she heard Mama leave. The clock said eight-thirty, but there was an unusual darkness in the bedroom, a strange muffled stillness. She put her barrow coat over her union suit and ran out in her stockings to stand by the range, which had been going long enough to be nice and warm, but the room, and especially the scuffed linoleum floor, was still cold. Viola pulled up a chair and let down the oven door and put her feet almost into it. She drew the barrow coat around her and looked out the window.

Snow. Lots of snow. Falling hard.

Vacation had started.

"Whoooeee!" Viola shouted out loud in the quiet house.

Then louder, just to hear herself do it, "Whoooeee!"

And there was the dance.

And Christmas.

And more vacation.

"Whooeeeeeeeee!"

Viola danced around the range. How nice to make all the noise she wanted, act as silly as she wanted, do anything she wanted, even if she was already fourteen, and going on fifteen, and getting her breasts finally, which bounced, just a little, when she danced, which made her feel vaguely guilty.

What should she do? If Mama were here she would recommend using any extra time to work on Christmas gifts, embroidering of handkerchiefs still to be done, but Mama wasn't here. She was alone. At last.

One of the things she often did on the rare occasions when she was alone in the house was get out *Dr. Gillvaray's Common Sense Medical Adviser.* Last year, Mama had used the book to explain about menstruation, but there were other things that called Viola back again and again. There were forty-six fascinating black and white plates of things like cross sections of the male and female urinary and generative systems, and a testicle wasted by onanism. She read about leucorrhoea and vaginitis and pruritus vulvae and stared with horrified fascination at figure #20, an expanding uterine speculum. Dr. Gillvaray cautioned again and again against excessive sexual activity, citing that and onanism as the causes of many female and male illnesses.

Viola was thankful that she displayed no signs of any of the female disorders Dr. Gillvaray described in his vivid language, but she knew that she might have to watch out for nervous debility, about which, Dr. Gillvaray said, "...*a patient may glory in a wild intellectual exaltation, a sense of mental power, with an almost uncontrollable brain activity, followed by periods of depression.*" That was disturbingly familiar.

But today, before she dug out the Medical Advisor, Viola wanted to find the dress Mama had been sewing as a Christmas gift. Viola knew right where it had to be, since there was no place to hide anything in the two-room house. She'd seen Mama working on it once when she'd come home early from Lutheran League, and caught a glimpse of the fabric. It was the color of heavy cream and had small, pale-blue flowers on it the size of quarters.

I wouldn't ordinarily do this, Viola told herself, as she slid Mama's sewing box out from under the bed and opened it up. She spent some time memorizing the exact order of things and their positions in the box, and then she began removing items one by one until there, at the bottom, was the dress. She took it out and unfolded it on the bed and then held it up.

It had a dark blue collar and darker blue trim on the cuffs of the half sleeves. It was pretty, but it looked more like a church dress than a party dress. "Damn!" Viola said.

Viola took off her barrow coat and union suit and put on the dress, though her legs and arms goose-bumped in the cold. The dress flattened her and made her look like a tall ten-year-old. She wanted a party dress that would make her look sixteen. Or seventeen. She would rip a seam if she tried to dance the Charleston in this dress.

"Damn, damn, DAMN!" she said, and took it off and folded it up just so and put everything back as she'd found it and slid Mama's sewing box back under the bed.

"Damn."

She wanted a dress with a long loose skirt that would fly up when she twirled. She'd mentioned this often enough that Mama should have gotten the hint. She wanted a party dress. A party dress was all in the world she wanted. And she wanted it for the Christmas dance so she could dance the Charleston in a line with Clara and Margaret and Leona.

Wearing the union suit and barrow coat and several layers of socks, Viola practiced the Charleston. When the Fulps had played it at the Thanksgiving dance, Viola went out on the floor all by herself and danced. People clapped and threw dimes. It was her first attempt at standing out in Sage Prairie, and it had turned out fine. Some of the kids even seemed to like her more, she could see, because of it. Since then she'd gotten even better, inventing extra moves with her elbows and heels. She practiced on Main Grade Road when she was halfway home from school and too far away to be seen by anyone, or in the chicken house when she went to gather eggs, singing the song to herself.

"Charle-ston, Charle-ston. Everybody's doin' the Charle-ston. Don't care what you say. Wait and see, I'm gonna do it my way."

Viola sang and danced by the range until she heard the vehicle. Through the window she saw a truck of some kind driving very slowly on Main Grade Road, just a dark shadow in the falling snow. Viola heard a muffled musical sound, almost like bells, from the chains on the tires. She watched the truck slow almost to a stop and then turn into the driveway. There was a Christmas tree tied on top of the truck and some writing on the side. It drove right up to the house and Papa Swan got out.

Viola gasped. She couldn't believe it. Every Christmas she'd imagined him arriving at the last minute to bring something special for her, but this year she hadn't thought of him at all. And now here he was. Mama was right. When you quit wanting something, that's when you're most likely to get it.

"Papa!" Viola flew out the door and ran through the snow in her stockings and threw her arms around his neck.

"I'm here," he said, patting her on the back with his gloved hand. "I'm here."

"Oh, Papa."

"How are you my baby girl? My God, you've become grown up. Almost grown up."

"I'm so happy to see you. Oh, Papa."

"And I'm happy to see you. Oh, it's been so long. I'm here. I'm finally with my family again," he said. He squeezed her so hard she almost lost her breath.

"Where *were* you?" Viola said when he let her go.

"Oh, my dear! It's a long story. And one I look forward to telling. But not right now, Petunia. Let's go inside. Where's the Scottish princess?"

Viola explained that Mama had walked to Sage Prairie and Will was on a Christmas tree expedition.

"Poor Adelia," Papa said when he got in the house and looked around.

"Why do you say that, Papa?"

"Why because...because you have no Christmas tree. Put on your galoshes, girl. Did you see what I've got tied on the truck?"

Outside, the black truck stood gleaming with snow melting on the warm hood. Everything else was soft and white and perfect. Papa Swan removed a ladder from the side of the truck and used it to climb up the side of the box, the softly falling snow sticking to his hat and to the shoulders of his fine black coat. He untied the tree and carried it down.

"What do you think of that?" he asked, holding it out.

"Oh, Papa, it's beautiful. The most beautiful tree I've ever seen," Viola said, though in truth she thought it a bit spindly, especially on top. And, it was too wide at the bottom for the little cabin.

"Find me a couple of pieces of two-by-four and Mama's hammer and nails and I'll make a stand. But before you go, one more thing."

Papa held the ladder in front of himself. "Watch this," he said, and suddenly he folded it into a triangle and made a step ladder, which he placed on the ground before the back of the truck. He climbed up and flung open the doors and the stew of Baskin's odor poured out. Liniment and canvas and spices and coal oil and cigar and a hundred other things lined the many shelves. Papa disappeared up the narrow center aisle.

"You don't have a radio receiver, do you?" she heard him ask.

"No," Viola said. Could it be?

"There's no excuse for not having a receiver," Papa said. He appeared carrying a beautiful wooden box and walked down the stepladder with it. Viola came up and put the tips of her fingers on the rich wrinkly-grained wood. On the front was a small glass window and below it three knobs like tiny tractor tires. It was so new and shiny that snowflakes were hitting it and sliding off without sticking.

"For us?"

"For my family."

"Oh, Papa." Viola heard herself squeal like a little girl, and then remembered that she was almost grown up, and had to act like it.

"This is what's putting me out of business," he said. "But you know what? I love it. It's changing the whole world."

"I love it, too. Oh, Papa!" Viola said. "We listened once at the Sullivan's."

Papa Swan also carried in a blue and yellow battery. He connected some wires and soon the box began to crackle and then it began to speak. Papa snapped open his pocket watch. It was connected to his vest by a heavy gold chain. Viola remembered it from the last time he was home.

"Time for the news," he said, and the radio told the news while Papa made the stand for the Christmas tree. On the news everything was Roosevelt this and Roosevelt that. Roosevelt, Roosevelt, Roosevelt. Papa made her be quiet while he listened. He shook his head at what he heard, but Viola paid no attention. Once he said "Oh, for Christ sake," as though disgusted by something. When the news was over he turned off the radio and went out to the truck. The moment he was out the door, Viola raced over and turned on the radio just to hear it start to hum, feel the words and music gather in it, ready to pour out—all the songs, all the stories. She turned it off before Papa returned with a burlap sack.

"I don't have a fatted calf," he said. "But I do have a fatted hen." He withdrew a stiff plucked chicken from the sack.

"What do you think, Petunia? Shall we bake it up and surprise the Princess? I'll make my world-famous Norwegian stuffing. Well. Famous anyway in eastern Montana and western North Dakota."

Papa threw more pieces of coal into the firebox of the range, and then brought in an iron kettle from his truck. The kettle had three little legs that kept it just off the surface of the range. He used bread and egg and seasonings he got from his truck and stuffed the chicken while Viola started some oatmeal and toast.

"So why did Princess leave Cottonwood? I thought she was pretty settled there?" Papa asked. He sewed the stuffing into the chicken and tied the drumsticks together with string.

"Well, first it was Eddie, and then Ruby, you know. She's in Havre. Studying to be a nurse."

"A nurse, you say. That sounds unlikely to me. Do you hear from her?"

"Not since spring. That I know of, anyway."

Papa had an expression on his face as though he didn't like talking about Ruby.

Viola put the oatmeal and toast and milk on the table.

"Where's your sugar?" Papa Swan asked, and Viola didn't know what to say. They had some sugar, but they never used it for oatmeal or for anything except Mama's cooking. But it was Papa, so Viola got the quart jar the sugar was kept in and put it on the table. Papa started telling a story and one of his exaggerated gestures knocked the sugar jar off the table. It broke, spilling the last of their sugar on the floor.

That's when Mama walked in the door.

5

When Eddie stepped off the bus at Great Falls he was relieved that Stanley was not waiting for him. Stanley had a spooky way of knowing things he hadn't been told told, and he loved to make his little demonstrations, appearing in places he shouldn't be and knowing things he shouldn't know.

The bus station was exactly the same as the last time Eddie had seen it. He and Mama and the kids had arrived on a desperate search for one of Swan's sisters that lived in Great Falls. How they would find her they didn't know, and Mama was running a high temperature. Of course they had no money. Literally none. He and Ruby found a Lutheran Church who helped them find a place to stay, found food, and ultimately found Papa Swan's sister, though she was none too helpful. He'd been thirteen. Ruby eleven.

There was the bench Mama and the kids had sat on, surrounded by their few possessions, including the rocking chair she insisted on taking everywhere with them. Mama's face was pale and slick with sweat. Of all the hard and scary times they had, that was the worst. That was the year Mama couldn't find a job.

The strange snow continued to fall straight down out of the sky, so thick and heavy that it seemed like dusk, though it was only mid-afternoon. Eddie noticed it was already stacking deeply on the few automobiles parked by the station.

He carried his suitcase up First Avenue North looking for a hotel, his shoes quickly becoming wet. He was surprised at how many stores were boarded up. Those still open had Christmas displays in the windows, but there were few people in them and few cars on the street and not enough people on the sidewalks to keep the snow tramped down. Friday afternoon before Christmas. Nineteen thirty-two. Eddie'd heard that times were hard, but he had not imagined this. He remembered downtown Great Falls as full of bustling people and honking cars. He passed a men's store with a hand-painted "Going Out Of Business" banner in the window. Next to the banner was a mannequin wearing a double-breasted navy blue suit. It had wide long lapels and six dark buttons down the front under broad shoulders. Below the jacket wide-legged trousers hung down to almost cover new shoes. That was the suit that the prison should have given him when he was let out. It was the very suit he'd imagined himself wearing when he saw Mama and the kids.

Why not get a suit now? Could he get one for the twenty-five dollars he carried without breaking into his chessboard?

The clerk was a squat man with a thin moustache and a toothy false smile. When it became clear that Eddie had money to spend, he became quite solicitous. He brought dry socks for Eddie as he tried on new shoes. He even complimented Eddie on his "patrician" foot size. Meaning smaller than most, Eddie guessed. For all his wide shoulders he knew he had small hands and small feet.

Fifteen minutes later Eddie walked out of the store wearing new shoes, the first pair he had owned in his life. He also wore a navy blue double-breasted gabardine suit with a white shirt and a blue tie. He carried his old suit in a paper bag. It didn't seem right to wear the new suit under the stinking overcoat, but that couldn't be helped right now. The clerk brought out a fine coat, one with velvet lapels, but the shoes and suit took nearly twenty dollars, and he needed the rest of his ready cash for a room and a meal and a ticket on the Goose to Cottonwood. He didn't want to break into his chessboard in the store. It was a good way to carry the money till he bought a new wallet tomorrow at the Mercantile in Cottonwood. He added "galoshes" to his list.

At the Lincoln Hotel, throwing open his coat to reveal his new suit, he signed the register as Edward Anderson and tossed over two dollars as if he had no end of dollars. Which was how it seemed. Tomorrow he'd show up at the Mercantile and make old Meyer Stallcop eat a little crow. Locate Bobby Williams and break his nose. Then on to Havre and a night at the Honky Tonk. Then home to Mama and the kids for a few days, and finally to the induction center with his letter of introduction. Tonight he'd treat himself to a good meal and a long soak in a tub. Maybe a movie.

The room wasn't fancy, but it was sparkling clean and newly painted. A white enamel water basin with matching pitcher sat on the night table, beside a very white towel topped with a washcloth and a new bar of soap. In the drawer of the nightstand were some envelopes and sheets of writing paper with a picture of the hotel on their right top corner. The room was cold, and Eddie turned the valve on the radiator and heard the steam hiss in. A stiff wooden chair with a padded seat stood next to the radiator. The two-pillow bed was wider and softer than anything Eddie had ever slept in. Ever. Today was a day of many firsts.

There was a tub in the bathroom down the narrow hall, and Eddie filled it almost too full with water that was almost too hot, and lay in it a long time. He'd never been in a real tub before. He couldn't stop smiling.

Eddie wanted to wear the new suit, but knew that he couldn't wear it with the old shoes, and he couldn't wear the new shoes in the snow until he got galoshes, so he dressed in his release clothes and packed the new suit and shoes in the suitcase.

At the front desk he asked directions to the library.

Books. He had missed books. Word got around in Deer Lodge how much he desired reading material, and those who had any material exacted payment from him in cigarettes and candy bars. It was Eddie's one personal expense. Unexpected books came to him, and he read all of them—religious pamphlets, strange histories of strange places. What fiction came was pulp, and no poetry appeared at all till he discovered a set of finely bound volumes of Ralph Waldo Emerson's poems and essays in a glass case in Chaplain Pierson's office. They had come with the office, as part of its décor. The Chaplain himself had never read Emerson, but he let Eddie take the volumes one by one. Though he knew he was digesting only a part of it, Eddie read the books hungrily, page by page, and even memorized the whole "Alphonso of Castile."

In Deer Lodge he had dreamed often about the library in Havre, which had been the destination of some of his longest trips with Mama and the kids. To him it had been a place of wonder, its huge quiet rooms filled with more books than could be read in a lifetime, though Mama said there were much much bigger libraries than the one in Havre. She had mentioned the one in Great Falls.

The Great Falls Library was grand and cold and empty. Eddie took his shoes off and sat with his feet close to a radiator and read back issues of *Life* and *Collier's*. Jack Sharkey had knocked out Max Schmelling, and the heavyweight title came back to the U.S. They were still writing about Jimmy Foxx missing Ruth's record by only two home runs. Even in prison everybody had heard about that. It looked like they were going to repeal prohibition this time for sure, which would ruin the bootlegging trade. Editorials discussed the New Deal and nobody believed Roosevelt could do any better than Hoover. Industry was running at sixty percent of four years ago. Racketeers ruled Chicago and the nation was in the grip of a crime wave.

What shocked Eddie the most were the wheat prices. Since he'd been in Deer Lodge, wheat prices had dropped from three dollars and a quarter a bushel to thirty-two cents. Thirty-two cents! That was less than it cost to get the bushel out of the ground. Which meant the wheat farmers where Mama was teaching would be having a hard time. Which meant hard times for Mama as well.

Eddie decided to take out a library card so he could check out some books for the rest of the trip home. He could return them when he came back for induction after Christmas. He wanted some Coleridge and John Stuart Mill, since Emerson had mentioned them again and again but the librarian said he had to have identification to get a library card. A driver's license. A birth certificate. All he had was the letter from the Chaplain, and she would not accept it.

It was late afternoon and still snowing heavily out of

the lead-gray sky, the fluffy snow now a foot deep as Eddie tramped toward the Lincoln in his soaked prison shoes. There were only a few cars on the street, all with steamed-up windows. Eddie walked until he found a movie theater. There was a short line waiting for tickets, and Eddie joined it. Once inside, he bought a sack of popped corn.

The theater was cold, and Eddie kept his big coat on. There were only a scattering of people, a few young couples probably on dates, and a scattering of single men. Eddie chose a seat toward the back. He watched Paul Muni play a gangster. He noticed that Muni wore an overcoat with the same pointed velvet lapels as the one he'd tried on at the clothing store, and a wide-legged suit. In the movie Muni had a girlfriend, a beautiful blonde who wore dresses that hugged her behind. She betrayed the gang. Muni's gang thought he betrayed them, and there was a long chase and a gunfight in which Muni was wounded but got away. Everybody was after him.

It seemed there was no way for Muni to get away, but he did, driving through bad weather on hard roads and arriving, finally, weak with loss of blood, at an old farm. Inside was his Mother. Eddie's chin unexpectedly puckered and tears started when Muni and his mother first saw each other, and he was glad nobody was close to see him dab his eyes with his sleeve.

Muni's mother nursed him to health and he came back to settle all the scores and prove his innocence. In the end Muni gave up gangstering and bought a house full of modern conveniences for his mother.

When Eddie left the theater, it was still snowing heavily out of a pitch-dark sky, the streetlights dim glowing dots.

In the hall outside his room at the Lincoln, Eddie, key in his hand, looked at the light coming through the transom. He knew he hadn't left the light on. He turned the knob. The door was unlocked. Eddie opened it to find Stanley sitting in a chair by the writing table, a felt hat drooping on his square head, wearing his half-lidded, self-satisfied smile. Beside him on the bureau was a pint of blackleg and two glasses. One of the glasses contained an inch of the dark whiskey. Next to the glass was Eddie's chessboard. He'd been playing a game against himself and was in the process of lifting a black knight off the board.

Eddie was careful not to show how shocked he was. He came into the room without a word and hung his coat on the back of the door.

"You said you'd git in touch," Stanley said. He was wearing an ill-fitting single-breasted suit with lumpy shoulder pads that did not hide his sloped shoulders. "You didn't even let me know you were gittin' out." He poured an inch of whiskey in the second glass and handed it to Eddie.

Eddie didn't reach for the glass. "Looks like I didn't need to."

"Since when do you refuse good Canadian?"

"I'm off. For now."

"Kid Anderson, the teetotaler," Stanley said. He poured the second glass into his own and took a pull, looking at Eddie with his indolent, self-satisfied expression. He tipped back his felt hat. "Brought ya a popper," he said, and reached into his waistband and withdrew a short-nosed handgun. He held it out but Eddie didn't take it. Eddie reached into his pocket for a Lucky. Stanley tossed the pistol on the bed where it sank into the soft comforter.

"Don't you know that parolees aren't supposed to be in possession of firearms?" Eddie asked.

"I'm on a huntin' trip."

"Hunting what? They even put Capone's bodyguard away for carrying concealed. I read about it."

"Well they were after Scarface. They ain't after me."

"Yet."

Stanley laughed his dumb-shit laugh and took another sip. "This is real Canadian," he said.

"I don't care if it's real French champagne," Eddie said. Before he got out Eddie had decided there would be no liquor this time. None.

"Look at the label." Stanley held out the bottle for Eddie to see close up. "Nobody could fake that label."

"If they can fake a fiver, they can fake a label," Eddie said. He didn't like the pistol, didn't like it that Stanley had found him. At Deer Lodge, Eddie had waited impatiently for Stanley to be released, eager to be left, finally, alone. He'd made the mistake of befriending Stanley because he could play chess, and now the fool was tailing him, checking up on him.

"What's goin' on?" Stanley said.

"I got plans."

"Yeah? Like what? I heard the chaplain and the warden cut a deal with you. Become a soldier boy."

"Like my own personal plans, Pigeon. Which don't include you." In prison they called him "Pigeon" because he was always talking about how he was going to fly the coop.

"Well my plans include you, Preacherman. What if I told you I know how to make a lot of money? Fast." Stanley was always full of money-making plans. In prison Eddie had humored him, pretending to go along, agreeing to get together after they got out.

"Crime doesn't pay. Haven't you heard?" Eddie picked

the shiny pistol off the bed. It was cold, and heavier than it looked. Must be loaded. "Get this thing out of sight," Eddie said, and handed it back.

Stanley put it in his waistband. "Yeah! Mr. Righteous. You already spent most of your twenty-five bucks trying to look like a millionaire. You must have managed to slip your stash past old Snodgrass."

"He got thirty-eight bucks."

"Where you got the rest? It's in your chess board, right?"

"Don't be so interested in what I have and where," Eddie said.

Stanley slowly smiled. "So what are your brilliant plans, Preacherman?"

"Hard work. Clean living."

"Do you know what a pint of true Canadian sells for?" Stanley asked. "I know this guy. Friend a mine. He'll pay a hundred twenty-five a case for true Canadian."

"So?"

"So we get a Packard. Make some modifications. Take out the back seats. Extra leaf springs to carry the weight on back roads. Pick up twelve cases at Grovenlock across the border. We buy for forty-five a case. Sell for a hundred and a quarter. I know you can do the math, Preacherman."

"I can do the math, but I'm not going to do the time. Agents are waiting beside every road and every bridge on the border."

Stanley leaned forward and spoke in a low voice. "There's other places to cross. I grew up in the Milk River country. I know all the back roads. I can see it all. Think about it. When the river freezes we'll be ready to roll. Chains on the tires. I know five or six places where we could cross. Places we can stash the cases. Hey, booze don't freeze. We keep makin' runs. The deal is fifteen hundred Yankee dollars for every load. That's a thousand bucks clear profit. Five hundred for you. Five hundred for me. Cash in hand."

"Sure, sure." Eddie said contemptuously. "You got the Packard? You got the buy money?"

"My contact in Havre will advance the necessary capital."

"Somebody's going to give you five hundred dollars and trust you to come back with it? Where is this guy? Have I got a deal for him!"

"Don't you worry," Stanley said with his sneer.

"Don't tell me it's Shorty Young."

Stanley sat back, seeming hurt. "Yeah, it's Shorty Young, so what?"

"Jesus Christ," Eddie exclaimed. Of course. He should have known. Everybody in the pen knew about Shorty Young; how he made a fortune out of prohibition. How he outsmarted the law at every turn and how he ran the town of Havre. How he was supposed to have bought the support of everybody—judges, cops, businessmen. And how—with gambling, prostitution, and bootlegging—Shorty Young had kept the Havre economy booming right through the worst of the crop failures and depression.

"Shorty Young offer you this deal face to face?" Eddie asked.

"Nobody talks to Shorty Young face to face" Stanley said. "But the deal is there to be made. I got a guy. Friend of mine."

"Then why do you need me?"

"You get the Packard. You're the car guy. I'll provide the muscle and the money."

"Here's the way I see it," Eddie said. Like Paul Muni. "You go get your own car and run your own Canadian, since you know the roads so well. And provide your own muscle and keep all the ill-gotten gains for yourself. You don't need me in this."

Eddie considered for the hundredth time how Stanley was pathetically ignorant of his own pathetic ignorance. Eddie had heard that Shorty Young distilled his own whiskey in caverns under the city of Havre, caverns dug out by smuggled Chinamen. He even printed his own Canadian labels and seals. Occasionally he bought a bootlegged load of real Canadian whiskey just to keep the price up and keep the attention of the feds on the smugglers.

"You think it over, Preacherman. Maybe you got a good stash from yer little business there on the inside, selling cigarettes and candy. I don't know. But one thing I do know is that five hundred bucks is a lot of money. A whole lot of money."

"And ten years is a lot of time. I'd rather be a shave-tail lieutenant. Steady pay. Exotic places."

"Well," Stanley said getting up. "I know you haven't had any dinner. Neither have I. Let's go. Steaks. On me. We used to talk about this, remember?"

Eddie wanted to get his money out of the chess board, but not in front of Stanley. If Stanley was buying, he was okay.

Across First Street and just up a side avenue was a nearly empty restaurant with white cloths and candles on the tables. The waitress was a thin, starchy, middle-aged woman who brought them glasses of water and then coffee. Both Eddie and Stanley ordered T-bones, well done. The steaks came with baked potatoes, which had perfect balls of butter melting in the middle, and steamed caramelized carrots on separate plates.

Stanley talked the whole time, whispering across the table

about the jobs he'd pulled, places he'd broken into. Stanley extolled the virtues of something he called a flashlight. It was a light you could hold in your hand, which ran on small batteries. It turned on and off with a switch.

"A man who owns a flashlight and knows how to pick a lock is a man living on easy street," Stanley said. He had the steak bone in his hands and was chewing the last of the gristle from it, his lazy eyelids hanging like he was half asleep.

"Till he gets caught. Then it's back to Deer Lodge," Eddie said. "Snodgrass told me to tell you he's keeping your old cell ready for you."

"They'll never take me," Stanley said, and patted his waist where the .32 was tucked under his belt. He pushed back from the table and took out two cigars from the inner pocket of his coat. He handed one to Eddie.

"Play a couple games? It's not late."

"It's after ten, Pigeon. I can't wait to get into a real bed with feather pillows. I didn't sleep much last night."

"So what you doing tomorrow."

"I'm taking the Goose home."

"Where's that?"

"Little town on the Hi-Line you never heard of. Where my mother teaches school."

"I know all those Hi-Line towns. Maybe I'll pick up a car and drive you there."

"The last thing I want is a ride in a stolen car with an ex-con carrying a gun. I'm telling you. I'm on the straight."

"So it's no go on the Canadian?"

"No go."

"You're really going in the Army?"

"It's my deal with the chaplain. It's the Army or Deer Lodge."

"Hell, just go to Canada."

"I'm going home for Christmas, Pigeon. That's all I have on my mind right now."

"I'll come by in the morning and we'll have some breakfast before you leave, okay?" When Eddie didn't respond, he insisted. "Okay?"

"Okay," Eddie said.

Walking back to the Lincoln, Eddie worried about Stanley. He didn't like it that Stanley'd found him so quickly and so easily, that he was carrying a .32, that he bragged publicly about his crimes. That someone so stupid could play a good game of chess. One thing he knew, though, was that he did not want to see Stanley in the morning. As much as he wanted to sleep in his bed at the Lincoln, he should take the night Goose to Cottonwood. It was just a half-hour ride. And it left in three hours. He'd get a room at the Steamboat Hotel. Have breakfast there in the morning alone, and then make his purchases at Meyer Stallcop's Mercantile. Necklace for Viola. Jackknife for Will. A nice set of kitchen knives for Mama. For himself, galoshes, a wallet, gloves, and a new overcoat. He would shop slowly, asking Meyer Stallcop to help him find things.

Mr. Stallcop, he would say as he shopped, Mr. Stallcop you might not remember me. I'm Eddie Anderson. I stole a few items from your store some years back. In fact, I stole the same items I'm purchasing from you today. They were to be gifts then, and they are to be gifts again. I'm here to apologize for that. It was wrong. I'd like to hear you apologize to me, now, for claiming much more was stolen than really was. The amount you claimed made it look like a

major robbery instead of a kid stunt. I'm sure it got
you a nice insurance settlement, but it got me sent to
reform school and then to Deer Lodge. Do you know
the meaning of the word mendacious? Pusillanimous?
Look them up. They describe what you are.

Back in his room, packing to leave on the night Goose, Eddie climbed onto the bed, just to see what a spring mattress felt like, what two pillows felt like, what really clean sheets smelled like. He didn't stay there long because he knew he would fall into blissful sleep. He got up, dressed in his new suit and shoes, and played games of chess with himself till midnight rolled around, finally, and it was time to catch the Goose.

When he attempted to tie on his new tie, Eddie found to his surprise that he could not duplicate the knot the clerk had made. He spent a good time trying before he put the tie in his pocket. He'd work on it in Cottonwood.

6

Cecil woke them up at earliest light. They rose from their beds under the wagon into the softly falling snow, now as deep as the top of their galoshes. While Pastor Bakke made a fire for coffee, Will and Cecil took the wheels off the wagon and bolted the runners to the axle with a clever contraption Cecil had made. He'd also bent strap metal to hold the wheels on the wagon's sideboards, making an even higher box for the trees. Before it was fully dawn they began the final drive up into the hills where the trees started, the wagon now sliding on the runners, the ride much smoother than with the wheels.

Pastor Bakke had a handsaw and Cecil an axe, and they cut the first trees they found. They worked as quickly as they could. Will and Chopper hauled the trees to the wagon and loaded them carefully so as to get as many on the wagon as possible. Will had heard that Pastor Bakke usually took special pains to find the perfect tree for the church and that he made a ceremony out of bringing this tree to the wagon, not letting it touch the ground, but it looked to Will as though Pastor Bakke cut down the first one that was big enough and dragged it over to be tossed on the wagon like any other tree.

The falling snow seemed to absorb sound and even discourage it, and they worked wordlessly. Will didn't notice the cold, bundled up and moving steadily as he was. He did notice that no matter how carefully he handled the trees, his leather gloves were getting pitch stains. It was all he could do to keep the pitch from getting on his new coat.

As soon as they had the number of trees they'd come for, they immediately turned the team toward the prairie. Will was disappointed. The only thing he had looked forward to about this trip was the chance to look across the hundred miles of prairie from the Sweetgrass toward the Bear Paws, but there would be no chance of long views now, with all the falling snow.

Will hadn't seen anyone eat anything or chew anything since the good stew Cecil fixed for last night's late supper, though he knew that the others, like himself, were slyly eating their private food without drawing attention to themselves. In addition to half a pocketful of bulgar, Will still had one apple, half an egg sandwich, and most of the cheese. Now and then, when he was the one walking behind the wagon, he would eat a bite of cheese from his coat pocket to supplement the continued flow of mouth-softened bulgur grains, two or three at a time.

The trees were another disappointment. When they lived at Cottonwood, they'd always found beautiful, perfectly shaped Christmas trees in the Bear Paws. These Sweetgrass trees were a different kind altogether, thinly branched, with short, spiky needles. He supposed that Cecil and Pastor Bakke were also unsatisfied with the trees, but neither said so. Both seemed rather grim. There was no small talk on the driver's bench. Since the wagon was full of trees, two of them took turns riding on the bench and the other two followed along behind, each walking in one of the narrow furrows made by the wagon runners.

On the trip across they had been able to see the rare fence lines and avoid them. Now when they came to a fence hidden by the snow, they had to follow it to its end or to a gate.

Whoever happened to be holding the reins just left them slack, counting on the horses to find the direction home. The team was well trained and young and strong, and the wagon slid easily. Will was sure they were making better time than yesterday. All he could hear as he walked behind the wagon, sometimes having to trot, was the tinkle of rigging and the squeak of the hitch and the puffing of the horses. Will wasn't able to see much farther than he could throw a snowball, but inside the bowl of dim light that surrounded them, he saw the snow was stacking straight up on surface irregularities. A badger mound, when they passed one, was still a badger mound, and the occasional rock pile signaling a section corner was recognizable as a rock pile, but the differences between things were smoothed together in a way that was pleasing to look at, the edges gone.

Will liked sitting on the driver's bench with Cecil since he could count on being left to himself. Once or twice last summer Will had tried to find out what Cecil thought about this or that, but he discovered that Cecil did not like to discuss things like Mama did. Everything Cecil said was short and to the point, and when he did answer a question he seemed annoyed by the interruption unless it was about the immediate work at hand. Watching him for the whole threshing season, Will learned that Cecil only smiled for his daughters. Then rarely. Years ago Cecil's only son had shot himself to death while trying to crawl through a barbed-wire fence with a loaded shotgun.

Will couldn't see the sun in the sky, but he guessed they'd been traveling for six or eight hours when a wind began to blow erratically in small puffs, making the falling snow swirl in one direction and then in another. The snowflakes were smaller and sharper, and the air seemed colder. The horses' breath produced thicker clouds. No one mentioned this, so Will held his tongue as well, but he wanted to ask if either Cecil or Pastor Bakke had done this trip in a blizzard. Though he had seen blizzards, he'd had never been out in one, and he didn't know anyone who had, though he'd heard many stories about toes and ears and fingers freezing clear off. When blizzards came you got indoors and stayed there until it was over. Everybody knew stories of people disappearing in blizzards just walking in from their barn or outhouse, and their bodies not being found till the next chinook winds blew in.

The wind flurried for a while and then settled on one direction, growing stronger and steadier. Wind-blown snow slid across the ground like a thick layer of smoke. Will buttoned the sheepskin flap across his face and kept one hand on the wagon as he walked. He felt his feet getting very cold; they felt wet, though they shouldn't be, buckled in heavy galoshes.

The wind increased and the falling snow sliced sideways, stinging exposed flesh and coating windward surfaces. The horses shook their heads but still the snow clung to them. Ice rimmed their nostrils and eyes. The horses walked slower, struggling to find their way through the thickening white curtain.

Cecil stopped the wagon and gestured for Will to help him. Judging by the silent, grim expressions on Cecil and Pastor Bakke's faces, Will knew they were in trouble. Cecil and Will unhitched the horses, tied them to the wagon, and let them turn their tails to the growing wind. The whole surface of the snow was blurring around them and thickening higher and higher in the air. It quickly drifted into mounds behind the wagon runners and even around Will's legs as he stood there.

Without a word, the four of them unloaded the trees, removed the wheels from the side of the box, and then tipped over the wagon so the bottom of the box was against the wind. The lower sideboard made a kind of seat above the snow, and the other formed a little roof that Cecil covered with a tarp and then piled trees on it to keep it in place. They leaned the wagon wheels at an angle against the sideboard roof and put smaller trees on the wheels, making a kind of cave protected from the blizzard's blast. The temperature dropped even more, and Will heard the high-pitched, whistling sound of frozen snow breaking into smaller and smaller pieces, and moving, all of it moving, shifting and sliding before the wind.

As snow whipped over the top of the tipped-up wagon, some of it drifted into the layer of trees, and Cecil used the shovel to throw more and more snow on the trees until the wind couldn't blow through them anymore. They stripped smaller limbs from some of the trees to make a floor inside their cave. There was just room for the four of them with their backs against the bed of the wagon, two on each side of a small opening they left in the middle of the stacked trees.

There was no talk.

Cecil spent a long time with his hands out of his gloves trying to start a fire. The fire needed to be near the opening so the smoke could escape, and several wooden matches blew out in his hand before he could light the scrap of paper and kindling. Once he had, he slowly built up the flame with slivers he had whittled with his jackknife from the sideboard wood.

The bone-dry sideboard burned hot and quick and didn't produce much heat, and the acrid smell of smoke inside the shelter stung their noses. No one mentioned it. Cecil opened the canvas kitchen bag, filled a pot with snow and hung it on its little tripod over the fire.

Will's feet had sweated inside his shoes and heavy galoshes when he'd been trotting behind the wagon. Now his wet socks felt frozen and his feet ached with the cold. It was difficult to move in the little cave enclosure, so Will went outside. He stood with his back to the wind and stamped his feet for a long time and moved his toes in his shoes to get circulation going, but it didn't seem to help. Now the wind was not blowing hard, but it was blowing steadily, and all around him was a landscape of moving snow.

Stubb and Jubal were huddled at one end of the tipped wagon, tails to the wind and heads down. Will went over and took a gloved hand out of his pocket and rubbed them behind the ears and murmured to them. They responded by pressing their faces into his new coat, and he let them do it.

After everyone had a drink of warm water, Cecil melted snow for the horses. Jubal got his muzzle in first and drank all of it. Stubb had to wait for another pot of snow to melt.

They sat inside, two on each side of the fire, wrapped in their bedrolls, their knees drawn up, breathing the smoky air. The steady wind continued.

"Shouldn't we be thinking about supper?" Chopper asked, finally, in a quavering voice. "Mom didn't send enough to eat, and I haven't had a thing all day."

"Perhaps it's time to make the stew," Pastor Bakke said to Cecil, and Cecil heated another pot of water. Pastor Bakke cut the potatoes and parsnips and turnips right into the pot without taking off the peelings, and then put in a handful of dried meat, a packet of flour, and some seasonings. Will took the rest of the bulgur out of his pocket and dropped it into the stewpot as well. It seemed like the thing to do. The wind howled over the wagon the whole time.

"I thought only Bohunks ate bulgur," Chopper said, and managed a grin, but nobody looked at him. "Do you have a lard sandwich too?" Chopper said, and still nobody looked at him. "Actually, I'd eat a lard sandwich myself right now." His jaunty, cocky expression was not working for him. His chin puckered. "We're not going to freeze to death, are we?" he asked in the direction of Cecil and Pastor Bakke.

"You get some stew in you, things'll look better," Cecil said. He continued to whittle slivers and feed them one by one into the small fire under the pot. Chopper drew up his knees under his bedroll and buried his face into his circled arms and shivered.

"Will, why don't you come on outside, if you don't mind." Cecil asked. "We need to do something for the horses."

Outside, the conditions were the same, a close bowl of dim light filled with the thin eerie whistle of snow, the ground surface sliding by. Stubb and Jubal looked miserable, their snow-crusted backs humped. Every time Will had come out to try to stamp some feeling into his feet or to piss he'd rubbed their foreheads and spoken in their ears, and he knew that Cecil had as well. Now Cecil was using the shovel to cut square blocks of the hard drift-snow that had built up around the shelter. Will saw at once what he intended. As Cecil cut squares, Will built the windbreak. When the wall was high enough, they made a bed of tree boughs. It took some coaxing, but they finally got Jubal and Stubb to lay down out of the brunt of the wind. After the horses were settled, the stew was ready.

"All powerful and all merciful Father in heaven thank you for this food that you have given us. Thank you for the bounty of your blessings and keep us all in health, amen." It was the same prayer Pastor Bakke always gave over food. Will thought a special prayer might be in order on this occasion, eating their last food, the wood going fast, and no letup in the blizzard.

Every time Will heard pastors address God as all-powerful and all-merciful, Will remembered what Papa Swan once said after a Lutheran service: "If God lets the innocent suffer, then He's not all-merciful. If He wants to end their suffering and cannot, then He's not all-powerful. One or the other, but not both."

Mama, Will remembered, had argued long with Papa Swan after he said this, one of the few times he could remember her doing that. Suffering was just another of God's gifts, she insisted. In His mercy He allows us to make our own mistakes and be punished for them, as a parent does to a child by letting them take the consequences for actions they themselves have chosen. And by this we purify our souls and make them presentable to God, she said.

"Like Eddie?" Papa Swan had asked, and Will had known that was the end of the discussion about God. They would begin to fight about Eddie.

Ruby was still living at home during that visit by Papa Swan. She was crazy for dances and would travel hours to them, sometimes getting back home after dawn. She and Papa had terrible fights about this, which would make Mama cry. Will didn't ever remember seeing Mama cry except when Papa Swan was home. Will remembered wishing he would just go away and stay away.

The turnips weren't cooked all the way through, but the potatoes were, and they were hot, and the broth delicious and satisfying. Will thought there was a lot of stew in the pot, but it was soon gone, long before his hunger had been fully satisfied. Chopper took more than his share, of course, and everybody pretended not to notice.

Will was more concerned about his feet than his hunger. He'd been able to tuck his fingers into his armpits and stop their tingling, but he was having a hard time making his toes work. He took off his galoshes and put his shoes as close to the fire as possible, but the heat didn't seem to be getting past the frozen socks. He needed dry stockings. In the future he must always remember to bring an extra pair of socks.

He got the shovel and put it next to the fire, thinking that when the shovel blade was warm he would take off his socks and put them on it to dry. He couldn't feel the three smallest toes on his left foot no matter how hard he pinched them.

While Will waited for the shovel to get warm, he massaged his feet with his cold hands and amused himself by imagining himself as a Pastor, Pastor William Anderson, and he imagined the blessing Pastor Anderson might give on such an occasion as this.

Dear God,

I'm supposed to thank you for this last meal and beg for your blessings, except that I don't like to beg, and you really didn't put this food in our pot, anyway. I've also noticed that those who beg and genuflect aren't

*getting any more prayers answered than those who
don't. So I'm just going to eat this food and hope the
storm is over soon, knowing that you really don't give
a fiddler's fart one way or the other about any of us. If
you're even there.*

Putting on the hot socks when they were finally dry felt
blissful for a few minutes, but it didn't bring back the feeling
in his toes.

Wacky Bakke tried to interest them in playing a twenty-
question Bible game, but soon it was clear that Will was the
only one who could answer the questions, much to Cecil's
embarrassment. Chopper quit trying as soon as he saw he
couldn't win and wrapped himself in his bedroll.

"I see you've read your Bible," Bakke said at one point,
with the faintest of smiles.

"Mama read it to us. Most of it."

"You'd do well at Concordia, William. You would find
yourself challenged."

*I'd be challenged, all right. I'd be challenged to keep my mouth
shut and to keep from laughing.*

"Having a mother who reads the Bible is the greatest blessing a young man can have," Bakke said fervently. "Did your
father join you for Bible readings?"

"When he was home," Will said, and then he pulled his
head into his bed roll.

Will found himself filled with gloomy memories of Papa
Swan. As a boy he'd always delighted in his arrival, his presents and songs and games, but now he realized that Papa used
Mama, used them all, took pleasure in the family but bore
none of its responsibilities. Those he left first to Eddie and
then to Will.

Mama. Mama and her expectations. Why was it up to him to make up for Eddie going bad? How good did he have to be?

Dear Mama,

Let's be clear about some things. First: I'm almost eighteen and I'm able to care for myself and no longer wish to be a burden to you. Second, you don't need me anymore. Viola can learn to milk, as each of us had to.

I've decided to move back to Cottonwood, and so I'm going to need the rest of my summer wages. I'm going to graduate with my friends. I don't want you to think that I'm abandoning you, Mama. But I'm ready to start out on my own. I still have college in mind, but I'm planning to join the Marines after graduation.

Your loving son,
William

Will didn't sleep well that night, waking over and over to the whistling of the wind and a flapping corner of the canvas tarp that had somehow come loose. Once he woke from a vivid dream in which he was flying high above the Sweetgrass on his way to someplace where many people waited for him, someplace important, but then he was falling to earth, to land at Cottonwood where his friends were tipping over an out-house and laughing at someone's terror who was inside as it rolled down a long hill. Every time Will woke up, Cecil was tending the fire.

In the morning the storm continued around them. Everybody stayed in their bedrolls as long as possible before they went out to relieve themselves. When Will went out, he saw that Cecil had shoveled the drifting snow out of the barricade they'd built for the horses, who were standing again, looking as miserable as before. Will shoveled out their drifted-in windbreak and made them lay down. He rubbed them down till he couldn't stand the cold any more.

The day was long. There was hot water to drink, which helped, and the shovel to heat the socks on over and over. All of them had begun to do this. Will and Cecil took turns rubbing down the horses and clearing away the drifted snow.

Chopper slept an amazing amount that day. Will liked it when Chopper was asleep because when he was awake he talked constantly about food. Pastor Bakke slept a lot too, or pretended to. When he was awake he put his glasses on and read his New Testament in the dim light. Every once in a while he'd put it down and close his eyes for a second, then he'd clear his throat and read a passage that he thought was meaningful and maybe worth discussion. William realized that this, for Bakke, was fellowship.

"So it is not of him that willeth, nor of him that runneth, but of God that sheweth mercy. Therefore he hath mercy on whom he will have mercy, and whom he will he hardeneth."

"So what do you think Paul is saying to the Romans in this passage, Will?"

"Sounds to me like he's telling them that it doesn't matter much what you do. God either gives you mercy or he hardens you."

Will heard Chopper's snort and knew he was thinking about what God was hardening.

"I think Paul means that God allows some to harden themselves," Bakke said at last. Chopper's bedroll shook as he tried to restrain his laughter.

"Whom he 'will' he hardeneth. Sounds to me like God is doing the hardening. Paul seems to believe it anyway."

"Why would God harden you?" Bakke asked, seeming genuinely puzzled.

"I don't know. Why would he?"

"God hardens those who wish to be hardened. They chose it for themselves."

If something bad happened or was happening, Pastor Bakke's answer was always that God was testing you or was paying you back for something you might not even know you did wrong. For Pastor Bakke, life was all about God's lessons. And if something good happened to you, it was because of God's grace, and was almost always pretty much undeserved. If you thought you deserved it, then for sure you didn't, according to Pastor Bakke. He seemed to believe that you were never going to be happy till you were in heaven, and it was selfish to try to be happy since it showed too much self-interest, a conceit which could be more rightly directed to doing God's work. To him, the world was a kind of reform school where we were all sent, and we should all feel bad about being there and work endlessly on correcting our bad behavior.

Will thought maybe he should be more diplomatic with Bakke. Mama had insisted that he join Lutheran League when they arrived last summer at Sage Prairie. The league, pretty much all ten of the Lutheran kids in high school, met every other week on Tuesdays after school in the church basement, where Bakke told Bible stories and then pointed out the lessons in them. At first Will asked questions when they occurred to him, but it was soon clear that this annoyed the pastor, who finally said sharply that he was not going to argue about God's word.

Bakke had been a disappointment after Pastor Griggs, the pastor of the Lutheran Church at Cottonwood. Pastor Griggs preached about Bible stories concerning people having everyday problems, and he looked at them from all sides. Pastor Griggs was good at talking about the stories so that you discovered the lesson on your own. Job, for example. Didn't he have good reason to complain? Abraham and Isaac. How could a father do that to his son? Pastor Griggs' sermons were about questions. Bakke's were about answers. Will wondered if Father Piletti talked about the same parts of the Bible as the Protestants, and in the same way.

"When I was in the War," Cecil said out of the blue, "we got stuck in a camp once like this. No food. But we also had no tarp and no fire, and it was raining. And they were shooting at us and spraying poison gas. This is nothing." Cecil gave everybody a full-toothed grin and a rare hearty laugh, and it made Will feel like laughing too, and Chopper and Bakke joined in.

"I only came close to dying once," Pastor Bakke said after a time. "I had an acquaintance at Concordia. We were assigned as roommates. He was from Nebraska and I was from Chicago. At first I thought he was the most offensive person I'd ever met." Bakke's face seemed to get soft and kind as he talked, looking down at his gloved hands. "He disagreed with everything I'd ever believed. He wouldn't let me alone. He made me defend everything I said, everything I did. I started to hate him. I began to think of him as a personal devil, assigned by God as just retribution for my many failings." He looked up and met Will's eyes. "Then something happened.

We were riding in a car. He was driving too fast. A tire blew out and we rolled over and he was killed. It turned out that he was the greatest influence on my life. An influence for the good."

Nobody said anything for a time. Will was puzzled about why Bakke had told that story, but he saw it was someone else's turn.

"The scaredest I ever was," Will found himself saying, "was when I fell through the ice at Cottonwood. I was crossing a little creek, following a trap line I had, and I went right into a big hole. Over my head. I thought I was dead for sure. I couldn't pull myself out, but I was able to break the ice piece by piece till I got to shore. Then I ran two miles home, and I knew all the way that if I just stopped and laid down I'd be dead in half an hour."

"I just can't get enough of those Cottonwood stories," Chopper said, grinning.

"You've probably never been scared in your life, have you, Rolph?"

"I'm actually about as scared right now as I've ever been." He tried an unsuccessful laugh. "It sure is as hungry as I've ever been. I wish we had some of those rabbits I shot," Chopper said for the tenth or twentieth time.

"Why don't you just shut up about food?" Will asked.

"I'm hungry."

"We all are, Rolph."

"Stop calling me Rolph."

"Isn't that your name, Rolph?"

"Boys!" Pastor Bakke said irritably, not looking up from his New Testament. Cecil continued to methodically slice dry wood into thinner and thinner slices, keeping the tiniest of fires going, just enough to keep water warm in the pot.

"There're probably rabbits all over the place. Right outside," Chopper said.

"Why don't you go shoot one, then?"

"I might, Cottonwood. I might."

"Go, then, Rolph, or shut up about it."

"Come with me?"

"Afraid of getting lost?"

"Boys!"

Dear Chopper,

I always wanted to tell you how truly ignorant you are, what a cretinous mongoloid you are, playing your stupid games. Why do you think you're so much better, you lout, because you have a father? Because he has money?

Your life is already over. You've already shot your wad. It'll never get any better for you than it is already. Star of Sage Prairie High School. All that's left for you is to marry a stupid wife and raise stupid children and drive a tractor around and around in a circle for the rest of your life. You're stuck in Sage Prairie, and I'm going to go around the world.

Yours truly,
Cottonwood.

It was Will's turn to rub down the horses. He went out into the storm, his hat pulled low over his ears and the sheepskin flap buttoned across his face. He'd promised himself that he'd let himself eat the last of the second egg sandwich, but when he did, it didn't touch his hunger. With the cheese and the bulgur gone, Will had only the small apple, which he kept close to his body so it would not freeze.

He was sure the horse's feet were as bad of as his own, and so he was giving Stubb's fetlocks a workout. He was crouched down and didn't see the jackrabbit until it was hopping right in front of him. He could have hit it with a baseball bat. It was hopping slowly, one hop at a time, putting its nose down into the snow as if sniffing for something. After it passed, Will moved very slowly and went to the opening of the wagon shelter.

"There's a rabbit out there," he whispered. "Here's your big chance, Rolph."

Chopper got out of his bedroll and put on his shoes without lacing them and then his galoshes without buckling them and followed Will. He didn't even take his scarf or gloves. The jack had continued to take one measured hop at a time. Chopper and Will followed it away from the tipped wagon and the horses. Chopper loaded a shell in the .22 and shot. The rabbit leapt into the air and fell quivering like so many of those Chopper had shot earlier, and Chopper gave a shout of triumph and ran toward it. Will stopped and looked back. He could still see the wagon. When he turned back he saw the rabbit leaping crazily in all direction. Chopper was chasing it, and in a moment he was out of sight.

"Hey!" Will almost shouted. "Hey Chopper!" But he didn't shout. He waited for a minute, then two, then three, sure that any moment Chopper would come back with the rabbit, full of his false superiority.

"Rolph. Hey Rolph!" Will shouted through cupped hands. Nothing.

"I'm going in, Rolph. Olly Olly oxen free," he shouted, and then went back into the shelter.

"Where's Chopper?" Pastor Bakke asked.

"He shot a rabbit. He chased it. I don't know. I think....I think he might be lost."

Will saw Pastor Bakke and Cecil exchange a look, then both of them put on their scarves and galoshes and went out into the storm.

After they had all shouted for some time, Cecil suggested they fan out in a line from the wagon, making sure that the one closest to the wagon kept it in sight, and the next person keep the first person in sight so that the last person could go as far as possible into the storm.

Will stayed just in sight of the wagon and team. Cecil was the one farthest out. Will could barely make out Pastor Bakke, twenty feet away, the wind whipping his cocoa colored pants around his skinny legs.

"Chopperrrrr! Chopperrrrr!" he heard Cecil shouting faintly.

Will was frightened. Why hadn't he gone farther into the storm to call for Chopper? Why had he waited so long? Was it his fault that Chopper was lost? How long had he been out there? A half hour? Would Chopper have been so stupid that he didn't stop when he knew he was lost? Would he have gone farther and farther away from the team and wagon?

"Chopperrrr! Chopperrrrr!" Will slowly walked in a circle around the wagon and horses, while Pastor Bakke and Cecil swung in a wider circle.

Maybe he had come back and was in their cave by the wagon already, smirking to himself.

Maybe he was out there hearing his name but just waiting, making everybody worry.

What if he was really lost? What if they couldn't find him? What if it was his fault?

"Chopperrrrr! Chopperrrrr!"

They hadn't made a complete circle when Will realized he didn't hear Cecil's shouts any more. Then he saw three figures coming towards him, and it was all he could do not to run to them.

Chopper did not have the rabbit or his .22. He was held up at the elbows by Cecil and Bakke, and he did not seem to notice Will at all. His mouth hung open and his face was dead white. His eyebrows were full of snow, his face too cold to melt it.

Inside the dark enclosure Cecil had Chopper drink some warm water. It looked like he'd never handled a cup before. His white hands didn't work and he needed help holding the cup. When he was done drinking he just stared straight ahead, as if he didn't know where he was, or care. Pastor Bakke pulled off Choppers galoshes. They were full of snow. He took off Chopper's shoes and socks and rubbed his white feet and wrapped them in his bedroll. He put the socks on the shovel. Chopper didn't seem to notice what Bakke was doing. Nobody had anything to say.

"I lost my gun," Chopper said finally in a faint way. "I'm so hungry."

"I've got an apple, Chopper," Will heard himself say. He had not known he was going to say it.

Chopper couldn't wrap his fingers around the apple. He had to clasp it between his palms, his white fingers sticking out stiffly, but he was able to eat it, staring straight ahead as if trying very hard to remember something important.

7

The night Goose was an engine, a freight car, a passenger car, and a caboose. The caboose stopped right in front of Eddie in a swirl of snow. There were three porters in the caboose. Two of them came down the metal ladder to the platform and opened the freight car. The third stationed himself at the door of the passenger car to collect tickets. Considering the late hour, Eddie was surprised at the number of people who got out and at the size of the crowd that gathered at the passenger car, ready to board.

By the time he gave his ticket to the scowling porter and entered the smoky car, every seat appeared taken. There were people crowding up behind him. There was one empty seat at the very back next to a fat man who was sleeping with his mouth open, his hands cupping his crotch. The front of the man's shirt was stained with something that Eddie didn't want to look at closely, but he took the seat.

When Eddie felt the Goose lurch and heard the door fold

shut, the aisle was still full of people holding suitcases and looking annoyed. The man beside him began to snore and massage his crotch.

A tall, thin, middle-aged women pushed her way down the aisle, using a thick leather valise to wedge her way past the others. She held money in her hand and was offering to buy anyone's seat, but nobody paid any attention.

Eddie took the chess bag out of his suitcase, set the suitcase flat on his lap, unfolded the board, spilled the pieces from their deer-skin sack, and started setting up the heavy, green-stone pieces. Though he knew them to be crude, he was proud of them since he'd chipped and chiseled and filed them out of soft serpentine himself. He made several quick introductory moves. Mid-game was where it became complex and interesting.

The woman with the valise stopped next to Eddie. "How about you, son. Sell your seat?"

Eddie looked at the woman. She had a long horse-face and wore thick round glasses that magnified her green eyes. Her nose came to a small, sharp point, as if when she was born the doctor had taken his thumb and a finger and pinched the end of her nose, and it had stayed that way.

Eddie smiled his barely interested, Paul Muni smile. "What are you offering?"

"Four dollars. The price of a ticket around the whole damn triangle. And nobody here will take it. And they talk about all the poor people." She snorted.

"It isn't enough," Eddie said.

"Well, what would it take, son?"

"Probably more than you're carrying."

She snorted again. "Seriously. What would it take?" She slurred "seriously" just enough that Eddie realized she was drunk. She set the big valise on the floor and grabbed one of the handrails along the ceiling of the car, steadying herself. Eddie wondered why a lady would carry a man's valise and not a purse. Could she be a man, dressed up like a woman? He gave her a glance, long enough to see that she was not a man. Just a tall, skinny, ugly woman.

"Are you making me an offer for my seat?" he asked her.

"Are you selling or not?" she said. "Four dollars is a day's wages for Chrissake."

"Standing up in a smoky train? Right before Christmas? Even poor people value their comfort." Eddie had established a quick pawn exchange and defensive positions for both sides, black and white. Now he began to take his time with the moves. The train shook as it rolled along, but the stone pieces held their places on the board.

"How much?" The tall woman said after a time.

"Now I, myself, am not interested in selling this fairly choice seat," Eddie said. "But your first question to me was how much. My best guess is—ten dollars, probably. Though that's no cinch. It's late at night. Folks are tired."

"Okay, wise guy. Would you take ten dollars to give up your choice seat?"

"I didn't say that, lady. I'm not sure what this seat might be worth in another hour. Later on, might be more."

"Here's your ten dollars. Let me sit down." She placed a ten-dollar bill on edge on the chessboard like a wall between black and white positions. Eddie picked up the ten, thinking how long it took to make ten dollars brokering cigarettes and candy bars in prison. This would pay for his room at the Steamboat in Cottonwood, for breakfast, and for his ticket on to Havre. He wouldn't need to break into his chessboard till tomorrow. He swept the chess pieces into their leather bag, folded the board, and stood. She slipped into the seat. Several people in neighboring seats looked at him and grinned.

"That's the best money I've spent in a long time," the woman sighed, shifting herself into the seat. She put her valise on the floor between her legs and stuck out a rawboned hand. "Lynn Strawn. From Havre." Her handshake was surprisingly firm.

"Edward," Eddie said. "Edward Kinkell." He was pretty sure he'd never shaken hands with a woman before. He placed his suitcase on one end in the aisle and sat on it.

The woman threw back the snap on the bulky valise and removed a delicately curved silver flask. "I," she said, "...am going to have a holiday toddy without further delay. Merry Christmas, Edward Kinkell." She poured a shot into the cap and tossed it back like a man. For a moment Eddie thought she would offer him a capful, but she didn't. She exhaled loudly and settled back into the seat.

"I see you're a chess player, Edward," the woman said, "and a good negotiator." She dropped the flask into the valise.

Eddie nodded slightly. He didn't want to get into any conversations with anybody.

"You have the look of a college boy headed home for the holidays, Edward. Am I right?"

"I just graduated," Eddie said. "You are perspicacious."

She laughed. "Yes. I've been called that before. Where do you call home?"

"Hi-Line. My family has a spread there."

"What part?"

"Middle part. North of Sage Prairie.

"And you're studying...?"

"Philosophy."

"Well. Philosophy is an unusual choice for a son of the soil. What do you plan to do for...ahh, employment? Who's hiring philosophers these days?" She turned her beacon glasses and swimming green eyes directly on him. She no longer seemed drunk, but finely focused on him, and Eddie looked away.

"I will probably take over management of the family farm," he heard himself say. "But this spring I'm going to Scotland to visit my mother's family at Kinkell Castle. It's at Ombrie, on the Rhy,"

"Ahh."

"The trip's a graduation present from my father."

"Ahh. Indeed."

"James J. Hill's mother was a Kinkell, too."

"Well."

"He built the Great Northern Railway."

"Yes, I'm aware." Little wrinkles came to the corners of her eyes and across her dry-looking cheeks. "Your father must be doing well," she said. "Most farmers are having a hard time, wheat prices where they are. What are they? Do you remember the latest grain report?"

"Thirty-two cents for number one hard northern," Eddie said, glad that he had seen the papers. He knew she was testing him.

"You're from Havre, do you by any chance know Shorty Young?" He had no idea why he'd asked that question or why Lynn Strawn made him nervous. He took out a Lucky.

"Mr. Young is, ahh.., shall we say, 'widely-known.' He and his myriad enterprises are often the subject of stories in my newspaper."

"So what's Shorty been up to?" Eddie said.

Lynn Strawn looked at Eddie for a moment, then a small

smile crossed her thin lips. "Oh, let's see," she said, numbering off on her fingers. "Prostitution. Gambling. Bootlegging. Smuggling. Fraud. Intimidation."

"That's Shorty," Eddie said, and he and Lynn Strawn laughed.

"Shorty and I are acquainted because he makes it a point to, ahh...discourage my reporters from pursuing certain stories."

She continued to look at him as if she saw something very subtle and amusing about the situation and was waiting for him to see it. It made Eddie nervous. He made himself stop tapping his fingers on his knee.

"So you work for a newspaper?" he asked.

He knew several passengers were listening.

"My husband and I have the *Havre Promoter*," Strawn said. "Or you could say it has us. In any case I just came from Great Falls where I was trying to, ahh...steal a writer from the *Tribune*, but alas, the gentleman was reluctant to come to Havre even for a recompense far in excess of his current salary. Partly, I think, because he, ahh...also knew of your friend Shorty Young."

"Really, he's not my friend. I haven't actually even met him," Eddie said. "Just heard his name."

"I was counting on being able to entice this fellow away," Strawn continued. "Alas. It's amazing how difficult it is to find someone who can, ahh...actually write in the English language." She leaned toward him and whispered, as though telling a secret. "Even some graduates of the university."

"Writing is one of the things I do well," Eddie said, wondering why he was blathering on to this strange woman. "Having my Latin helps."

"Oh, I fully agree. So you have your Latin?"

"My mother believed every gentleman should have Latin and a fine hand."

"A philosopher with Latin and a fine hand. And a good writer," Strawn said. "Come work for me. Just imagine the dashing romantic life of an investigative reporter."

Eddie could not help but look at her.

"You want to hire me as a reporter?"

"Somehow you don't seem a good fit for farm management."

"I'm flattered. I really am."

"If you haven't ever seen a printing press in full flow, you should. Stop by."

"Maybe I will."

"Scotland will always be there. Some opportunities are once in a lifetime."

"I'll think about it," Eddie said.

"Good. Now, young Mr. Kinkell, future newspaper reporter, please do not be shocked or alarmed or dismayed, but I am going to have one more helping of holiday spirits. Ahhh," she said, when she was finished. "And now, in the comfort of my ten-dollar seat, I am going to go to sleep. God speed," she said, and closed her eyes.

Eddie wished she wouldn't sleep. She had a way of listening that made him want to talk, and he felt embarrassed to have fallen so easily into telling lies about who he was. Emerson would not have approved. Strawn began snoring softly. Eddie settled on his suitcase.

Okay, he told himself. No more lies. He imagined getting to start over, telling the truth. If he did, where would he start? With the Scaramouch gang, which was not really a gang at all? Or did it start when he stole the Ford? In any case, it was his sixteenth year:

Papa Swan arrived at Cottonwood to show off his first truck, a Ford with a custom built box for the Baskin's Products. After Papa broke his big toe kicking a dog, he couldn't manage the foot pedals, so he taught Eddie to drive and took him along on his sales trip.

It was the most exciting summer of Eddie's life. They visited farm after farm where Papa Swan was well known and welcomed as he delivered goods and took orders. He would tell his stories and bring the news and talk about economics and politics and business, and sometimes, especially if liquor was served after supper, he would play his fiddle. Eddie could tell that the farmers who gave Papa lodging and meals considered themselves lucky. The wives served supper on their best dinnerware and everyone seemed to buy things and make orders for the next trip. Papa always had a bunkhouse or a guest room to sleep in. Eddie always slept in his bedroll on the front seat of the Ford.

The Ford had a tendency to break down, but Papa Swan refused to learn anything about mechanics. "The greasy part of the Ford," he said, "is not the part that interests me." So over the long summer Eddie learned how to clean plugs and set tappets and adjust the float valve in the carburetor and blow out fuel lines. He fixed flats, changed the oil, learned to double clutch and drive with an elbow on the windowsill while Papa Swan slept. He also learned to siphon fuel from farm machinery at night and to increase Papa's tool collection when an opportunity presented itself. Most of all he watched how Papa Swan talked to people, how he told his flamboyant stories, how when things began not to go his way in a conversation, or when he wanted to get away from someone, he began to talk religion, asking people if they were saved. This device had served Eddie well ever since.

Eddie was surprised at the amount of kitchen products that Papa Swan sold. Fresh supplies were ordered and delivered along the Great Northern Hi-Line, and every week or so they drove to restock at Devon and Shelby, sometimes staying at a hotel and eating supper in a restaurant. When they were in town, Papa would play cards and drink whiskey in the evenings, and sometimes Eddie was allowed to stay up and watch the poker games, and sometimes Papa would buy him a soda. He thought of himself telling Bobby Williams and the Scaramouch gang about life on the road with Papa Swan, but after Papa Swan's toe got better, he seemed irritated with having Eddie along and sent him home to Cottonwood on the Goose.

On the way to Cottonwood, the train stopped at Havre, and Eddie saw there was freight to be loaded and unloaded before it would take off again, so he got off to have a look around. Even then Havre was famous for Shorty Young and his Montana European Hotel and Grill, better known as the Honky Tonk. Men played Fan Tan there with hundreds of dollars on the table for a single hand. Whiskey was smuggled from Canada. Beautiful girls were available for a price. Sixteen-year-old Eddie wondered what the price was.

Eddie walked a few blocks and headed back to the station. When he got there, the Goose was gone. For a few minutes he just sat on one of the wooden benches wondering what to do. He'd left his bedroll and everything on the train. His suitcase of clothes.

There were Fords parked everywhere, and Eddie knew he could walk up to any one of them, start it up, and drive away. He could drive to Cottonwood and probably beat the Goose there. If he acted quickly, he'd be there when it arrived and could just step onboard the train and get his stuff.

He'd been lucky to select a Ford that had plenty of gas, and he did beat the Goose to Cottonwood, and he did get his suitcase. Then, with a Ford to drive, he quickly became the hero of the Scaramouch gang.

The Scaramouch gang had started in the eighth grade after studying *The Three Musketeers* in English class. Bobby Williams and some of the other boys began wielding imaginary swords and saying "Scaramouch!" to one another, and over time the word took on many inflections of meaning. By the time they were sophomores, they were widely known as tough and mean, even though the worst they ever did was tip over outhouses on Halloween and put Ty Carlson's Model A Ford on the roof of his chicken house. Still, they swaggered, and kids made way for them. Eddie liked their style and longed to be accepted, and when he came back from Havre with the Ford, he was.

Those had been the headiest of times for Eddie. He told everyone, including Mama, that Papa Swan had bought the Ford for him. He was big for his age and already starting to get whiskers. He began to smoke cigarettes. He and the gang took the Ford on long weekend trips, and often returned with items they hadn't left with, which they stored in an abandoned homestead. In its most ambitious undertaking, the gang ambushed a bootlegger at the Canadian border. The driver had no money, so they took several cases of Canadian whiskey.

The thing about the Scaramouch gang that never came out was that after the Canadian heist, they were drunk every weekend, each one carrying a flask that was often replenished from the bootlegged cases.

About a month later Sheriff Haugen found out about the car. Eddie was threatened with being sent to the state industrial school at Miles City for auto theft, but he was given one more chance.

By this time Eddie was not only a Scaramouch, he was their leader. Mama was unhappy with him being away so much. It meant that Ruby had to take care of Viola, and Will had to take care of the firewood and water. But in Eddie's mind he'd already done his share, and it was his turn to be a kid. In fact, that's what they came to call him around Cottonwood, "Kid" Anderson. Kid Anderson and the Scaramouch gang.

It was Bobby Williams' idea to break into the Mercantile. They were drunk, of course, and it was on a dare, just Bobby and Eddie. It wasn't till later that Eddie understood that Bobby had planned for them to get caught. Bobby knew he'd be released as a first-time offender, but Eddie would be sent away. That would make Bobby the leader, again, of the Scaramouch gang. It was hard for Eddie to admit, but Bobby Williams turned out to be way cleverer than he seemed.

The Goose began to slow down, and Eddie knew they were at Cottonwood. It was still several hours till dawn. Those few who were getting off stood and began to get their belongings from the overhead rack. Toward the front of the car someone who'd been sitting on the floor turned to look back. He caught Eddie's eyes and smiled his satisfied smile.

Stanley.

Eddie felt himself go cold. This was bad. This was very bad.

This was very, very bad.

Stanley was waiting for him when he walked down the steel steps of the car. Eddie did not acknowledge him as he walked across the platform to the waiting room, but Stanley was on his shoulder every step of the way. Behind them the Goose rumbled away.

"What're you up to, Preacherman? I thought we were gonna have breakfast."

"You fool," Eddie said, finally. The others who had gotten off the train had disappeared into waiting vehicles, leaving many deep footprints on the depot platform.

"Might be a fool, but you're the one looks fooled. To me. Who's the woman? She's ugly as a badger," Stanley was drunk and bare headed.

"Why are you following me?" Eddie asked in a voice he barely recognized.

"Cause it's so easy. Besides. I couldn't let you set up your own smuggle with Shorty Young. You think you're so smart. Haw!" He laughed his stupid hiccupy laugh, then he touched his head. "Aw, Goddammit all to hell. I left my hat on the Goose."

Then Eddie realized he did not have his chessboard.

8

The chicken got dark brown and crispy inside the Dutch oven, and the smell was heavenly. Papa turned on the radio while they played cribbage, but it kept fading in and out and there was so much static that Mama turned it off. Viola had heard the market report three times already, all the prices of grains and cattle, and the same news about Roosevelt, since Papa always turned on the radio for the news broadcasts.

Mama didn't seem happy about the radio. Her first question to Papa was how much the batteries cost, and she began to make rules right away. It would be turned on only for special programs. No exceptions. She wasn't going to have their lives taken over by the drivel that came out of radios.

After he beat her three games in a row at cribbage, Papa asked to look at Viola's teeth.

"What?" Viola said.

"Come here and open up," Papa said. "I want to look at your teeth."

Viola stepped close and opened her mouth.

"Does your mother make you brush your teeth?" he asked sternly.

"No," Viola said.

"I do too," Mama said. "Viola!"

Papa showed no sign of having heard Mama. "Do you have your own toothbrush?" he asked.

Viola glanced what she knew to be a guilty look at Mama.

"She loses them," Mama said.

"You should have one," Papa said. "Wait here." He slipped on his galoshes and went out, not fully closing the door. Mama rose from the Singer and shut the door harder than usual.

"I wish you weren't so mad at Papa," Viola said.

"He is a thoughtless, selfish man," Mama said.

"He's nice to me," Viola said.

When Papa came back in, he had a toothbrush in his hand. He shut the door behind himself very gently.

"Now Petunia," he said. "It's time you got used to the idea that you are responsible for taking care of your own self. If you brush regularly you will avoid the sheer misery of tooth-ache, which is one of the worst pains the gods inflict on man. Now, when you brush, what do you brush with?"

"Soda," Viola said promptly.

"No,"

"Salt?"

"No. Not salt." Papa shook his head and produced a metal squeeze tube from one of the many pockets of his big black coat. "Tooth paste," he said, "a new line of ours. You have beautiful teeth, Petunia, but they are, I'm afraid, a bit stained. A lady should keep her teeth clean and very white." He held out the tube to her. It had a red, white, and blue Baskin's label on it. "May this be the start of a new habit for you. Healthy habits lead to healthy lives," Papa said. Mama stopped treadling the Singer and turned to look at him as if she hadn't heard right.

Viola brushed her teeth with the new toothpaste, which tasted a little like spearmint chewing gum, thinking how nice it was that Will wasn't here and she had Papa Swan all to herself. Lots of memories about him had been swirling into her mind. She remembered being very small and looking up at him while he sharpened a razor blade by rubbing it back and forth inside a drinking glass, his suspenders hanging down. She remembered that he saved the bands from his cigars in a box and gave her one to wear on her finger. He gave her a whole cigar box once, which she still had and kept arrowheads in it. And a brightly painted china doll which now had one hand missing. She remembered he wanted Mama to rub his sore muscles with Baskin's liniment, and he liked to have his wavy black hair brushed. She remembered that he had many pockets inside his overcoat and would produce things unexpectedly: a honing stone for sharpening knives or a safety pin or a cough drop.

"Papa, would you like to have your hair brushed?"

"What a sweet girl you are, Petunia, to remember. But don't leave that toothbrush and paste there and walk away from them. You put them away in a special place and always put them back there."

Viola was surprised that she was so shy around Papa. She remembered that the last time he was home she sat in his lap with her arms around his neck and her head on his shoulder, which is what she still wanted to do now, but knew she was too big.

"Sweetheart, go bring me my suitcase. It's under Mama's bed," he said.

Papa's suitcase was made of thick, black leather, held together by two wide belts with brass buckles. Rough use had worn the leather smooth in several places, leaving white islands in the pebbly black. It was so heavy that it banged against Viola's legs as she carried it. She stood next to Papa, anxious to see what might be in there when he opened it up.

"Daughter! It's not polite to be nosy," he said in a stern way, and Viola felt so embarrassed that she had to roll up her eyes as she walked away to keep tears from starting. Papa reached into the suitcase and withdrew a leather case. Even across the room Viola could see his initials branded into it. S.A. She remembered the case with a rush of pleasure, the smooth, wooden-handled brush she knew was inside, the brown bristles all full of his black hairs.

Papa Swan's hair was thick and wavy like Ruby's. He had to stiffen his neck so his head wouldn't be pulled back as Viola stood behind him and drew the brush through it. The Singer buzzed and hummed when Mama treadled it, and Papa Swan had a big coal fire hissing in the range. The air still smelled of roast chicken and Viola felt happy and blessed. There was the Christmas tree, all decorated and beautiful with her angel on the top. Here were her mother and father.

She knew the very things she would buy for everyone if she had the money. For Papa Swan, a toenail clipper. Clippers weren't that expensive, and he clearly needed one. Almost as soon as he had settled in at the house, he sat in Mama's rocking chair next to the fire and took off his shoes and socks and began to peel off the sticking-out ends of his long toenails one by one. He stacked the ragged white slivers on the top of the crate by the chair. Mama eventually came and swept them off into her hand and tossed them into the range.

For Will, a magnifying glass.

For Mama...? A fan. Sitting in her rocker sometimes, even when it seemed cold in the room, Mama would fan herself.

"What a pleasure," Papa Swan said. He had his eyes closed as Viola drew the brush through his hair. He was talking so loudly that Viola knew he was really speaking to Mama, who had her back turned. "I can't help think of the winter of twenty-seven, remember, Princess? Before you got the job in Cottonwood? The wind howling like wolves at the door? All of us bundled up in bed day after day to keep warm?"

Mama said nothing and gave no sign that she had heard.

"I remember," Viola said.

"Those are my fondest memories. Being with my family."

"Mine too," Viola said. "My best Christmas memories are when you're home, Papa." This wasn't really true, but Viola said it anyway because she knew it would make Papa feel good.

"Which are yours, Adelia?" Papa asked.

The range creaked as the fire cooled and Viola held her breath, hoping Mama would talk nice.

"If you mean fond Christmas memories, then probably that winter of '27 is one of the best."

"I barely beat the storm getting there. Like this time. Remember? Just like this time. That was when you were teaching in...."

"Whitewater."

"That's right."

"I remember," Mama said. She still had her back turned, and Viola tried to will her to turn around and smile, just imagine it hard enough so that she'd have to, but Mama did not turn around. Mama always smiled lots, and made the best out of things, and was cheerful, but she hadn't smiled once or been cheerful since Papa came home.

"At the time we thought it was the bottom of the pot." Papa chuckled, and Mama actually laughed a little, though she still didn't turn.

"The winter of twenty-seven was the last time we were all together," Mama said. "I just realized that."

"The whole family," Papa said. Mama didn't say anything.

After Viola washed the supper dishes, Papa went out to the truck and got his violin. He played *Peg-o-My Heart* and *Stardust* and *Mood Indigo,* and then he began playing some Scottish songs that Viola remembered him playing in the past. She knew he was playing them because Mama liked them. Mama worked on the Singer and didn't seem to notice.

Viola asked him if he could play the Charleston.

"I can play anything I ever heard," Papa said. He tucked the violin under his neck, closed his eyes, and began to play.

Viola began to dance.

"Look at my baby girl," Papa said, and Viola saw that even Mama had turned around and was smiling at her. She danced till she was out of breath, listening to Papa laugh as he played. "I don't believe I've ever seen anybody dance the Charleston in long johns and wool socks before," he said. "If Mr. Ziegfeld saw you he would sign you to a contract on the spot. And now," he said, playing a fancy introductory piece on the violin, "introducing that phenomenon from the Montana plains, Petunia Anderson in the long johns review!"

Papa laughed so hard at his joke that he couldn't keep playing, but Viola didn't think it was all that funny. Someday, she knew, something very like that was actually going to happen.

"A nice warm fire when there's a blizzard out," Papa said. "I bet it's going to be cold in the bedroom tonight, don't you think, Petunia?"

"Probably," Viola said.

"When I was a boy and the weather was like this, I liked to sleep near the fire. I'd just bring my tick in, and my blankets, and sleep right there, and be so cozy and warm."

"I'm warm in bed even when it's cold," Viola said.

"Listening to the fire is so soothing when there's a storm out," he said, and then began playing classical music, with lots of fancy bow work, his fingers flying across the neck of the violin. Viola was not so interested in the classical playing, though it was very impressive. She was trying to work up the courage to ask him to play *Bye Bye Blackbird* so she could sing along with him, but before he finished playing Viola suddenly realized why Papa wanted her to sleep in the living room. She blushed and turned her head away from Papa and Mama.

When Papa had finished and put the violin away, Viola said, "Maybe I will sleep out here tonight."

"Sleep in your own bed, Viola," Mama said quickly. "The floor is going to be too cold. You take my bed, Swan."

Papa sat for a moment. "I think I will," he said. "Thank you for your generosity."

9

Adelia never knew how to act when Swan was home. She knew how he expected her to act, like an obedient wife who was so grateful that her man was home that she was ready to do special service in his honor, but she could not deny that her real feelings were anger and disgust and fear. Anger that he would come back fully expecting to be treated with deference, the man of the family returning to set things straight, disgust at his personal habits and his smoking, fear at what she knew he wanted and would take if given the opportunity.

Earlier Swan had sat in Adelia's rocking chair near the stove and told stories as he watched her and Viola decorate the tree. His stories were full of comic exaggeration, and he did funny voices for his characters, and he used wide hand gestures and broad facial expressions. Viola laughed so hard she was almost no help with the tree, but long ago Adelia had seen that Swan's stories, however well told and no matter how humorous, always showed himself to be more clever, or more honest, or more perceptive than others, and she had come to see his storytelling as just another of his many forms of self-indulgence.

Adelia forced those thoughts from her mind, only to have them replaced by a growing sense of impending disaster.

Please, God, please hold back the wind until William comes home. If they had turned back when they first noticed the snow they would be back by now. They must have gone on. Don't let them be lost in the blizzard.

She set up the Singer so she could watch the road for William or Edward as she worked. She had decided to cut a shirt for Edward out of a remnant of flannel she had been saving for something else. She could sew it up and buttonhole it now, and when Edward arrived home she would measure him for arm length and collar size and sew it together. She'd wrap it in Christmas wrapping and put it under the tree so he would have something to open. Viola could hem a handkerchief. Then he'd have two presents.

Swan made a trip to the truck and returned with gifts for Viola and Will, each wrapped in colorful paper and tied with wide bright ribbons. He put them under the tree with great drama. Viola made a fuss about her present. Even across the room Adelia could hear it rattle. She observed coldly that there was no present for her. She supposed he would say the radio was for her.

She clearly remembered the last gift he had given her, though how many years ago she couldn't recall. It had been a smallish box, and Adelia got it in her head that it was a piece of jewelry of some kind. A nice pin, perhaps, something pretty, but when she opened the box on Christmas morning, she discovered instead a small sampler of spices, the same item he was giving away to all the customers on his route that year.

Swan made another trip to the truck and returned with the biggest orange Adelia had ever seen, though in truth she had not seen many oranges at all. She knew he had a bottle of whiskey in the truck and it was making his cheeks glow. He peeled and sectioned the orange with great flourish and gave a piece to Viola. Then he went to the cupboard and got a small plate and placed half the sections on it and brought the plate to the end table next to the Singer.

"For you, Princess," he said.

"Say 'Thank you,' Mama," Viola said after a moment.

"Thank you, Swan," Adelia said, and hated him for the way he manipulated these situations to make the children think that he was the injured party, the neglected partner. Swan rose and rattled the grate on the range, shaking a perfectly good fire to pieces and then adding too much new coal, not asking anyone or mentioning it in any way, just taking the coal and burning it. Adelia's heart raced with the purest hatred she had ever allowed herself to feel.

She would not yield this time. She would not. There had been times when Swan returned unexpectedly that she had fought her feelings and had tried to be a good Christian woman and wife. Not this time.

The day passed slowly for Adelia. As she washed clothes and strung up the drying lines in the house, her ears stayed tuned for the sound of a wagon or a vehicle, her sense of foreboding gathering. Swan and Viola played cribbage, pulling the small table next to the stove, and Swan took a long nap on Mama's bed while Viola edged squares of linen for handkerchiefs.

There were many things to worry about other than Christmas gifts. There was bedding. There was food. What was she going to do about food? Tonight they would have Swan's chicken. Then it would be chicken soup with the bones and scraps, the most meager of meals and the right message for Swan but the wrong one for Edward. Then, perhaps, potato soup and dumplings. Thank goodness for the milk from Sullivan's cow.

Sullivan's cow, Millie, needed to be milked before dark, and Adelia decided to take along Viola for the milking since she needed to talk to her about Edward, an embarrassing prospect.

Adelia washed the milk pail, utterly unable to eliminate the feeling that something inevitable was happening, something dreadful. And it wasn't just the prospect of her talk with Viola. This feeling had come upon her many times since she was a child, and she had come to believe it should be taken seriously.

"Something bad is going to happen," she heard herself mutter aloud, and then realized that Sawn was there reading and would think she was speaking to him.

"Something bad?" Swan said immediately. "Are you casting a spell, or..." Adelia observed the high color on Swan's cheeks and the whiskey brightness in his eyes. He smiled his most charming smile, but Adelia did not return it.

"It's nothing."

"An augury, perhaps? From the oracle?"

Adelia said nothing, but Viola looked up from the handkerchief she was edge-stitching. "Is it Will?" she asked.

"I'm just worried," Adelia said.

"Mama has second sight," Viola explained to Papa. "She really does."

"Superstition," Swan pronounced, "is the refuge of little minds," and he went back to his book. "Your mother has always been a worrier."

"There's a difference between legitimate concern and worry, I suspect," Adelia said.

"Viola, don't you see that second-sight implies a foreknowledge of the future, which implies a future which is predestined. So if the future is already written on some cosmic blackboard, then there is no use to worry."

"I don't know what you just said," Viola said, smiling "But it sounded nice."

"Viola, you and I need to go milk."

Viola immediately started to complain and try to talk her way into staying, but Adelia did not even let her get started. "Come along, now, Viola," she said, "I need your help."

Adelia had not mentioned Edward's letter to Viola or Swan, but she saw that she could no longer delay bringing it up. "Swan," she said. "Do you want to meet the Goose with us tomorrow? It may be that Edward will be arriving."

"Eddie?" Swan said, coming alive behind his book. "Eddie might be coming?"

"I had a letter from him saying he was on his way to be here for Christmas."

"Eddie? When? Why didn't you say so before?" Viola said.

"Eddie," Swan said with great satisfaction. "How wonderful."

"Mama!" Viola said. "You should have told us before."

"I just got the letter this morning. I don't think you need to get too excited, Petunia. He probably won't get here till tomorrow."

"If that boy decides to do it, by God he'll do it," Swan declared. "That boy had no quit in him, remember? Wouldn't cry."

"You always told him he'd better not," Adelia said.

"What? Are we going to get into this?" Swan said, astonished. "Are you now going to try to make me feel like Eddie was my fault? Don't you try to blame Eddie on me," he said. "You're the one sent him away to reform school, Princess."

"She didn't either," Viola explained. "Eddie robbed the Mercantile. In Cottonwood."

"Well I happen to know Winfred Haugen, who happens to be the sheriff of Cottonwood, and he told me that it was up to the Scottish princess here whether Eddie went to the industrial school at Miles City or no. And she recommended that it be so. 'Take him away,' she said."

"He was going bad," Adelia said. "He was uncontrollable."

"Somebody let him go bad. Somebody didn't control him."

"A father who wasn't there." Adelia said.

"Here we go," Swan said. "Yep! Here we go again." He opened his book.

Adelia, her faced flushed and her pulse pounding, handed the milk pail to Viola. "Let's be on our way," she said.

Outside the snow was light and not difficult to walk through, though it was deep. It had already stacked higher on the tops of fence posts than she had ever seen, and it was still thick in the air, flakes spinning like tiny white butterflies. Soon the wind would blow the post tops clean and all the loose snow would start to move, as inevitable as sundown. There would be a blizzard.

Please Cecil. Please arrive back home soon.

Viola carried the pail and lagged behind, saying nothing.

"I didn't want to send Edward away, Viola," Adelia said after a time. "He was my first born. I loved him. But he became...heedless. I was the *teacher*."

Viola walked slightly behind, hands in her pockets, face out of sight behind the scarf she had pulled over her cap and tucked into the front of her coat.

"It wasn't just the Mercantile," Adelia continued. "He stole that car in Havre. There was all that wildness with that foolish Scaramouch gang. Stealing from the Mercantile was just the one last thing. It couldn't go on. I honestly thought the industrial school would give him some opportunity. Would be good for him."

Adelia wanted to say more, but she was without words to explain so that Viola would understand how it had truly been. Edward had started out being a Kinkell, but he had become an Anderson. He became coarse and undisciplined. Like his father, he had been given great gifts, but somehow she had been unable to prevent him from corrupting them with selfish behavior, as his father had corrupted his. There had been a time when Adelia would have found the words to explain it all to Viola, but today her mind felt too tired.

"I don't know why I had to come," Viola said finally. She had reached an age when she was taking stands. It worried Adelia. It was exactly what Rubyann had done.

"Because I have to talk to you about Edward," Adelia said. "When he gets here it would be impolite to ask him about.... things. About his life. About what he has been doing."

"Because he hasn't been going to college like you said?"

"Well...well, he has been taking college classes, Viola, but...."

"Because he was in prison instead?"

Adelia stopped and turned around, "Were you and William reading my letters?"

"Yes. We were."

"I'm disappointed," Adelia said and turned back to trudge along the fence line between her little teacherage and the Sullivan place. They walked two posts before Viola spoke.

"So were we," she said.

"It was a white lie. To protect your feelings."

"I know."

They didn't say anything the rest of the way.

At Sullivan's barn Millie, the blond Jersey, was already waiting by the stall with a full bag, tossing her head and tail to show her impatience. Her calf tried to climb out of its pen, hearing the clank of the milk pail. Adelia slid open the lock-rod on the feed-room door and ripped the string to open a new sack of ground barley. She poured two quarts into the box behind the stanchion, threw in some hay, slid the one-legged stool under Millie, and began to milk into the bucket. Millie had short small teats, but she always let her milk down quick and heavy. Of all the cows that Adelia had milked, Millie was one of the easiest milkers.

With her head resting against Millie's warm flank, Adelia thought about cows, about how important they had been in her life. Starting with the Durris cow, Effie, all that time ago. Effie's sharp curved horns were normally balled at the end, but one of the balls came off during the crossing from Scotland and was trampled beyond repair. Mr. Durris worried that Effie might accidentally gore one of the other animals as the three families journeyed overland from Boston to Blue Earth, Minnesota, but there were no incidents until that morning when Adelia's mother braved a blizzard to go to the barn to milk. Somehow, Effie, the gentlest Holstein cow anybody ever had, Mr. Durris would always say when he told the story: somehow Effie swung her head just at the wrong moment, and the unballed horn ripped open Adelia's mother, with Adelia inside her, not nearly full term.

Helen Kinkell's husband, Hugh, brought the doctor from town by pistol point, forcing him to ford his horse through a swollen river. The doctor was unable to stop the flow of blood, and finally he rose and shook his head and said nothing could be done for the mother and that the child, also, was likely doomed. That was when Hugh Kinkell walked outside the cabin and shot a ball from his pistol into his own brain.

Three Doukhobors, a woman and two men on her way to a community of her kind in Saskatchewan, had been waiting out the storm in the barn and had witnessed the original injury. The Doukhobor woman said that she was a midwife and begged the doctor to remove the living child from the dying mother, saying that it could be saved. To the amazement of all present, the doctor did this, and the Doukhobor woman cut a large swath from Adelia's mother's skirt and wrapped Adelia in it and put her in a tin breadbox to be kept warm by the stove.

Adelia heard Mr. Durris tell the story of her miraculous birth many times. He always began the story with the Atlantic crossing that the three young couples had made with their animals from Ombrie on the Rhy, the prettiest and poorest part of Scotland. The McAddens were ill-equipped and Helen Kinkell was helpless with her pregnancy during the whole overland journey to Blue Earth. Only the Durris family, Mr. Durris never failed to point out, had put down roots and sent back for others of their clan. With meaningfully raised eyebrow, he always described Hugh Kinkell as a "nervous type" and left that to account for his extreme reaction to his wife's impending death. Mr. Durris made no attempt to disguise, though, his fascination with Hugh Kinkell, who was descended from ruined Scottish Royalty. In her earliest childhood, hearing this story, Adelia was thankful for her luck in being adopted by Harold and Nellie Durris instead of being taken by the Bohunk Doukhobors or the shiftless McAddens.

As she grew older, Adelia often had a dream so vivid as to seem prophetic. She and a woman she knew to be her sister were together at Ombrie on the Rhy. They were grown women wearing white dresses and lacy bonnets, surrounded by frolicking children. White geese floated on the wide Rhy, which flowed by the green field where they played, and now, the milk ringing in the bucket, Adelia dreamed of that place.

Millie's swishing tail brought her back to the present and she remembered her dread. *William. William. Please be home when we get back.* Finished milking, Adelia threw some extra ground barley and hay into the manger to help tide over Millie if a blizzard blew in.

On their way back, Viola complained bitterly about having to carry the heavy awkward pail of milk, and she continued to pout. The first wind began to gust in little puffs, and by the time they arrived at the house the little stacks of snow on the fence posts had all blown off.

Adelia ironed quietly with her back to Swan. She used two flat irons with well-worn wooden handles. She ironed with one while the other iron heated on the stove. Even though the handles were wooden, they became hot after a time, and she used the end of her apron as a glove as she drew the hot iron back and forth across the laundry. In the Durris house it was assumed that a gentlewoman would iron all washed items. All. In Adelia's household that meant the dishcloths, tablecloths, underclothes, sheets, and the one or two sets of clothes everyone wore during the week. She had been taught that ironing was also an important sanitary measure, and in the winter it helped with the drying.

Viola, still pouting, took a book into the bedroom and closed the door. Now it would come, Adelia knew, and she braced herself, acknowledging and even stoking the fires of hatred as she ironed by the stove. She hated how he made the kids all love him every time he came home. He did not appear to understand the havoc he created in their lives with his false and empty promises. There had been a time when she herself believed the promises, when she did not want him to go, when she gave herself to his songs, but that had been long ago.

"You are still a fine-looking woman, princess. You always have been," Swan said in a jovial tone.

Adelia steeled herself.

"The gray looks good. So do the extra pounds. You're quite the matron."

Adelia had promised herself that she would not make any more cutting remarks to Swan while he was here, but instead would suffer him, if not gladly, at least silently.

"How have the children been? Tell me about that Will. I can hardly wait to see him."

She wanted to say that William was fine because he displayed none of Swan's characteristics or attitudes or proclivities. "He's a wonderful young man," Mama said. "He makes me very proud."

"Pride goeth," Swan said, "before the fall."

"I have faith that God will suffer my pride in William," Adelia said. She discovered that her lips were pressed together, and she made herself relax them.

"I intend to suggest to him that he enter the military," Swan said.

"So," Adelia said, feeling a flash of anger. "You've come home to make sure your son's career gets started in the proper direction?" She stopped ironing and turned to look at him.

"He is my business. He's my son," Swan said, hurt. "I know you would like to see him in college, and there's nothing I would like better than to see him there. As I believe I've informed you, I've already lost one fortune. In the crash. It was big enough to send them all to college."

Adelia glanced at his expensive shoes and his modern puffed-sleeve shirt.

"But I've got something ready to go. It could be big." Swan had been talking loud, but now he lowered his voice, as if this were a secret he was sharing just with her. "If everything goes as I hope, I'll be able to help him go to college, and Viola too. Later on. I am eager to tell you about it."

"You've always been a generous man," Adelia said, "with your promises."

"Where did you get that Singer," Swan asked.

"You bought it, Swan," She admitted. He had. And he had already used it as leverage a dozen times, brought it up dozens more.

"What was it? I don't recall. Was it Christmas? Or perhaps your birthday?"

"It was just a gift. On no occasion."

"So. Do we concede that you exaggerate my failings?"
Adelia said nothing.

"Can it be that you are punishing me, with this vitriol, because you do not see a gift under the tree with your name on it?"

"Punishing you?" Adelia exclaimed. "Vitriol? I'm not sure I would accept any gift from you at all, Swan. Wrapped or unwrapped."

"What?" he said incredulously.

"I've learned that when I accept a gift from you, however paltry it is, you want something from me in return. That's not a gift. It's an exchange. And frankly, I don't want to give you anything. Or exchange anything either."

"How outrageous. How outrageous. Didn't I send you money two years ago?" Swan was having a hard time keeping his voice low, to not disturb Viola.

"Eighteen dollars."

"Yes. Eighteen dollars. For which I was never thanked," Swan hissed. "Do you know how difficult it was to raise? Do you know how difficult it was to part with? What did I ask from you in return?"

"That I accept it as your payment on half ownership in this family, so that I must accept you back whenever you chose to arrive. Feed you, wash your clothes, give you my bed and pretend that the father of the family is home," Adelia said in a louder voice than she had intended. She wondered if Viola had her ear to the door.

"The father of the family *is* home," Swan said in a low level voice. "I am home." He leaned back in the rocker, turned up the kerosene lamp, and read quietly for a time.

When the ironing was all folded, Adelia put it away neatly in the apple-crate boxes that served as dressers and end-tables, each with a tacked-up, flour-sack curtain, lye-soap bleached and hand-scrubbed till the red Guilford Grain Mill stamp was no longer readable.

Adelia heard a vehicle on the High Grade Road and ran to the frosted window. She rubbed a clear spot and watched the lights come slowly through the blowing snow. She could hear chains on the rear tires. When it turned into the driveway, she knew it must be Cecil's truck. William was safe. She had known he was safe, and so he was.

"It's William," Adelia said to Swan.

"How can you know that?" Swan asked. "They'd have burned you for a witch in Inquisition times."

The vehicle stopped, its lights pointed directly at the window where Adelia watched, and she could see nothing but the swirling snow. The vehicle sat with its lights on, and at last a figure carrying a suitcase crossed the beams of light as the vehicle backed away. A moment later there was a knock on the door.

Even as she went to the door, her heart pounding, she knew it couldn't be William. He would not have knocked. He would not have a suitcase. It had to be Edward. How did he find his way? He was so willful. Had always been so willful. Adelia looked for some gladness in herself that she could greet Edward with, but she could not find it. She was tired. All she could think of was that the figure in the lights did not carry a bedroll. Where would she find the bedding?

She opened the door and a figure in a snow-blown, hooded coat, carrying a blond leather suitcase, stepped inside. A thick red scarf covered the bottom of the face, but Adelia knew the eyes. Rubyann.

Rubyann unwrapped the muffler and grandly threw back her hood. With a big smile, she said, "Merry Christmas, Mama," and held out her hand. Adelia felt herself short of breath as she shook hands with her daughter. Rubyann had lightened and bobbed her hair and wore a bright beret. She had darkened her eyebrows and painted her face, but the bright, quick eyes were the same as when she was a child, and it was comforting to see them. Adelia loved Rubyann, her first daughter. She loved her but did not understand her. Hadn't since Rubyann turned thirteen.

"Rubyann," was all she had breath to say. Rubyann put down her suitcase and walked into the room.

"Haven't laid eyes on you for a while, old man," she said, glancing at her father.

"How have you been, my darling daughter," Swan said with his smile, but he didn't get up from the rocker.

The bedroom door burst open and Viola ran out and hugged Rubyann.

"I prayed and prayed," she said. "I really did. And here you are. Oh Rubyann, I'm so glad to see you."

"I caught a ride from Havre," Rubyann explained casually, as though it were something she did all the time. "They told me at the tavern where you were living, Mama." She removed her coat and thick red scarf and hung them by the door. "That was one slow trip," she said. She was wearing a wool skirt snug around her hips and a sweater tight across her bust. The suitcase was made of thick palomino-colored leather, with a wide strap and brass buckle. She opened it and brought out three cheerfully wrapped presents and placed them ceremoniously under the tree.

"Have you been well?" Adelia asked.

"Fabulous," Rubyann said. "Just fabulous. I've been living in the absolute lap of luxury. Living on easy street." She opened a slim silver case and lit a tailor-made cigarette. She held the cigarette away from herself in a languid way, one hand supporting the elbow of her smoking arm. She had a small white purse on a long white strap over her shoulder. Adelia wondered why she didn't hang it up.

"Why haven't I heard from you? Why didn't you write?"

Adelia heard herself say, knowing as she said it that it was a dangerous thing to say. She had to be cautious with Rubyann and try not to do or say anything that would set her off. She always seemed so ready to fight, as though holding an old grudge.

"Letters are too important to you, Mama. I just wanted to be on my own. It's only been a year. Or so. Don't start right in, all right? I just need a little rest. Where's Will?"

"Will's on a Christmas tree trip to the Sweetgrass Hills, with the pastor."

"Can I use his cot, then?" Rubyann asked.

"Of course," Adelia said. She nodded to where it was folded in a corner. Adelia felt perspiration on her forehead and could feel her heart still pounding from the confrontation with Swan. She tried to take deep calming breaths, but she couldn't seem to get enough air in her lungs. She hoped she would not have another sinking spell when Swan was there to see it. The sinking spells had been happening more and more. She would feel her heart fluttering and missing beats, and she would need to sit down right away. If she sat and regulated her breathing for a time she was soon all right, but it was frightening nevertheless.

"You don't look well, Mama."

"I haven't been well," she said, and realized that she had not said this to anyone, not even to herself. "I haven't been well," she said again. Yes, it was true.

"Well I'm here and I'll take care of you, Mama. So it's all right," Rubyann said, and hugged her briefly, smelling of cigarettes. "Ruby's back to take care of everybody again. For a little while anyway."

10

Eddie lit the kerosene lamp in the Cottonwood waiting room and used the same match to light his next-to-last cigarette. The match trembled between his fingers. All the money he had was the ten dollars from selling his train seat and what he had left from his shopping spree in Great Falls. He could not afford a hotel room and a ticket through to Havre and then on to Sage Prairie.

Stanley stood watching him, snow sticking to his thick hair and the shoulders of his lumpy overcoat. "I thought you were going to Havre."

"I wasn't."

"So what are we here for?"

"I'm going to wait for the afternoon Goose."

"Twelve hours from now?"

"That's when it comes," Eddie said.

"Then what?"

"Then I'm going home for Christmas."

"If this ain't your home, why'd you come here?"

"To settle a couple of scores," Eddie said.

"In the middle of the night?"

"Basically I came here in the middle of the night to get away from you, Pigeon. Isn't that funny?"

Stanley squinted at Eddie for a moment. "Where's home, then? Where you going?"

"Where my mother teaches school. Little town you never heard of."

"I know all those little towns."

Eddie didn't answer. He pretended to adjust the lantern's wick.

"You're jist gonna *sit* here for twelve hours? In the freezing cold?"

"I just sat for eighteen months. I can sit for twelve hours."

"Let's split a room. We'll play a few games."

"I'm going to sit here."

"It's midnight. You'll freeze your ass."

"That's my problem."

"Are you really so broke you can't afford a room?"

"Yeah. I'm so broke I can't afford a room."

Stanley looked at him for a moment. "Hah." he said. "Your money was in the board, wasn't it?"

Eddie took a drag of his cigarette and said nothing.

"I knew it. When I was playing on it in your room there at the Rainbow it looked funny to me and I thought, here's where his money is. I know you had money. Everybody knew you had money, Preacherman."

Eddie said nothing.

"Know what I do? When I need a room? And it's late? I go to the hotel. Pick the back door. Find an empty room. Never been caught yet. Hah."

"I'm out of Deer Lodge one day and I'm caught breaking and entering. Can you see why your plan might not appeal to me?"

"I'll do it alone. I'll get a room and signal you." He took off one of his gloves and reached a hand into his lumpy coat and took out a round yellow tube with a headlight on it. He turned a switch on the tube and a strong beam of light came out. "I'll flash this out a window. The door will be open. You just come on up."

"You pay for a room and I'll share it," Eddie said. "But I can't afford a room and I won't poach one."

"Yer jist gonna sit here then?"

"I'm just going to sit here. By myself. All alone."

Stanley stood for a time, then he turned away and, with his flashlight, walked in the snow toward downtown.

The waiting room contained a long wooden bench along one wall and a potbellied stove. Eddie'd hoped to find ready kindling and some lumps of coal in the stove, but there was nothing but cold ash inside, and the coal bucket was empty. Eddie sat on the bench and opened his suitcase to make sure, but he knew he had not put the chessboard in there. The board must have folded up and slipped to the floor when he saw Stanley on the train, and he'd been so shaken that he lost track of what he was doing.

Eddie lifted the collar of the stinking coat as high as he could. The slouch hat was no good at keeping the ears warm. He needed a scarf. Lord, how he needed a scarf. Could he really sit here all night without a fire, and the temperature dropping? He opened his suitcase again and took out his prison-issue pants and shirt. He took off his shoes and wrapped the pants around his feet. He used the shirt as a scarf to cover his ears and neck.

His ears began to warm, but his feet did not. Should he walk downtown and try to find some place still open before it got too late? What would be open? Nothing but the hotel, which would close after any Goose passengers checked in.

Eddie tried curling up on the bench, bunching the shirt under his head for a pillow, but he could not get comfortable enough to sleep. He let out a long stream of frosty breath, letting his plans go. His little revenge wasn't going to happen, and it probably never needed to. Just jailhouse dreams.

Eddie put the kerosene lamp on the floor between his feet and rubbed his hands over it. He'd shaken it so he knew it was only about a quarter full. It would last a couple of hours at best. He turned it down to its lowest level and tried to think how he could warm his feet with it.

Automobile lights pierced the falling snow. They came slowly, turned into one of the parking spaces in front of the platform, and someone got out.

Stanley walked up, his hair wet from melted snow.

"I decided to just drive back to Great Falls," he said, grinning his dumb grin, as if entirely pleased with himself. "You have a room back there, as I recall. Tomorrow you can have them check the Goose for your board when it comes."

"You just stole a car?"

"Borrowed," he said happily. "Had a sign on it said 'Take Me.' It'll be waiting for them in Great Falls. Studebaker. Got a good heater. Plumb full of fuel. C'mon. In an hour we'll be in Black Eagle for some early breakfast."

Eddie felt the cold around him and again considered the consequences of sitting there till morning, weighed against being with Stanley in a stolen car for one hour. There was a soft warm bed and a warm room waiting for him at the

Lincoln. He picked up his suitcase and got in the Studebaker, knowing it was the wrong thing to do but there seemed no alternative.

The car's headlights showed untracked snow on the streets as Stanley drove back and forth, trying to find the road out of Cottonwood to the highway. The falling snow was thick enough that anything not directly in front of the headlights, including road signs, was almost impossible to see. Even knowing the town as well as he did in his memory, Eddie found it difficult to tell exactly where they were. They backtracked through downtown, searching for the road. Turning a corner, the headlights illuminated Meyer Stallcop's Mercantile. Stanley slammed on the brakes to keep the headlights on the storefront. In the window were a number of men and women's hats.

"Whoa," Stanley said. "I need a hat." He turned off the car lights and withdrew the flashlight from his pocket. "I'll just be a minute," he said, opening the door.

"Jesus, Pigeon. No. This is stupid."

"Flashlight and a pick is all a guy needs."

"I'll drive away without you," Eddie hissed. "I will, by God."

"No you won't," Stanley said. He reached in and took the key out of the ignition, shut the car door, and stepped into the darkness. A moment later the flashlight briefly flared on the front door lock, and then Eddie saw the light moving around inside the store. After a moment Stanley was in the store's front window. He put on a hat and turned the flashlight on himself so Eddie could see him. Then the light moved away and disappeared into the store. Eddie waited for what seemed like a long, long time. His heart was beating hard inside his coat. Finally he could stand it no longer and got out of the car.

The Mercantile door was wide open. Eddie was immediately hit with the familiar odors. He knew where everything was, items on his long composed list, the necklace for Viola, the kitchen knives for Mama, the pocket knife for Will; and the gloves, the galoshes, the wallet; but all he wanted was to get Stanley out of there. He saw the light flickering on polished metal toward the back of the store and got there just in time to see Stanley opening the cash register.

"Nothing but change," Stanley said. "Nothing but pennies and goddamn nickels."

Eddie reached over to grab him and get him out of there when the alarm went off, filling the building with a hysterical clanging. Eddie raced to the car. Just as he got in he saw a kerosene light flaring up in the apartment above the store.

Where was Stanley? Stanley, for God's sake!

Through the thin curtains on the upstairs window, Eddie saw someone throwing on a robe, moving fast. Stanley emerged from the snow wearing a hat, and Eddie could see the pockets of his coat were stuffed. A moment later Stanley was in the driver's seat but couldn't find the ignition key in his pocket. He swore steadily in a higher and higher pitch, going through his pockets again and again until he finally found the key. Suddenly, out of the darkness, a shape appeared and jerked open Eddie's door. An instant later Stanley started the car and the lights came on. Eddie saw a pistol pointing at his head and a face behind the pistol. In despair, Eddie saw it was old Meyer Stallcop.

"It's you!" Stallcop shouted. "You little shit! Get out of the car."

Something exploded near Eddie's ear, and for a moment

he thought he'd been shot in the face. Stallcop and the pistol had vanished. Eddie turned to see Stanley holding his .32, smoke snaking out of the barrel.

"I shot him," Stanley said in a kind of wonder.

Eddie staggered out of the car, his head pounding from the blast. Meyer Stallcop was laying on his back in the snow next to the Studebaker. The car's taillights cast a scarlet glow on Stallcop's face. Eddie saw a small red hole above Stallcop's left eye and reddening snow under his head. His robe had fallen open, revealing a gray union suit. One bare foot had pulled out of his overshoe.

Eddie heard a car door slam and felt the Studebaker moving away. It was only by lunging at the door handle that Eddie was able to swing himself into the car. Stanley's face was stricken, his eyes wide. He seemed unaware of Eddie screaming at him.

It was only after Eddie came to himself a second time, while lighting his last Lucky with shaking hands, that he became aware of the painful ringing in his ear, the burn on his cheek, and that Stanley was not going to Great Falls. He was headed north toward Havre.

"You're going the wrong way," Eddie shouted. "You're going the wrong direction. *You fool!*"

"*I'm no fool,*" Stanley yelled. "I'm going to Canada, and I'm not going to stop till I get there."

Stanley gripped the steering wheel with white-knuckled hands as the Studebaker sped through the snow.

"For Chrissake, slow down," Eddie said.

"I'm not slowing down. They're gonna be after us soon enough, and we're leaving tracks."

Stanley was going so fast that Eddie could barely see out

the windshield as the snow whipped against it. He could just make out the borrow pits on both sides of the road.

"This road is as straight as a barbed wire fence all the way to the badlands just outside Havre," Stanley said. "We're gonna be in Canada by the time the sun comes up. You used to talk about Canada yourself." He reached in one of his bulging pockets and took out a nearly full pint of Four Roses. His hand was shaking so badly he could hardly get it to his mouth. "Blow, wind," he said. "Blow wind, blow."

The ringing in Eddie's ear reminded him of the alarm bell in the Mercantile. How did it all go so wrong? What did he deserve Stanley? How could he get rid of him?

For a moment Eddie considered just getting off at Havre and picking up the Goose again, going back around the triangle to Great Falls. Start again. See if his chessboard was in the lost and found. Was that even possible now? Could he even go home now? Would they be looking for him? Had he been seen getting off at Cottonwood?

Eddie decided there was no possibility he could see Mama and the kids now. He'd have to send her a telegram. Could he even do that? Would his name soon be in the papers, humiliating Mama again? Oh, God, no. Please don't let that happen. It isn't fair. It isn't fair.

Canada was the best choice. Stanley was right about that. But the minute they got to a town up there where he could shake Stanley, he would do it. But he would be without money. His ten dollars would be gone in no time. Could he stop in Havre and see if Lynn Strawn had noticed his chessboard and picked it up? Would she know that he had gotten off at Cottonwood? Could he still appear for induction? Thank God he had not told her his real story.

Before long the headlights showed the snow streaming

across the surface of the road like a thick white river. Stanley whooped and gave himself another drink. "We're safe," he said. "We're safe. We're safe. We're safe."

Twice they met cars coming the other way, and both times Stanley slowed so that they passed each other at a safe crawl. Eddie crouched down in the seat so he would not be seen. Then Stanley would speed up again. "If we're safe, why do you have to drive so fast? Slow down, Goddammit."

Stanley was still driving fast when the road made its first sharp curve into the badlands. Eddie felt the Studebaker start to slide. By the time Stanley tried to correct, the Studebaker was already twisting sideways, gathering momentum, and starting to roll. That was the last thing Eddie remembered.

DECEMBER 23

11

The storm whistled and howled through the night, whipping at the canvas door, and it still howled when daylight came. Every time he woke in the night, many, many times, Will saw Cecil, wrapped in his buffalo robe, tending the fire. He'd begun sawing spokes out of the wheels. The oaken spokes were too tough for the ax to split, so Cecil used the saw to slice silver-dollar-sized pieces to feed the fire, just barely keeping it glowing under the pot of warm water. Several times Will woke to the sound of sawing.

Will had been hungry in his life, but he had never been a day and a half without a bite of food, and his stomach was cramping, growling and twisting on itself. How long could this go on? Would they burn the wagon bed as well, and if they did, how would they stay out of the wind? And if they didn't keep burning the wagon, how would they keep from freezing? And how long could Stubb and Jubal last?

There was no reason for any of them to get out of their

bedrolls except to relieve themselves. When they came back inside, they held their hands to the little fire, or put them on the sides of the warm pot, and drank some warm water.

Chopper kept his gloveless hands in his pockets, or tucked under his armpits. When he put his own hands on the pot to warm up, Will saw that his fingers above the second knuckle were waxy white like the toes of Will's one foot, and his face had become red as a beet except for the end of his nose and his ears, which remained white. But Chopper didn't seem to notice his hands or his face, and he didn't talk about food or anything. His attention seemed to be someplace other than where he was.

Not long after everyone was awake and had a morning cup of hot water, Cecil spoke: "Stubb and Jubal aren't gonna make it unless they can get moving. We got no choice but to move on. If we go north we'll eventually hit the railroad tracks and can follow it. There's farms out here. Maybe we can stumble on one." No one protested. Will wondered if he had ever heard Cecil speak at such length, as he had twice now on this trip.

They worked as quickly as they could in the cold, shoveling the wagon out of the snowdrift it was buried in, setting it on its runners, and putting the remaining trees in the wagon bed to make a kind of nest for Chopper. Then they covered him with the tarp.

Stubb and Jubal were shivering badly. Will helped Cecil re-hitch the animals, and then he used the shovel and scooped the remaining coals from the fire into the stew pot and put the pot under the tarp for Chopper.

Wrapped head to foot in his buffalo robe, Cecil sat on the wagon seat, snapped the reins, and set out into the storm. Stubb and Jubal walked stiffly and reluctantly with their heads

down into the wind, the snow whipping directly into their
eyes. This young team was Cecil's pride, and he had treated
them gently on the trip to the Hills, but now he showed them
no quarter. He had a long-handled buggy whip, and when
the two slowed or tried to turn out of the wind, he would give
a shout and a snap with the end of the whip.

Pastor Bakke and Will walked behind the wagon in the
sled tracks, staying within arm's length of the wagon, and
they continued that way for what seemed like hours.

Stubb and Jubal struggled through endless snowdrifts,
forced on by Cecil's shouts and whip, but at a large drift they
stopped and would not go on. Cecil snapped them smartly
with the whip, but they just hunched their backs and refused
to move.

Will went forward and discovered why the horses stopped.
"It's a fence," he shouted over the wind. Hundreds of tum-
bleweeds caught in the fence had trapped the snow, burying
the fence.

Cecil turned the team and followed close along the fence,
and it was not long until a graceful two-story barn loomed
out of the swirling snow. Behind the barn was an immense
drift of snow.

Except for an outhouse, there were no other buildings, but
there were two matching bureaus with framed mirrors near
the door of the barn, half covered with snow, creating drifts
nearly as high as themselves. That seemed very odd to Will,
but he was elated. They were saved.

When they stepped into the barn, they found the air heavy
and wet and much warmer than outside. The straw floor was
muddy, not frozen, and a row of neat stalls ran along one wall
with a feed room boxed in at the far end, much like Cecil's
barn. Animals moved in some of the stalls. That meant there

would be feed for the horses. And water. If there was hay in the loft, they could all burrow in it to get warm.

Even through the thick dank barn odors, Will smelled wood smoke. Cecil must have smelled it too because he shouted a greeting. After a moment the door on the feed room swung open and a man stepped out holding a lantern, followed by a thin cloud of smoke. He appeared to be dressed in all the clothing he owned and there was a muffler around his face, which he unwrapped to display thick lips surrounded by a black beard.

"Good afternoon," the man said, and Will could tell at once that he was a Bohemian.

They all stared at one another for a moment.

"I have horses that need water. Is your pump working?" Cecil asked.

"Certainly," the man said. "Certainly I have plenty of water." He did not move, and Will knew there was someone else in the feed room.

"We're from Sage Prairie," Cecil explained. "Caught in the storm."

"Peter Bolechek," the Bohunk said, and stood there holding the lantern.

"Cecil Halstead," Cecil said. "This is Martin Bakke, and these boys are Will and Chopper." Will knew that Cecil had called Pastor Bakke by his first name, which nobody ever used, to spare the Catholic Bohunk any uneasiness about being in the presence of a Lutheran pastor.

"The house burned," Peter Bolechek explained, and now a woman and two very young girls, so bundled up that their arms rode out at angles from their bodies, came out of the feed room into the lantern light, their eyes wide.

"Ah," Cecil said. "Bad luck."

"Yes. It burned just yesterday," Mr. Bolechek said. "But we have plenty of water." He smiled broadly, showing many teeth through his beard, and gestured the woman and girls back into the feed room and shut the door on them.

"It's bad weather to be out," Mr. Bolechek observed, and took two tin pails from a shelf against the wall. He went out the door and showed Cecil where the pump stood solitary in the wind. Cecil and Will pumped water for Stubb and Jubal until they no longer wanted to drink while Mr. Bolechek, Pastor Bakke and Chopper stood braced against the wind and watched.

"Do you know where Sage Prairie is from here?" Cecil asked.

"Heard of it," The Bohunk said helpfully, "...I tink."

"Umm," Cecil said, and gave a small nod toward Will.

"You might want to tink about maybe taking the animals inside," Mr. Bolechek said finally. "Let me give you some feed for them."

"That is very generous," Cecil said.

Two of the stalls contained milk cows, one a big-bagged Jersey. Mr. Bolechek put Cecil's horses in an empty stall and gave them a generous amount of grain and some hay, and then the rest of them watched as Cecil and Will rubbed down Stubb and Jubal with dry gunnysacks that the Bohunk provided.

"Do you have anything to eat?" Chopper asked.

After only a tiny hesitation Peter Bolechek said that he would ask his wife, and he disappeared into the feed room, and after what seemed to be a long time came back out and with a gesture invited them inside.

The small smoky room was made smaller because Peter Bolechek had piled grain sacks against the walls. Bedding was carefully folded on the sacks. A nativity scene was set up on one grain sack with a picture of the Virgin Mary. Peter Bo-lechek and his wife had managed to bring the kitchen stove into the feed room, though it was blackened from having been in the fire. Pieces of burned and sooty stovepipe angled up to a crude hole they had cut into the loft above. The stove was leaking smoke from cracks in its firebox, but the air was not nearly as smoky as the tree-cave had been, and much, much warmer. Cecil and Pastor Bakke and Will and Chop-per all sat on grain sacks, and the small room was very full of people trying not to touch one another, except for the two girls who huddled with the mother. There was a coal fire in the stove and on the warming shelf there was a covered pot, also blackened, with a cast iron lid. The wife brought it down and opened it.

"Would you like some oatmeal?" she asked shyly. She had a Bohunk accent. Cecil and Pastor Bakke declined, so Will declined as well.

"No, but thank you very much anyway," he heard himself saying. Nothing he had ever laid his eyes on looked better than the hot, steaming oatmeal. Will could see there were raisins and nuts and seeds in it.

"I do," Chopper said, and Will saw in his eyes that Chop-per knew better but simply could not help himself.

The wife looked much younger than her husband. She had dark hair, and so did the two young girls. Like their mother, they had wide, frightened-looking eyes, but the wife smiled determinedly as she produced a bowl and dropped a large sticky dollop of oatmeal into it. Then she poured milk from a pitcher on it, added a spoon, and gave it to Chopper. Chop-per had a hard time holding the spoon, but he found a way to get the oatmeal into his mouth. Will had to look away.

"Too bad about your house," Pastor Bakke allowed.

"It was a nice house," Peter Bolechek said. "I built it."

Peter Bolechek's wife looked at him. "Along with your cousin John," she reminded him.

Peter Bolechek grinned. "She doesn't like living with the animals," he said. "But I don't mind."

The two little girls stayed close to their mother. "Ask the gentlemen if they would like a cup of coffee," the mother said.

"Oh, ya," Peter Bolechek said with a smile and got up and opened one of the smaller sacks. He reached in and took out some coffee beans and ground them in a small hand grinder. The smell of coffee beans almost overcame the garlic and smoke in the air. Will saw that many of the sacks didn't contain animal feed, as he thought. Some of the sacks contained dried beans and bulgur and potatoes and onions and rutabagas. Will had never seen so much food in one place in his life, except in stores. He looked at Chopper to see if he recognized what he was sitting on, but Chopper did not seem to notice anything but the oatmeal.

"Flue fire?" Cecil asked.

"Ya," Peter Bolechek said, and gave the ground coffee to his wife. "Jist got away. First the roof, and then...." He sat with his hands gripping his knees.

"Once they get going. No stopping them."

"Ya."

"Is there more?" Chopper asked, smiling, even before he had completely finished his oatmeal. Pastor Bakke's face got very red.

"Certainly," the woman said, and she dropped another dollop in Chopper's bowl and poured in more milk. She put the coffee pot near the middle of the blackened range. It had been a very nice range with several porcelain panels, which were cracked now and blistered.

The ends of Will's fingers were still bloodless and white, and his toes were so cold they ached. He longed to take his feet out of his boots and put them near the wood stove. He hoped that the coffee, when it came, would enter his system and go directly to the ends of his fingers and toes and warm them up.

"We were after Christmas trees," Cecil said.

"At the Sweetgrass?"

"Yes. For...for our friends in Sage Prairie," Pastor Bakke explained.

"We had a Christmas tree," the younger of the girls stepped forward to say, eyes wide.

"Shhhhhh," the mother said.

"We did," the girl insisted, and then went back to her sister and mother.

"The one that burned I got at the Sweetgrass," Mr. Bolechek confessed, his hands still gripping his knees.

When the coffee had boiled for a time, the wife poured in a little cold water and dropped in an eggshell she took from a plate on the warming tray above the firebox. They all watched the pot steep again for a minute before she finally poured the fresh hot coffee into the preheated cups. Pastor Bakke had always preached against stimulants, including tea, but he did not refuse the coffee. Will would have liked some milk and sugar in his, but he did not ask for it. He had never really liked coffee the few times he had been offered to him, but he looked forward to swallowing this hot coffee, however it tasted. He looked forward to holding the warm cup with his fingers. He wished he could take off his boots and wet socks and put the cup against his feet. Outside he heard the wind heave against the barn as if it had no intention of letting up. "Any crop to speak of?" Cecil asked after a time.

"Damn little," Peter Bolechek said, and Will couldn't help but smile that the Catholic was unknowingly swearing in front of a Lutheran minister.

"How many acres are you harvesting?"

"Two hundred or so. With my cousin."

"Any crop?"

"Saved seed. A little cash."

"Cutworm?"

"Ya. Cutworm."

"Same where we were. Hoppers before that. Before that the rust."

"I had some pretty decent crops in the field."

"Me too," Cecil said. "Do you get hail?"

"Hail...!" Peter Bolechek said, and laughed as though the word brought up hilarious images, though he did not give up his grip on his knees. He looked at his wife and she laughed too.

They drank the coffee for a while.

"How far is the Hi-Line?" Will asked, and Peter Bolechek looked at him in a startled way, as if he had just noticed Will for the first time and wondered how he got there.

"What?"

"The Jim Hill Railroad," Will said.

"Bout twenty miles," Peter Bolechek said, talking to Cecil. "...or so."

"What town?" Will asked, when nobody else did.

"Simpson."

Cecil nodded to Will. "We made better time than I thought," he said.

"Let us give you another Christmas tree," Will said. The idea seemed so good and natural to him that he didn't even think about checking with Cecil or Pastor Bakke.

"Oh! No, no, no," the wife said.

"You got the trees for your friends," Peter Bolechek said. He let go his knees and waved his hands.

Will left the feed room and went out to the wagon. Immediately he saw and felt that the wind was dying and that the temperature was getting even colder. It was almost completely dark, but he knew where to find the tree that he had set aside to take home to Mama. He shook the snow out of it as best he could and brought it in. Peter Bolechek nailed a couple of braces on the bottom and they set it up outside the feed room since there wasn't enough room inside. The little girls put bits of ribbon on it and the wife began rolling out dough for bread and Will volunteered to churn up some butter.

The wife made a potato soup with cream and onions and black pepper sprinkled with paprika, and she made fresh bread. It was one of the best meals Will could ever remember in his life. There was a moment of uncertainty when Peter Bolechek said the supper prayers, and the whole family crossed themselves. Will hoped that Pastor Bakke would not say his food prayer as well, and he didn't. He just said a small "amen." Hearing it, Will said a soft "amen" and so did Cecil.

After supper Peter Bolechek went out of the feed room and came back with an accordion strapped on. Without an introduction he began to play and sing songs that made them all smile, even Cecil. He sang in a language that Will thought he heard Latin in, but not enough to make sense of them. The wife peeked proudly at him as she did the dishes in a big pot of hot water on the stove.

After a good while, Peter Bolechek finished playing. "Looks like the fire has died down," he said, nodding to the range. "Maybe you'd like to sleep in the loft?"

Will and the others climbed the ladder to the loft and burrowed into separate places in Peter Bolechek's hay. Will listened for the wind but did not hear it. In a moment he was asleep.

12

Eddie lay in confusion for a moment before opening his eyes to the peppering snow and the blackness. His body hurt and he gingerly experimented with arms and legs, fingers and feet. After a moment he got to his knees, then stood, the horror of it coming back to him. He saw two dim spots of light and walked toward them through the wind.

The Studebaker had ended up on its wheels and sat there, snow blowing sideways past the headlights, as if waiting to be driven away. The driver's side door was open. There was no sign of Stanley.

"Pigeon!" Eddie shouted into the wind. "Pigeon!" But there was no sound or movement. Eddie slid into the driver's seat and found the switch for the interior lights. The roof was dented in and most of the windows were broken. The back seat had come loose and was sitting crossways. Stanley's yellow flashlight was on the floorboards. Eddie turned it on and went into the snow.

He found Stanley's body halfway back toward the road. Snow was blowing into his open eyes and blood dripped from his nose and ears. His wrist was warm when Eddie felt for his pulse. There was none.

Stanley's overcoat was thrown forward to expose a bulge in an inside pocket. Eddie took out the wallet and was surprised to find two twenties, two tens, two fives and four ones. He took everything but the four ones and put the wallet back. He removed Stanley's gloves and galoshes and put them on. Eddie's whole body was trembling violently.

Back at the car he found Stanley's scarf. He pulled his slouch cap over his ears and wrapped the scarf around his face. He became aware again of the ringing in his left ear. Again he saw the blood spreading on the snow under Meyer Stallcop's head and recalled the long, seemingly slow, inevitable skid of the Studebaker into the ditch. Eddie turned off the headlights and sat there with his face in his hands, sobbing.

"All I wanted to do was get home to mama," he moaned over and over. "I'm sorry," he said. "I'm sorry."

Eddie's suitcase was wedged under the dislodged back seat. He jerked it free and checked the car with Stanley's flashlight to see if there was anything else that was his. Then he started walking through the blasting wind past the lump of Stanley's body and back toward the highway.

Eddie had steeled himself for a long walk, but somehow, just at dawn, he stood across the street from the burned-out remains of the Havre Hotel and Honky Tonk. Inside his galoshes, his feet felt like wooden stumps.

Up the street the thin electric sign of another hotel, the Palace, blinked dimly through the blasting snow. Eddie plodded toward it. Once inside he set down the suitcase and looked around the empty lobby, stamping his numb feet. The insides of the big front windows were all iced over. There were lamps along both walls, but none of them were turned on, just one bright bulb behind the counter. In front of the double doors to the restaurant, a velvet rope dangled with a sign that said *Open at 7 A.M.* A chrome and leather barber chair sat between a shoeshine stand and an empty newspaper rack. A clock hung on the wall over the barber chair. Eddie could just read it in the dim light. It was five forty-five in the morning.

At the hotel counter he couldn't straighten his fingers and had to bang the bell with the side of his hand. After a moment a beefy man appeared behind the counter trying to look alert and cheerful, though one side of his hair was sticking up. He was pulling on a rumpled jacket. "Sorry," he said. "It's early." The nametag on his jacket said *Patrick Pickett, Manager.*

"A room," was all Eddie could say.

"I have one on the third floor," Patrick Picket said. He looked at the frosted front windows and yawned. "Got our storm, looks like." He turned the large registration book toward Eddie and handed him a pen. "Up from the Falls?"

"Yeah," Eddie said. He couldn't stop shaking, and it was difficult to write the name, *Edward Kinkell.* Why he wrote this name he did not know. He only knew that he could not use his own.

"You look like you walked the whole way."

"Had a flat on my Ford, and then the heater went out. Do you have a room with a radio?"

"Got a favorite program, Mister Kinkell?" Pickett said. "I can bring one up, but it's fifty cents more. Per day."

Eddie was struggling to make his cold fingers clasp the money in his pocket. He finally put two dollars and fifty cents on the counter.

"Three dollars for the room, Mr. Kinkell."

"Three?"

"So it'll be three fifty for the room and the radio."

Someone burst through the front doors, and Eddie turned to see a sour looking old woman on the arm of a short burly man. Their cheeks were red and their coats crusted with snow. The burly man carried a suitcase in each hand and was smiling as if he'd just seen something outside that amused him. He wore a flat-brim Stockman's hat nearly as wide as his shoulders and a long overcoat with velvet collars. Eddie had never seen Shorty Young before, but he knew at once that's who it was.

"Morning, Mr. Young," Patrick Pickett said.

Shorty Young set the suitcases on the floor of the lobby as if glad to be done with them. "Damn! Never had a drive from the Falls like that before. Some of it was fifteen miles an hour. Hard to see a damn thing. Bring those up, would you Pickett?"

Pickett literally clicked his heels together and made a small bow. "Of course, Mr. Young," he said.

"Here we are, Mama," Shorty Young said to the old woman. "It's the best I can do at this particular moment."

Eddie was shocked to hear that Shorty had a thin, high, almost girlish voice. He swept past Eddie, looking him over, and started up the stairs, followed by the old woman.

"Don't be in such a hurry," the old woman said.

"Pickett," Shorty said, chewing a short unlit cigar and glancing at Eddie again, "Don't let anybody get to me till later. I know Kravik wants to talk about the goddamned fire some more, but keep him off if you can."

"Yes sir. I'll make sure." Pickett said, making another head duck.

"Was that Shorty Young?" Eddie asked when the two were out of sight.

"Shorty Young?"

"Yeah."

"What's it to ya?" Pickett seemed to have recovered some self-importance since Shorty left.

"He stays *here?*"

"Since the Honky Tonk and the Havre Hotel burned, everybody stays here. This room you're getting is my only room, and yesterday I didn't have it. You're a lucky man, Mr. Kinkell, to have any kind of room for any price." He slid a key across the counter.

"By the way, what room is Shorty staying in?"

"Unless you know him, I'd strongly advise that you leave Mr. Young be." He picked up Shorty Young's suitcases and carried them up the stairs.

"And the afternoon Goose leaves...?"

"Scheduled for three twelve for the last twenty-two years and hasn't hit that number once," Pickett said, "but it's always close." Eddie could tell this was a well-used chestnut.

When Eddie arrived at his third floor room he realized he should have told Pickett to wake him by two if he slept that long, but he didn't have the energy to go downstairs and then climb up the three flights again. All he wanted was to get warm, sleep, and have something to eat. Then get on the Goose and be gone.

The room was small, but it had a bed as big and soft as the one he'd paid for and hadn't slept in at Great Falls. He hung up his rank coat and took off his new suit. Inside the overshoes his new shoes were soaked, and he put them near the radiator. Then he sunk into the softest bed he'd ever slept in.

Eddie woke under heavy blankets in an unfamiliar room that wasn't a cell. He heard snow pelting against a window and for a moment dreamed he was in the teacherage at Cottonwood, still a kid, just waking up from a bad dream about being in prison. Eddie let himself doze in that Cottonwood memory, his tree house on the riverbank, Papa Swan coming home for his birthday. Mama's laugh.

And then he woke fully to his room in the Palace Hotel in Havre, the tips of his ears burning and a ringing in his left ear.

What time was it? How long had he slept? When he swung his legs out of bed he felt aches all over his body, especially in his left hip and shoulder. He had a powerful hunger.

There was a radio and a washbasin on the dresser, apparently brought in by Pickett while he was asleep. Eddie was a light sleeper—prison had taught him that—and he wouldn't have believed a man could enter his room and not wake him, but it had clearly happened.

Eddie dialed two Canadian stations before he found one in Montana. A county agent talked about wheat rust control in a nasal monotone. Finally the time was mentioned. Almost noon.

...extended cold front...Alberta Clipper...thirty-four below at Cut Bank... roads closed...power out...telephone lines down. In local news, the murderer of Cottonwood Businessman Meyer Stallcop is still at large, believed to be driving a black Studebaker sedan with Montana license plate number nineteen, twenty two, eleven. Anyone having knowledge....

Eddie was wide awake now. Who could have known that he had been with Stanley? Nobody. He was going to get away. Going to get away. Nobody could prove he'd been in Cottonwood. Nobody could connect him to Stanley. His ticket was through to Havre. He was going to go home to Mama after all.

Eddie looked at himself in the mirror. He looked like a bum. He brushed his hair with his hands. He needed a haircut. He needed a razor. A toothbrush. He needed to have the suit pressed. But he had his life back. It was all going to be all right.

His new leather shoes were dried stiff by the radiator, the toes curled up. He could barely get them on. His eyes fell on the galoshes. He picked one up and opened it to the light. Inside, on the felt lining, written in ink, was *James Stanley.* Eddie searched for a pen in the drawer with the envelopes and stationary, something to smear out the name, but there was nothing. He would ask for a pen at the desk.

As he went down the stairs to the lobby, dressed in his new suit, the tie still in the pocket, Eddie smelled the food in the restaurant and felt raw inside with hunger.

Across the lobby the barber, a man with almost no hair, was putting on his coat and galoshes, but when he saw Eddie walking toward him he stopped.

"Shave and a haircut," Eddie said, and the barber took off his galoshes.

"You're a lucky man. I was getting ready to go home. Normally before Christmas in regular weather, I have two or three waiting on the bench all day. I don't get time for lunch. Throw a blizzard into the mix and I get four." He snapped open a barber's apron and placed it over Eddie. "You're five, and the last cut I give till after Christmas."

The barber chair faced a large mirror on the wall. Eddie could see the lobby in the mirror and through the open doors of the restaurant he could hear the clink of silverware. The smell of fried meat made him aware of how long it had been since he'd eaten. Almost twenty-four hours. Could he order a meal brought to his room?

Just as the barber began whipping up the hot lather, the hotel door opened, letting in a blast of frigid wind. In the mirror Eddie was surprised to see Lynn Strawn walk in, carrying her big valise. She was followed by two men.

"Lo, Wyatt," she said to the barber.

"Lo, Lynn," the barber said.

Strawn saw Eddie's face in the mirror. "Well my goodness, it's Mr. Edward Kinkell."

"Hello, Mrs. Strawn," Eddie said, gulping under the shaving cream.

She walked toward him. "This is the young student I mentioned," she said to the two men. "The philosopher." They both nodded towards Eddie.

"Edward, this is my husband, Glen, and our managing editor, Marvin Warner.

Eddie awkwardly held his hand out from under the barber's apron, and they awkwardly shook it. "A pleasure," they both said. Eddie nodded back. Her husband had a kind smile. The barber was trying to shave Eddie's Adam's apple but it was difficult since he could not stop swallowing over and over.

"I had a feeling I'd see you again," she said. "I've got your chessboard."

Eddie never moved, though his heart was racing. He managed to mumble a thanks, though his mouth was dry.

"I'm hoping you thought over my offer."

Eddie held up his hand to stop the barber so he could talk. "I think I'd like being a reporter, but the time just isn't...just isn't right."

"Do you have a room here?"

"Yes."

"I'll send the board over."

"Thank you," Eddie managed to choke out. "I do have a sentimental attachment to it. I'm leaving on the afternoon Goose, so...."

"I'll make sure it gets here. When the time is right, Edward Kinkell, there's a job waiting for you at the *Havre Promoter*. I have a good feeling about you." Strawn picked up her valise and turned toward the restaurant.

Eddie felt like laughing. He felt like crying. He felt like throwing up.

"You a philosopher?" The barber asked after a time.

"You could say that," Eddie said.

"How do you know Mrs. Strawn?"

"We did some business together," Eddie said.

The barber droned on about the big fire at the Honky Tonk, the weather, last year's crops. When the shave and haircut were finally done, Eddie paid his six bits with a dollar and didn't wait for the change. At the desk he finally got Pickett's attention and ordered coffee and the blue plate special sent to his room. And a pen, please.

In his room Eddie turned on the radio to find he had just missed the first part of the news.

....fingerprints taken at the scene have been sent to the FBI for possible identification. The fugitive is believed to be traveling in a black Studebaker, Montana license number twelve, twenty two, eleven....

Eddie paced back and forth with a slight limp, his shoulder and hip very sore. Four paces one way. Four paces the other. Always in the past when he caught himself pacing and anxious, he played chess to calm down, and it always did the job. The linoleum was patterned with small squares. They would work. He was deep into his game when a knock on the door startled him.

"Here's your supper, Mr. Kinkell. And your pen," Pickett said through the door.

"Just set it down outside. I'm...I'm occupied at the moment."

"There's somebody here wants to visit with you, Mr. Kinkell."

Stanley, Eddie thought. He knew it could not be, but still the fear went through him like an icy knife. When Eddie opened the door, Pickett entered with his tray and behind him was a broad shouldered man in a sheepskin coat whose blazing jug ears were red from the cold. His large hands held an enormous hat in front of him.

"This is Sheriff Kravik, Mr. Kinkell," Pickett said, bowing. "He wanted to ask you a couple of questions."

13

Viola woke to the sound of snoring. It was black dark in the bedroom. The snoring came from Mama's bed, and it took a second before she remembered that Papa Swan was there. Somehow she couldn't picture Mama there with him. She listened to see if she could hear two breaths, but the sound of the blizzard howling outside was too loud. Snow blasted against the frosted bedroom window like blowing sand. Better the blizzard should come now than later, Viola thought. Now the question was, would it end soon enough for the Christmas dance to still take place? She thought about praying for this but decided it wouldn't be fair to God, since others might be praying for there to be no dance. It was safe to pray for Will to be all right, though, since nobody would be asking God to hurt him.

She listened as the wind lessened, withdrew, and then rushed again in gusts that rose to a shriek. The frail building creaked and seemed to lean with the force of it. It was a good old blizzard, all right. And it was nice to be warm in bed.

Viola heard the grating squeak of the bedroom door opening. Was it Mama? Would she get in bed with Papa? Would they have intercourse? Viola pulled her blanket over her head.

The sound of socks sliding on linoleum came toward her, and a hand patted the covers until it found Viola's shoulder and shook her.

"Mama?" Viola whispered.

"No, Petunia. It's me."

"Ruby?"

"Yeah. Say. I can't get to sleep on Will's cot, and Mama can't sleep in the rocker. And I'm cold. Is there room in there with you? Then Mama can have Will's cot."

Viola made space. In years past, when Viola was smaller, they had slept on this tick together many times, but now there was barely room for the two of them.

Across the room Papa Swan shifted on the bed and stopped snoring.

"I haven't had a wink of sleep. Oh. You're warm," Ruby said, and then she was asleep.

Papa Swan grandly made pancakes for breakfast while the blizzard whipped around the house outside, and Ruby slept in. He beat the whites of four fresh eggs and folded them into a batter that had buckwheat in it, along with oats and regular flour. He added a bit of yeast and let the batter rise a little before he fried up the cakes, the whole time telling stories to Viola that made her laugh so hard that tears came to her eyes. She should not have done it, she knew, but she out got Mama's sugar, the part they had saved by whisking it up from the floor, and gave it to Papa Swan when he whispered a request for it. He put some into the batter and explained to Viola that it would "put a brown crisp" on the cakes. Then he boiled most of the rest of the sugar with water and mixed in a few drops of Baskin's Maple Extract to make a syrup.

Viola went into the bedroom to wake Ruby for the pancakes, but Ruby snapped at her and said she wanted to sleep in.

The pancakes Papa Swan made were the fluffiest and most delicious Viola had ever eaten, and she told him so right at the table even though she knew her praise would hurt Mama's feelings. After breakfast Papa Swan made real coffee. He offered Mama some but she refused. Viola hoped that he would offer some to her since she had never had a real cup of fresh hot coffee. Of course she'd tasted it before, leftovers at the dances when she helped Mama clean up after the suppers. The first time she tasted it she was nearly sick. She thought she had drunk some dreadful tobacco spit, but that turned out to be the way coffee tasted. Horrible. Which was why, Viola supposed, people put sugar and cream in it. She was sure it wasn't good for you. In fact Pastor Bakke made it seem downright evil. Certainly it was too expensive for Mama to buy for herself, though Viola knew that Mama had some coffee hidden away, to be brewed and sold at the dance. Along with some orange extract for punch.

After breakfast Papa sat in Mama's rocker by the stove and filled his pipe with good-smelling tobacco from a leather pouch. Then he said gravely that he was going to read and did not want to be disturbed.

Nobody replied except Ruby who shouted from the bedroom, "Does that mean I won't have to be kept awake by any more damn yakking?"

Papa pretended he didn't hear. He put on his round glasses, set his feet in their long polished shoes up on the crate by the stove, and opened his book.

Viola was surprised that Ruby would talk to Papa like that when they hadn't seen each other for so long. It was rude. First Mama was mad at him and acted like she wished he hadn't come home, and now Ruby was treating him mean. Right after he comes home for Christmas with a nice tree and bringing a radio and presents and making a chicken supper and then the wonderful pancake breakfast.

Papa Swan's long black shoes looked like they'd never even been wet. His pipe smelled good. Viola began to brush his hair again, and while she brushed from behind the rocking chair she read over his shoulder. The book was called *A Treatise on Money* by John Maynard Kenyes. She could see it was a library book by the stamp on the side. It didn't hold Viola's interest for very long. She wondered why Papa would read such a book when there were novels.

Mama seemed angrier with Papa Swan than she should be, over the sugar. Viola thought that probably Mama was also mad at him because he had been gone so long and hadn't written, and it was true that it had been at least three Christmases since they'd seen him. And there'd been only a few letters that Viola knew about. But he was here now, and Viola was glad. Life was exciting again with everything that was going to happen. There was the dance. There was Christmas. There was Papa Swan here to go to church with them. He would easily be the handsomest man there, and Viola remembered how he used to shake hands with everybody and introduce himself as the father of the family. She thought about how proud he would be when he heard her sing. Viola decided she would sit right next to him in church. How much fun it would be if he would sing tenor and she would sing alto and Ruby would sing soprano and they would just sing out, but she knew they never would do such a thing. Not in a million years of singing together in Lutheran Church on Sunday. They would never live it down.

"Merry Christmas," Ruby's voice said from the bedroom, and she came out wearing a gray robe tied at the waist with a beautiful silk sash. She had on lovely warm-looking slippers. She used to have the most beautiful thick wavy hair, like the picture of Ophelia in Mama's book of Shakespeare's plays, but now it was cut short, and she wore a red beret tilted on the side of her head.

"Good morning, Rubyann," Mama said. "Did you manage to get some sleep?" Mama was washing clothes in the tub.

"Once you get used to feather mattresses, it's hard to sleep on a straw tick," Ruby replied. "I forgot they're so noisy. I thought I was coming home for a rest, but I got practically no sleep."

"The Princess and the Pea," Papa said dryly, without looking up from his book. For a moment Viola thought Ruby was going to say something back, but she didn't.

"How're you feeling this morning, Mama?" Ruby asked. "You don't look well."

"I didn't sleep well either," Mama said. Viola noticed the dark under her eyes. She did look tired.

Ruby carried the wash pan to the range but found no water in the copper pot. The water pail, too, was empty.

"There's no water? No hot? No cold?" she said, with a stricken face.

"We used it all for the wash," Viola said. "Guess we forgot about you."

"I can't even wash my face?" Clearly Ruby saw this as a severe irritation. She lifted the coffee pot and loudly set it near the middle of the stove to warm up what was left.

"I'll pump some more," Viola said. Mama had strictly forbidden going outside into the blizzard except to get the eggs, though Viola had asked several times just to keep testing her. This time Mama said nothing, continuing to plunge the clothes, so Viola picked up the pail and put on her scarf and galoshes and big coat.

"Viola. Just to the pump and back. Do you understand?" Mama said.

"That's my coffee, daughter, I see you getting ready to drink…," Papa Swan said to Ruby without looking up from his book. "…and there's a good cup left. But go ahead. You're welcome."

"So I'm supposed to thank you for the dregs?" Ruby said.

Viola looked at Papa to see if he would say something back, but he continued to read, and Viola was glad. She didn't like it when people bickered. She remembered that Ruby and Papa Swan both liked to bicker and have the last word.

Viola made two trips to the pump house to bring in enough water to fill the copper pot on the range, then she went to gather the new eggs. Though the snow seemed sharp when it hit her in the face, and her nostrils stung from the cold air, she was warm inside her clothes, and it was fun for her to stand in the blizzard and let it whip around her and yet know she was safe. She walked farther and farther into the storm until it was just her inside a circle of snow whizzing on all sides. But of course she was careful to remember which way was back to the house. She imagined what it must be like for Will, out there in the howling blizzard, right now. Somewhere. She tried to imagine Will being in desperate trouble, but she knew he would be warm in his new coat and new gloves and Mama's knit scarf, warm as she was right now. She knew blizzards didn't last forever. She wished she was out there with him. It would be an adventure. A real adventure.

She practiced the Charleston for a time, though it was difficult in the bulky clothes. Then, before she collected the eggs, she checked the chicken house drift to see if it was big enough for a snow cave. It looked like it was. When the blizzard was over she'd build a cave.

14

The windows were frosted over, a crystalline rim growing along their bottoms. The rise and fall of the shrieking wind was hypnotic. Adelia sat at the Singer assembling the pieces for Edward's shirt, letting her mind rummage in the trunk of memories about Swan, a trunk she'd kept shut for so long. Anything to keep from worrying about William.

The fact that Swan had not seemed to age annoyed her. His hair was still as rich and full and wavy as it had been that July afternoon twenty-five years ago in Minnesota, when she first saw him at the pavilion with his violin. Even his face seemed no more lined than the last time he'd come home, and his eyes still had their light and luster, and it could not be denied that he was a vibrant and handsome man. It had seemed impossible to her that he had sought her out after his performance that summer afternoon, and pursued her and lavished attention on her, and seduced her, and in truth she had willingly been seduced, had thought that their love was the reward for her life of studious virtue. He was everything she had imagined in a husband. No. He was more. Not only was he handsome, he read books. He could recite poetry and play music. He drew her out and listened to her when she talked and laughed at the clever things she said. He told her she was beautiful. He held her in his arms and invited her to dream with him of the life they would have together out West after they were married.

And so they were, quickly, married, and Swan's disappointments began. He'd thought, somehow, that she was an heiress of the Durris farms and lands and would be handsomely dowried. When he discovered she was not, he said nothing. When it was clear that all Mr. Durris was prepared to do was give them enough to make a bare start of homesteading, she could see that he felt betrayed and injured. Adelia had felt blessed that Mr. Durris had sent her to the teacher's college, and she'd never expected anything more. She blamed herself for Swan's disappointment and vowed to make him glad that he'd chosen her, dowry or not.

She remembered their train ride to Havre and the very long buggy ride in a biting spring wind to Randall, Montana, just a post office and an ill-provisioned store. Empty land stretched away in all directions, sun-blistered, wind-deviled, and treeless, just waiting to grow wheat. The store's owner, Mitch Peelman, was a locater, and he took them in his buggy to tour what was left of the unfiled land.

The two half sections they chose, one for each of them, were nearly an hour's buggy ride from Randall, passed over by others because a coulee ran through it, thus reducing plantable acreage. Swan believed it would be easier to find water there, and he was charmed by the Indian tipi rings on the low bluffs above the coulee, so they took it and filed their homestead and had a bare shack built there.

Adelia's hands became rough, and she developed hard muscles on her arms and legs. She was amazed to watch herself grow almost stout. She carried dirty kitchenware and soiled clothing in burlap sacks to the coulee, washing it there, and she hauled the milky, alkaline water back up to the shack in buckets. Before eating meals, to conserve water, she and Swan washed only their fingers.

She remembered the plans they made during those supper meals that first summer, the two-story house they would build with a covered porch all around. They would send to Minnesota for fruit trees and have an orchard by the slough in the coulee. Swan decided their first motorcar would be a Packard.

By the time the snows came that first winter, Swan had broken only thirty acres, a bitter disappointment. Other new homesteaders had broken twice that amount.

By February Adelia knew she was pregnant. Even in the winter cold she felt herself blooming in pregnancy and was truly happy and fulfilled for the first time in her life. She had her handsome husband. She had her own house. She was going to have her own family. Her own family.

And she did. First Edward and then Rubyann, and then... and then one bad year after the next until they lost their house and their two half sections to the bank and Swan left with a threshing crew and didn't come back for nearly a year and she took a teaching job at the new Randall School.

Adelia pricked a finger with her sewing needle to make herself stop thinking about the past and put her attention to what needed to be done right now. There was always something that needed to be done right now.

"Viola," she said. "Swan wanted to go meet Edward at the Goose. Will you wake him please?"

"Why won't you call him Papa? You used to."

Adelia thought for a way to answer this and was unsuccessful.

"I wish you weren't so mad at him," Viola said. She put down her sewing and went to wake Swan. He came out of the bedroom and put his hands to the range.

"So," he said in a cross and irritated way. "Did Eddie say specifically in his letter that he was going to be on this Goose?" He had always been out of sorts after a nap. He took his gold watch from his vest pocket, looked at it, and snapped it shut.

"No. He didn't."

"So now you want me to go out into the blizzard because of one of your hunches?"

"If you don't want to go, stay here," Adelia said, putting on her coat and scarf.

"Why can't I come?" Viola said.

"Please, Petunia, no more about it. Stop now."

"But I need to go to George's store."

"Enough, child!" Swan snapped. "Your mother and I need to talk." He went to the nails by the door and took down his own big coat and put it on.

The wind was loud and biting, and every part of Adelia's face had to be covered as they walked. It was clear immediately there would be no talk, and Adelia was glad. She was quickly cold through her clothes and could not keep from thinking about William, out there now for a full day and night.

It was just possible to see the slight elevation of the road through the blowing snow. Swan walked ahead at a brisk pace, and Adelia hurried along behind him, stepping in his tracks, quickly short of breath. She wanted to shout at him to slow down, but finally just let herself fall behind and walk at her own pace. Soon he was out of sight. Following along, Adelia realized she felt apprehensive about seeing Edward. He'd been so hard and bitter the last time she'd seen him, when he was paroled the first time. So angry. There was little left of the handsome, clever, exuberant boy she'd raised. Now, of course, she knew it had been wrong to let Edward be sent to the state reform school in Miles City, but at the time she'd believed it a heaven-sent solution, one which would be good for everybody in the end.

Before she expected to see them, the two grain elevators began to loom through the blowing snow, and then the roofline of George's General Store, and then the narrow white and green clapboard depot with its platform by the tracks. There were deep drifts across the tracks. Adelia wondered if the Goose would run at all.

The little depot was mostly a warehouse built to hold important shipments that never came, but a small waiting room in one corner contained a potbellied stove and a bench. The cubicle was always left unlocked to accommodate the infrequent Goose riders. When she arrived, Swan had the potbelly open and was trying to start a fire. She wondered where he got the fuel. Adelia pulled her coat around herself and sat on the bench to wait, trying not to let Swan hear how short her breath was. The round clock on the wall showed that if the Goose was on time, they were early by fifteen minutes.

Adelia had been building herself up to asking. It had never been easy for her to ask for anything. "Swan," she said at last. "I need help with paying down my credit at the general store."

"What? You've been here only a few months and you've already exceeded your credit?"

"Do not give me a lecture on economizing," Adelia said. "I need help."

"I don't have cash money to give you," Swan said. "I have accounts receivable from here to Fargo, but I have no cash money."

"You arrive with nothing? Again? Expecting to be taken care of?"

"I put a roast chicken on the table last night. We'll have chicken soup tonight, and I'll make dumplings. I made pancakes this morning. I brought the Christmas tree. I brought you a radio." He always spoke softly when his feelings were hurt, and Adelia suddenly felt ashamed of herself, of her anger and resentment.

"I'm sorry, Swan."

"I spent the last of my dollars on Christmas gifts for you and the children," he said. "Maybe it was foolishness, but how was I to know that you would be in dire straits?"

"Food is going to be an issue." Adelia said.

"After William is home he and I can scare up some rabbits for a stew."

"I don't know what I'm going to do," Adelia heard herself say, and for a moment thought she might lose control and start to weep.

"Princess, if you only knew—"

"I'm Adelia. Stop calling me that."

"Adelia. Please accept the truth. All that time I was working single-mindedly, thinking only of the day I would come home a success. You'll never know how hard I worked. I slept in my truck and saved and invested."

"You sent nothing home for your children."

"You don't understand investment, Prin....Adelia. Capital that is spent cannot be invested. I had six men working under me, just delivering orders. I put every penny back in stocks. I had to sacrifice. You had to sacrifice. The children had to sacrifice."

"I may not understand investments, but I do understand sacrifice," Adelia said.

"There's so much you don't know," Swan said, shaking his head sadly. "There's so much you'll never understand about what it's like to be a man out there in the world in these times. How dispiriting it is to come home to these complaints."

"Lord knows you have not had to hear many complaints from this family," Adelia said in a trembling voice.

"Oh, no!" Swan said hotly. "Except from the minute I come home till the minute I leave. Do you think I am insensitive to the subtle, insinuating things you do and say to make me feel guilty? I suppose you think that I ought to be sending you checks in the mail so that you can all live here like the royalty you believe yourself to be. We're in a depression, Princess. Perhaps you've heard of it. Perhaps you are aware that four million struggling, starving, desperate men are unemployed out there. There are abandoned homesteads from here to hell and back, and the ones still occupied have people in them who have little money to spare for necessities, let alone Baskin's condiments and spices and specialty culinary items." Swan leaned forward on the bench as he talked, stiff backed and stiff necked.

"There has certainly been no money to spare in this family, either," Adelia said with tight lips. "Not for tobacco. Not for coffee. Not for whiskey. Not for gold watches, and not for sugar."

"This is exactly the kind of insinuation I was talking about. How accommodating of you to illustrate it for me."

Adelia swallowed back several spiteful things that occurred to her and said nothing.

"All right! I've been away. I haven't written," Swan said in a resigned way. "I didn't write because what I would have told you would have given you false hope."

"False hope?" Adelia cried, in spite of herself.

"Just as it gave *me* false hope. You can't imagine how hard this is for me. To come home with nothing, again, after what I've been through. What I've sacrificed. I expected to come home this Christmas with *an eighth of a million dollars.* An eighth of a *million!* Enough to take you away from your hard life and give you the kind of house and comforts that you so richly deserve, and which I long to give you. Enough to send all the children to the kind of schools which would enrich their spirits and challenge their abilities. Enough to make us a family again. Enough to earn for me your love and respect." Swan paused and shook his head. "And I almost had it. I almost had it, but I lost it all, a fortune, in the crash. I bankrupted. And then I had to dig my way back out. So that's why I stayed away, working hard. I was going to come back a success. I came just that close. Just that close."

Adelia nodded toward the potbelly. "Your fire has gone out," she said. Somehow this gave her satisfaction.

"Let's put the past behind us, Adelia," Swan said. "I'm on to something with this new project. Will you listen to me for a moment?"

"I'll listen."

"A man named Irving Langmuir won the Nobel Prize this

year for a number of brilliant discoveries. One of them is that silver iodide will cause rain particles to form in clouds. Do you see? Cause rain to form in clouds. How many clouds have we seen, heavy, dark, wet, coming across the sky, and go right by to North Dakota and Wisconsin? Imagine putting silver iodide into the clouds from an airplane that would cause rain to fall. Silver iodide is just dry ice. Dry ice. Do you see?"

"You're going to fly an airplane?"

"No. No, of course not. Though I could if I wanted to. I'd be selling subscriptions to farmers. I already know them all. From here to Fargo. It's perfect. It could revolutionize farming. Finally, predictable rainfall. Dependable rainfall. Finally, abundance! For all!"

Adelia looked at him, at his exuberance and wild hope, and felt nothing. "Good luck with it, Swan. Selling hope to broke farmers."

"I would form co-operatives. Each farmer's contribution would be acreage-based. I have it all figured out. And I wouldn't have to be on the road. Others would do that for me. We could have a home. We could be a comfort to each other."

"A comfort?" Adelia asked, amazed at the word.

"A comfort. I want to come home."

"Well, where do you think 'home' is, Swan? Do you think your home is here in Sage Prairie?"

"I had such hopes," Swan said sadly, "that we would not fall so quickly to bickering."

"False hopes," Adelia said, and they heard the Goose. A moment later it sped by, plowing through the drifts, sending a shower of snow on the platform. Adelia glanced at the clock. The Goose was exactly on time.

They did not speak all the way back.

15

"Hope you don't mind," the sheriff said, and stepped into Eddie's room at the Palace. Ahead of him Pickett dodged the chess pieces on the floor and placed the supper tray on top of the bureau. He set the ink pen next to it, lined up as if it were a piece of silverware.

For a moment Eddie couldn't move or speak for a moment. He could see the sheriff was keeping the hat in front of himself to conceal the pistol he wore. "Patrick here says that you drove up from Great Falls last night," the sheriff said. He had a tired, rather kind face, a face that looked as if it smiled now and then.

"Yes I did. What's wrong?" Oh, God, Eddie thought. The galoshes. He could read Stanley's name from where he stood.

"Well I'm wondering if you remember seeing any traffic at all. There was a black Studebaker on that road last night. Thought maybe you mighta happened to see it."

"Excuse me, gentlemen," Pickett said. He put his heels together and made the smallest bow, then left the room, shutting the door behind him.

"It was pretty much eyes-on-the-road kind of driving, sheriff, in the storm. Middle of the night. I remember there were two or three cars, but I couldn't tell you if one was a Studebaker or not." Eddie knew he sounded calm, but his mouth was very dry.

"What're you driving?"

"Damn Ford with a bad heater," Eddie said. "Like to froze."

"May I ask your business here in town, son?" the sheriff said.

"I'm a reporter," Eddie said. It was the first thing he thought of. "Lynn Strawn offered me a job and I came down to have a look around."

"Oh?" the sheriff said, and offered his hand. "Welcome to Havre. Pretty small town, when you git down to it. Thanks for your time." He lifted his hat and put it above his glowing ears, then disappeared out the door and down the hall.

Eddie could hardly wait to shut the door, and when it was shut he began to ink out Stanley's name on the insides of the galoshes.

The steak was cold and tough, but he was able to get the eggs and toast into his stomach quickly. He chewed the last bits off the T-bone as he paced his four paces, recognizing that this was what he had done for the last two years. Four steps over. Four steps back.

There was a rap on the door and Pickett's voice said that he had a message. Eddie felt himself go cold. Was the sheriff out there again? This time with his gun drawn?

"A message?" Eddie said through the door.

"From Shorty Young."

Eddie opened the door and was handed a folded note. It was written in a rough hand.

Pickett says you're a chess player. Got time for a game? Room #300 Shorty Young.

Eddie carefully folded the note and put it in his pocket. Finally something was going right.

The sour-faced old woman opened the door when Eddie knocked. She looked Eddie up and down, then walked away as if disgusted by what she had just seen. She wore grey shapeless clothes and thick black shoes. Eddie walked in and shut the door.

"You're the frozen fellah," Shorty said in his high voice, coming to the door. "We seen you before. Remember, Mama?" He held out a thick, chapped hand and Eddie shook it, thinking, I'm shaking hands with Shorty Young.

"I'm Eddie Kinkell. Glad to meet you," Eddie said.

"Shorty Young. The same." He had thin, gray, receding hair and a bulbous pitted nose, but his eyes were sky-blue and clear. "This is my mother, Florence. She's here visiting for Christmas from North Dakota. Case of bad timing."

The old woman sat across the room in a straight-backed chair, and Eddie walked over to shake her hand. "Pleased to meet you," he said. She shook his hand and looked sternly at him without a word, as though she knew well his many faults and could not bring herself to forgive them. Eddie felt himself flush under that gaze.

Shorty's room had the same flowered wallpaper as his own room though it was bigger and had two bureaus instead of one. Along the wall were several uneven stacks of documents and ledgers. Shorty's chess set was on the table. The board was polished black and white squares of marble, surrounded with a thick inlayed wood frame. His white pieces were polished ivory, old and yellowed, beautifully carved. The knights sat with spears on rearing horses. The queens wore delicate crowns.

"I look forward to a game of chess with someone I haven't played before the same way bachelor farmers look forward to trips to town," Shorty said. "It doesn't happen that much, so I appreciate you coming by. Best two out of three?"

"Whatever you'd like, Mr. Young."

"Call me Shorty. Cigar?" He wore broad suspenders, delicately striped. His shirt was open at the neck where he sprouted gray hairs.

Eddie took the cigar, and Shorty flipped the lid back on a silver lighter and held out a flame.

After Shorty lit his own cigar, he took a black and white pawn and mixed them in his hands behind his back, then held out his two broad fists, one pawn concealed in each. Eddie chose left and got black, and Shorty made the first move with the white. Eddie stared. It was a very unconventional opening. He had never seen or imagined anything like it. He thought a long time before he made his standard king-pawn three move.

"Too bad about the Honky Tonk," Eddie offered after he had made his move.

"I'd prefer to just play and not talk, Eddie," Shorty said in his high, girlish voice, almost apologetically. "Especially about unpleasant topics. What people don't know is, I not only got burned out, I got robbed. Three thousand in cash. It ain't all I got, but it was a week's wages for a lot of my people."

Shorty quickly made his move and then drummed his fingers as Eddie took his time.

Shorty's opening cost him two pawns and a knight, but he was able to take a bishop and destroy Eddie's king defense before it even got set up. By mid-game Eddie was already playing defensively. He picked off Shorty's other knight and both bishops, but checkmate was soon inevitable. Eddie never really had a chance to win. His cheeks flushed, and he was glad Shorty didn't want to talk.

In the second game Eddie opened with the white and made his standard king-pawn first move. He was able to set up a good king defense and mount several attacks, but over and over he misjudged Shorty's response. Suddenly his queen was taken, and Shorty methodically proceeded to checkmate.

Eddie thought for something to say, but nothing came. Shorty leaned back and smoked his cigar contemplatively. "Where'd you learn to play?" he finally said.

"Around. Why?" Eddie said.

"You play jailhouse chess, Eddie. Guys who play a lot of chess with just a few people develop a certain style of game. Kind of predictable. What's your story?"

"I'm enlisting in Officer Training School."

"Yeah, but what's your story, Kinkell? At first I thought you might be an insurance dick, or a federal."

Eddie leaned back in his chair. "I just got released."

"And you came right to me for a job. They ought to just give everybody they release a ticket straight to Havre. Half of them come to me."

"I didn't—"

"The Honky Tonk days are over, Eddie. Over for good," Shorty said. "I'm out of business. Hear that, Mama? Out of business."

The old woman sat across the room with her hands in her lap. She gave no sign that she heard Shorty.

"Won't you rebuild? People will always want to drink, won't they?" Eddie said. It was Stanley's best argument.

"Sure they will. What's gonna happen, though, is the state's gonna take over the liquor trade. Sell the booze. Regulate the prices."

"Wouldn't prices go down?"

Shorty laughed a good hard laugh, as if genuinely amused. "Prices never go down," he said.

"Maybe they won't repeal."

"They're gonna repeal. Count on it. So certain kinds of… opportunities…will simply not be there anymore. Last week I paid in cash the wages of thirty-seven people who paid other people, who then paid other people. That money went into the community like water into an irrigation ditch. All produced by Canadian whiskey and Canadian beer. Well, that ditch is dried up. Now there's a couple hundred more people on the street needing a handout."

"Was it an accident?"

"Accident? Like the cow kicks over the kerosene lamp? No. Not an accident. Someone lit it during the middle of the night."

"Was it the federals?" Eddie asked, amazed that here he was, talking to Shorty Young like any other person.

"Could be. But I think it was a common thief. Accidentally burned down the building trying to cover stealing a few thousand. An employee, more than likely."

"Shorty. Can I ask you a question?"

"As long as it's not 'can I give you a loan or a job.'"

"Did you really hire Chinese to dig tunnels under the Honky Tonk?"

Shorty drew on his cigar. "I did indeed," he said. "But I didn't realize it was widely known."

"And print your own Canadian labels and brew your own whiskey and beer?"

Shorty pulled a long smoke, looking at Eddie. "Are you writing a book or something, Eddie? Or are you just the curious type." Shorty crushed out his cigar without taking his eyes off Eddie, and then turned to the old woman. "Are you ready for a steak, Mama?"

"I suppose," the old woman said.

Eddie rose from his chair and walked toward his jacket on the bed. He was still holding half a cigar. It had gone out.

There was a knock at the door.

"Goddammit," Shorty said.

Shorty Young opened the door and there stood the sheriff in his sheepskin coat, holding his enormous hat.

"Sorry to bother you, Mr. Young," Eddie heard the sheriff say. "But Pickett said it was all right to come up. Got a couple more questions about the fire and the robbery. Hope you don't mind?"

Shorty stepped aside and the sheriff walked into the room looking very uncomfortable. Shorty started placing his chess pieces into a wooden box that had a velvet-lined bed for each one. Eddie began to slide toward the door.

"Mother. This is Sheriff Kravik. Kravik, my mother, Florence."

The sheriff walked across the room to shake hand, and when he did she smiled and nodded and said 'pleased to meet you' and appeared to mean it. When Kravik turned around Eddie was almost out the door.

"Well, how about that." The sheriff held out his hand to Eddie. "Didn't expect to see you here. It's Kinkell, isn't it? Doesn't take you long to get around," he said in an admiring voice.

"Nice to see you sheriff," Eddie said. "I guess I'll be going,"

The sheriff didn't move. Grinning stupidly, he said to Shorty, "I thought you didn't give interviews to newspaper reporters."

"Newspaper reporters?"

"Mr. Kinkell, don't you work for Lynn Strawn?" the sheriff said.

"Why you little bastard," Shorty said. He took two very quick steps and grabbed Eddie by the front of his shirt and slammed him against the wall.

"Morris! You stop that right now!" the old woman said.

"I don't like reporters, get it?" Shorty said in a calm deadly way. "And I hate liars. Tell Lynn Strawn this better not happen again. And if I see a word of our conversation in print, you will come to deeply regret ever laying eyes on me. Deeply. Regret!"

"Sorry," Eddie said, and slipped out the door.

Back in his room Eddie looked at his white face in the mirror for a long time, taking deep breaths and trying to organize his thoughts. How many close calls could there be? Why hadn't they found Stanley?

He searched several channels for the news, but everyone was playing Christmas music, one song after the next. Eddie paced his four paces, waiting, and finally the news came on.

The statewide manhunt for the killer of well-known Cottonwood merchant Meyer Stallcop was called off earlier today when Montana State Patrol discovered the frozen body of James Charles Stanley and the stolen Studebaker. The vehicle apparently left the road south of Havre and rolled into a ravine. Recovered with the body were a number of items stolen in Cottonwood, along with what is believed to be the murder weapon. Stanley, twenty-four years old, has been a resident of Great Falls since his release two months ago from Deer Lodge Penitentiary and has been a suspect in a series of rural robberies. Officials say there is no evidence to suggest that accomplices were involved.

Eddie took a pillow and held it over his face to muffle the sound as he sobbed into it. *It was going to be all right. It was going to be all right.*

There was a knock on the door, and Eddie looked up, alarmed.

"Mr. Kinkell?" It was Pickett. "I have your chess board from Lynn Strawn."

16

When the water in the copper pot was finally hot enough to suit her, Ruby ladled some into the hand basin. She undid the buckle on her smooth leather suitcase and removed a small mirror and a very white washcloth and washed her face. Viola had put herself in a position to see what else was in the suitcase when Ruby opened it. It looked like there were some silk stockings, and a pair of high-heeled shoes.

Silk stockings. High-heeled shoes. Many times Viola had wondered what it would feel like to wear silk stockings and high-heeled shoes. She had seen a magazine advertisement of a long leg in a silk stocking and had instantly wanted to wear silk stockings more than any other thing in the world. Wear silk stockings and dance the Charleston in high-heeled shoes.

Viola watched Ruby smear some cream all over her face, using just the tips of her fingers. She put on a bright lipstick, pushing her lips out in a silly way at the mirror to do it, and then darkened her eyebrows with a pencil. With the beret over her short hair, she looked very grown up and brave. Viola wondered why she never took off her purse. She wondered what was in there.

Before Ruby left home, Viola had heard her say terrible things to Mama. Hard things. She and Will weren't supposed to know, but they knew everything. Ruby got herself pregnant. She wouldn't tell who the father was, but everybody knew it was Bobby Williams. Viola wondered what became of Ruby's baby and wondered if it was something she shouldn't ask about.

"Were those silk stockings in your suitcase?" Viola couldn't help but ask.

"Don't touch those stockings," Ruby said.

"Can't I even try them on?"

"Don't touch those stockings," Ruby said again.

"Why are you so cranky?"

"I'm not cranky. I just don't want you putting a run in my stockings. That's all."

"Where did you get them?" Viola asked.

Ruby turned and looked at her for a moment, then at Papa Swan, then she turned back to the mirror. "Shorty Young gave them to me," she said. "I dance in them."

Viola was surprised there was no reaction from Mama. Even Viola knew who Shorty Young was. Everybody did. He ran Havre. So Ruby wasn't a nurse after all.

"I won't put a run in them," Viola said.

"And he used to be rich." Ruby said to nobody in particular. "Till they burned the Havre Hotel down, Honky Tonk and all."

"What?" Papa said, lowering his book.

Ruby took out her cigarette case, lit another cigarette, and put her elbow in the palm of her hand. "Burned two days ago," she said, blowing out a stream.

"Who burned it," Papa Swan wanted to know.

"The Federals, is what everybody says. Since they couldn't get Shorty one way, they got him another." Ruby did not look at Papa when she talked to him, but kept her back turned. "It burned to the ground along with the buildings on both sides."

Viola was embarrassed for Ruby. Why was she so rude?

"Are you going to wear the silk stockings to the dance?" Viola asked.

"There's a dance?"

"Tomorrow night, if the blizzard lets up. Fulps."

"Really?" Ruby said. "The Fulps? Whoop de do."

Viola couldn't tell if Ruby was sarcastic or impressed.

"Please let me wear the stockings to the dance. I'll do anything. I'll be your slave."

"I'm not giving you my stockings and high heels, so forget it."

"I can't even try them on?"

"I don't want to hear any more about it," Ruby snapped, and when Viola got tears in her eyes she said she was sorry, that she hadn't gotten much sleep. But she'd brought a surprise, popcorn, which they popped immediately. What they didn't eat they strung with needles and thread and hung on Papa Swan's tree. Along with the ornaments and buttons and paper chains and the angel on top and the presents underneath, it was an almost beautiful tree. Ruby made popcorn soup for lunch, which was one of her own favorites, since she believed that she had invented it. Hearing Ruby call her "Petunia" and eating popcorn soup, seeing Papa Swan reading by the stove and Mama sewing at the Singer, made Viola feel just perfect. Now only Will had to come home to make them a family again.

She kept a spot rubbed clear in a window and watched the drifts grow. The one between the shed and house had been as high as the bottom of the window in the morning and was up to the middle of it by midday. She'd also been watching the growth of the icicles hanging from the eve, begging Mama to let her go outside, but Mama said no, and wouldn't discuss it.

They listened to the same news, over and over...*extended cold front...Alaska Express...thirty-four below at Cut Bank... roads closed...power out....*

Then there was something different.

Businessman Meyer Stallcop was found dead early today outside his business establishment in Cottonwood, apparently murdered during a robbery. An automobile from Cottonwood is also missing. The automobile is a black Studebaker sedan with Montana license plate number twelve, twenty two, eleven. Anyone seeing this vehicle should call....

Viola heard Mama suck in her breath as though she had pricked herself with a needle. Viola turned to see her sit heavily and awkwardly on the kitchen chair she had been standing near.

"Get me a glass of water," Mama said, out of breath. Saying it seemed to take all the air out of her. She put one hand to her throat and took tiny little breaths, concentrating very hard on each one. The hand was splotched with dark marks. It looked like the hand of a dead person, and Viola felt a chill.

"Mama needs her rocker," Ruby said to Papa Swan.

"What?"

"Give Mama the rocker!"

He got up with his book and Ruby and Viola helped Mama

to the rocker. Ruby ladled a tin cup of cold water from the bucket by the door. Mama drank the whole cup, and after a time her breathing evened out and she said she was beginning to feel better. "It was just a sinking spell," she said, and tried to smile, but she was still pale and her skin blotchy.

It was a good thing that Papa Swan was home, Viola thought.

By mid-afternoon the storm had cleared enough that Viola could see past the chicken coop. Though the wind still blew strong, most of the snow had collected in drifts, and the air began to clear. Finally Mama said she could go outside, and Ruby immediately wanted to go with her.

Viola and Ruby went out into the weather, Ruby wearing Mama's galoshes and milking coat. Viola saw that Ruby still wore her white purse under the coat. They broke off all the icicles hanging from the eve of the house and threw them like javelins into the drifts. They dug out the ladder and set it up on the lean-to part of the house and then took turns jumping farther and farther into the snowbank below. The snow was too cold and dry to roll a snowman, so they started to dig a snow cave in the chicken-house drift. The drift was firm, and it was easy to cut a crawl hole with the coal shovel. They kept at it until they had carved out enough snow to create a room where they could sit inside. They put down a layer of clean straw from Will's sack of nesting straw in the chicken coop and sat on it. It was intensely quiet and still in there and surprisingly light. Ruby lit a cigarette and passed it to Viola, and Viola smoked without hesitation, though she took only the smallest amounts into her lungs. She didn't want Ruby to know she had never smoked before.

Ruby began to talk about the amazing things she had seen and done in the last year, as though Viola were one of her oldest friends. Life at the Havre Hotel had been a party with constant music and intrigue. The cars. The clothes. The men.

Viola had been through Havre twice, once to a circus, and once last year on the way to Sage Prairie on the Goose from Cottonwood. Ruby was supposed to be in nurse's school at the Deaconess Hospital in Havre, and Viola wondered why they hadn't stopped to visit her, but instead went right on through to Sage Prairie.

"Great snow cave." Ruby said. It was nice to see her excited and grinning her big toothy grin and not trying to be a debutante. "I'll bet you don't remember the cave we made the blizzard of twenty-seven?"

"Yes I do," Viola said. "We slept out in it and everything. Eddie was there."

"How long has it been since you've seen Eddie?"

When she drew from the cigarette, Ruby narrowed her eyes to squints, and so Viola did too. "I think it was that year."

"He was fifteen or sixteen. I was fourteen. You were just..."

"I was nine," Viola said. "Or ten."

"What do you know about him, Petunia?"

"He's been in prison."

"How did you find out?"

"Will and I read the letters he sent."

"What did you think?"

"About what?" Even the tiny amount of tobacco made Viola feel clear in the head but woozy in the stomach.

"About Eddie supposedly being in college and everything."

Viola was uncomfortable with the question. She remembered that Ruby was always pointing out Mama's failings and inconsistencies and trying to get everybody to take sides against her. Ruby could be really hard, taking stands on things that didn't seem to make any difference.

"It's not really a lie," Viola said. "About Eddie."

"Oh, Petunia," Ruby said, and drew on her cigarette and looked away.

"Well it isn't. He was taking college classes. By correspondence. From the University of Montana. He's a chess champion, too, or something like that."

"What did she tell you about me?"

"Not much," Viola said. "You never wrote. Or if you did Mama hid the letters better than she hid Eddie's."

"But the last you heard...?"

"You were at the Deaconess Hospital. In Nurses' School."

Ruby passed the cigarette and gave Viola a look.

"Weren't you?"

"Hardly."

"Did you have a baby? What happened to it? Was it adopted?" The words spilled out of Viola.

After a small hesitation Ruby said, "...Yeah."

"Was it a boy or a girl?"

"What's the diff?"

Viola thought about this. It seemed to her that it did make a difference, but she didn't want to start disagreeing with Ruby. She knew how Ruby loved to argue, and this wasn't something she wanted to argue about.

"Lots of people get adopted," Ruby said.

"Sure. I know that."

"Mama was adopted, for Christ sake."

"I know."

"...and missed being a princess, so she raised us to be some kind of ... "

"That's just what Papa Swan says," Viola said. "It doesn't make it true."

This made Ruby laugh her delighted-sounding laugh. "Oh, Petunia. You are so sharp."

Viola reached for the cigarette and took a tiny puff. "I'm going to be a singer," she said, surprising herself for blurting this out to Ruby.

"Oh, baby," Ruby said, and shook her head.

"Except that I really am."

"Yeah. And I'm gonna be the Queen of Sheba."

Viola was surprised that Ruby would hurt her feelings like that and not support her. Mama always supported her.

"What are you doing, then, if you're not being a nurse?" Viola hadn't asked this question earlier, not wanting to risk hurting Ruby's feelings. But now she didn't care.

"Well. Actually. I guess if it's true Eddie is in college, then it's true that I'm a nurse," Ruby said, and they both laughed at that, though Viola wasn't quite sure what was funny. Then they were quiet, passing the last of the cigarette. Viola understood by the answer that Ruby didn't want to talk about her employment, and that was all right with Viola. She knew what some of the women who worked for Shorty Young did for a living. She hoped it wasn't that.

"Did Mama talk to you about boys?" Ruby asked.

"Sure. Sure she did."

"Did she tell you that you're going to want to make babies? Did she tell you that you're going to fall in love with some boy and all you'll be able to think about is making babies?"

"I doubt it," Viola giggled.

"You remember the prairie chickens we saw on the hike we took outside Cottonwood?" Ruby asked, and she started to grin, and that made Viola grin too. "You remember how we found them mating that time, and you could walk right up to them and they didn't even notice you? Strutting around? Showing off for each other? We thought it was so funny. And you remember Eddie's dog and the neighbor's dog? That Sunday when Pastor Griggs was visiting. How nobody could do anything to make them stop until Papa Swan kicked them and broke his toe. Remember?"

Viola rolled on the floor of the snow cave, laughing, tears in her eyes.

"People get like that. You'll get like that," Ruby said.

"Some people get like that. Maybe. But not me," Viola said finally, when she got her breath back. She knew that Ruby always exaggerated.

"*All* people get like that. It's called falling in love," Ruby said, getting serious. "And it's going to happen to you pretty soon."

"I'm not going to have a family till after my career as a singer is over."

'Oh, Petunia," Ruby said.

There was a long silence and then Viola asked the question she'd been wanting to ask. "Was it hard? Being pregnant and having a baby?"

"You're sick. You're fat. Nobody's interested in you. You can't go anyplace and dress up. Pregnancy is all they ever said it would be and way worse."

"Was it a boy or a girl?"

"Girl. So what?"

"Did you give her a name?"

"Why do you care?"

"It's my niece. It's Mama's granddaughter."

"You don't get to give it a name if you give it away."

"Who did you give it to? Were they nice?"

"They took care of it at the hospital. I don't know. I don't care. What I do know, baby sister, is that you'll get pregnant, too, if you don't take care of yourself. Do you know how?"

"How to what?"

"To take care of yourself. Mama never talked to me about any of this stuff. She probably didn't know herself."

"Know what?" Viola said.

"How to keep from getting knocked up."

"Rubyyyyy!" Viola covered her face

"Listen now. This is important. You take a piece of sponge about the size of your thumbnail and put two drops of Lysol on it and—"

"Rubyyyyy!"

"And you put it up there. Before. Not after. Some people say do it after, but that makes no sense. Are you listening?"

"Yes," Viola said, blushing. She could not imagine doing what Ruby suggested and knew she'd have no occasion to do so.

"So. You want to be a singer, you come to Great Falls," Ruby said. "I haven't told this to anyone, but I'm on my way to Great Falls. I'm going to start my own business down there." She patted her little white purse.

"You're going to open a business?" Viola said. That seemed extremely bold, and it made her proud of her sister.

"I kept my eyes open around Shorty Young. Don't kid yourself. They talk about the depression, but there's money out there, and I know how to make lots of it." She tossed her head and gave Viola an imperial look, then crawled out of the snow cave.

DECEMBER 24

17

At first light Adelia rose from her rocker to make up the fire with the last of the kindling, setting a few small pieces of coal into the firebox. Then she left for Sullivan's to take the calf off Millie so they would have milk tonight. She'd been awake most of the night, praying, sleeping in snatches, waking over and over to Swan's wall-rattling snores from the bedroom. As the hours passed she heard the wind begin to die, slowly subsiding until finally only stillness was left. Even under her blankets she felt the temperature drop. Even further.

Halfway to Sullivan's, walking on top of the solid, curved drifts, the sub-zero snow squeaking with every step and her nostrils stinging with the crisp, new-dawn air, Adelia felt surprisingly calm. The first rays were lightening the sky behind the Sweetgrass Hills. Someplace between here and there was her sweet William, but she knew with certainty, somehow, that he was all right. Something was wrong, but it was not with William.

Adelia wished she weren't so guarded around Rubyann, wished that so much of what her daughter did and said didn't seem callous. She longed to feel the swelling of the old love for her little Sweet Cakes, the name she called Rubyann as a child.

Rubyann seemed more irritable than ever, coiled to pounce on the first thing that annoyed her. She got up very late, and after a long time silently grooming herself, began to play solitaire on the table, one game after the next, slapping the cards, her slippered feet twitching under her chair, her cigarette butts filling a canning lid she used for an ashtray. She utterly ignored Swan, and Swan utterly ignored her.

"Why did you give him your bed?" Ruby had asked suddenly when Swan had gone out to the truck.

"Why, I'd offer my bed to any guest," Adelia said.

"Except that 'any guest' would not accept it."

"What are you saying?" Adelia heard herself ask sternly.

"I'll tell you why, Mama. Because he's a man, that's why, and men get to make all the rules."

Adelia thought it best to let the topic die without a response, and so she did. Along with the topic of what was the fate of Rubyann's baby. At least they hadn't started fighting yet, or exchanging hard words, as it had been so often before she left. Adelia was determined not to fight or exchange hard words during this visit. And not let Swan do it either. All she wanted was to keep the peace.

Rubyann appeared to be healthy and was certainly as feisty as ever. Though she'd just lost her job, she didn't appear to be concerned about that. Did she have some savings? It seemed unlikely. And what was she going to do about a gift for Rubyann? Here was her much-longed-for first-born daughter back home, and tomorrow was Christmas, and she didn't have a gift for her. With all the preparations for the dance tonight there would be little time to make anything, even to finish Edward's shirt, before he arrived today. If he arrived. She couldn't allow herself to think about her fears.

Adelia wondered if she dared talk to Rubyann about the dance. Remind her how things were in small towns. Remind her how hard teaching jobs were to get, and how easily they were lost. But Rubyann was always so defensive and ready to be offended. How could she say these things? How could she not say them? At least she had to think of a gift. Was there a book she could give her? Could she give Rubyann her copy of *Titcomb's Letters*?

The moment Adelia thought of it she knew it was the right gift. It was something that she had prized all her adult life. It was a part of herself, really. If only Rubyann would read it and take it to heart. She thought that she might leave bookmarks in the chapters on "Manners and Dress" and "Bad Habits."

Titcomb's Letters had been a source of comfort to her, an important guide in her own life. The book, leather bound with marbled paper inside the covers, had been a wedding gift from Mr. Durris.

She'd written to thank Mr. Durris for the book, one of a number of letters sent the first few years she and Swan were trying to learn to farm wheat, but they were all unanswered, and she knew she was no longer part of the Durris family. Still, she never opened the book without a sense of gratitude. Certain chapters had been required reading for each of her children as they reached different stages in life, and certain chapters were read again and again as punishment for misdeeds. Several times she had made Rubyann read "The Beauty and Blessedness of Female Piety," but she had never been successful in getting Swan to read "Special Duties of the Husband."

Swan. Adelia admitted to herself that there were things about Swan hidden away inside herself that she didn't want to think about: how it felt to be spooned in bed with him on cold nights, how he'd scratch her back sometimes when she couldn't sleep, rub her shoulders when they were sore, and she'd rub his back and bush his hair, and he'd braid hers, back when it was long and thick. How proud she had been of her family when they were together, how grateful when he would arrive with his plans and promises. She gloried when he was there to accompany them to church. His appearance cooled the ardor of the local bachelor farmers and stilled the tongues of the gossips, at least for a while.

The minute she opened the barn door Millie headed for the stanchion, waiting for her ground barley, the calf following her, butting the empty bag. Millie kicked fitfully at him. Adelia herded the calf into its separate pen and gave Millie a good ration of hay and went to the feed room and brought her an extra helping of ground barley. She went to the well and pumped two buckets for the water trough.

"You'll have to wait till tonight for more milk, Junior," Adelia told the calf. "We all will."

The radio was playing when she got back to the house. Viola had made oatmeal and was whipping up biscuits. The oven was almost hot enough to bake in, but just a few feet away it was very cold. Swan was wrapped in his overcoat, sitting in the rocking chair, drinking coffee. The stock report was followed by the long grain report, and then the weather forecast, which was for fair and warming with the possibility of chinook winds, a big change. The news reported the severity of the blizzard that had swept across the whole tier of northern states from Montana east. Then came the news Adelia had been waiting for.

> *The statewide manhunt for the killer of well-known Cottonwood merchant Meyer Stallcop was called off earlier today when Montana State Patrol discovered the frozen body of James Charles Stanley in the Stallcop's stolen Studebaker. The vehicle apparently left the road south of Havre and rolled into a ravine. Recovered with the body were a number of items stolen in Cottonwood, along with what is believed to be the murder weapon. Stanley, twenty-four years old, has been a resident of Great Falls since his release two months ago from Deer Lodge Penitentiary and has been a suspect in a series of rural robberies. There is no evidence to suggest that accomplices were involved, officials say.*

Adelia felt faint with relief. It wasn't Edward after all. He would be home.

18

Though he'd woken up over and over with a burning ache in his toes and on the side of his right foot, Will was almost warm under the thick layer of hay, his bedroll wrapped close with only his nose sticking out. In the night, waking over and over, he was aware of the dying wind, and towards dawn, the ringing silence.

He heard Cecil moving, and then Pastor Bakke. With the blizzard over, Will knew they would start home as soon as they could get the animals harnessed.

Downstairs, wordlessly, Will began to work on Stubb, and Cecil rubbed down Jubal. There was frost on every crack on the walls inside the barn, and the water in the troughs was frozen so thick Will had to stomp it with his good foot to break it out. Immediately the animals drank.

Pastor Bakke climbed down from the loft. He spoke softly to Cecil.

"Chopper's feet are swelled and blistered. He can't get his shoes on, and his hands are stiff."

"I'll help. Let's get him down the ladder," and at that moment Peter Bolechek stepped out of the feed room, letting out blue smoke and light, and invited them in for oatmeal and coffee.

Chopper could not hold a knife to butter his toast or a spoon to feed himself, so Will fed him before he ate his own oatmeal. The end of Chopper's nose was capped with a shiny black shell, and his cheeks were blistered in a way that indicated they too would soon have black caps. Still, Chopper didn't seem to be very aware of his condition. He was utterly focused on the oatmeal.

Outside, as earliest dawn pinked the edge of the Bear Paws, Mr. Bolechek poured half a pail of hot water on the pump to get the handle free, and then he primed with the rest, pouring steadily and slowly into the shaft to free the plunger deep in the pipe. The steam rose against the bright new morning sky.

Just as they were leaving, Mrs. Bolechek, all bundled up with a bright scarf around her neck, brought out a half dozen hot potatoes wrapped in a flour sack.

"We use them to keep warm on the buggy," she said. "Then you can eat."

They had been on the move for several hours before Will saw the tops of Sage Prairie's two grain elevators on the horizon. Stubb and Jubal seemed eager to get back and needed no encouragement to trot, and the wagon slipped easily over the hard snow, all of them riding. Soon Will could see the black dot of Mama's little house. Will knew Cecil would swing by to let him off.

As they neared, Will saw the outline of a truck half covered with a snowdrift in front of the house. He also saw someone standing on the front step and knew it was Mama. Even after he could read Baskin's Products on the side of the truck, it did not register immediately in Will's consciousness that the truck belonged to his father. When it did register, Will found himself immediately angry. He didn't want to see him, had assumed that he never would have to see him again.

Mama stood on the front step, bouncing up and down. She was waving as if he might not see her. Will had decided that it was best to tell her right away about his decision to go back to Cottonwood, to get it over with, and again he went over all the reasons why it was right and necessary. There wasn't going to be any Christmas to spoil anyway. He'd just blurt it out and have it done. That way he could start teaching Viola to milk. She should have learned a long time ago. He'd leave a few days after Christmas. He'd ask Mama for the rest of his harvest money and just get on the Goose and go. He'd be one less mouth for her to feed.

But seeing her there, so happy to see him, he began to weaken. How could he arrive and suddenly tell her he was going to leave? How could he scare her as he knew he just had, with her weak heart, and then abandon her? But how could he not?

And how could he not tell her about Pastor Bakke's unexpected offer? Will knew exactly how she would react. She would see it as heaven sent, the opportunity of a lifetime. How could he possibly say he's leaving and not taking Bakke's offer?

Papa Swan joined Mama on the step and waved as Will got off the wagon. He was wearing a gartered, puffed-sleeve white shirt and narrow black suspenders. "Hello, son," he shouted, his hands cupped around his mouth. "Bet you didn't expect to see me here!" Then he went inside the house and shut the door. Will turned and waved goodbye to Cecil and Pastor Bakke.

"Oh, Will," Mama said when he got to the step. "Are you're all right?" She hugged him harder than he could remember being hugged. She'd been baking and had flour on her apron. Some of it stayed on Will's new coat. He brushed it off.

"How long has he been here?"

"He got here just as the blizzard started. Ruby's here too."

"Ruby?" He wondered if she had her baby with her, but knew better than to ask. He wasn't supposed to know about the baby.

"And Eddie will probably be here on the afternoon Goose," Mama said.

"Eddie!" It seemed impossible.

When Eddie was sent to reform school, it broke Will's heart. In all their moving, Will had never made real friends, but Eddie had always been his friend. Eddie could make up stories almost as good as having a book read to you. He invented games. He made everything fun, somehow, even hard things like moving. He could always make Will laugh.

"Do you know how long he'll be here?"

"I just got a short letter saying he was on his way."

"How'll we do it?" Will asked. "Did Ruby bring a bedroll?"

"No."

"Let's hope Eddie does."

"We'll manage," Mama said. "We'll manage. We always do." She gave him another hug. "I'm so glad you're all right."

Inside the house the air was full of the rich, sweet smell of freshly baked bread. He'd eaten the Bohunk's hot potato, skin and all, before it had cooled, but it hadn't done much to ease his hunger.

Papa Swan was sitting in Mama's rocker by the range. "Come over here, son, and let me have a look at you," he said. "You've filled out. You've got your height. You turned into a man since the last time I looked." Viola stood behind Papa Swan, brushing his hair with a wooden handled brush.

"A handsome one, too," Ruby said. "How are you Billy Boy?" She was playing solitaire on a corner of the table.

"Cold, hungry, and tired," Will said. He looked at the egg basket and saw it was empty. "Are we out of eggs?" he asked. He'd been counting on frying up some eggs the minute he got home.

"I need every egg for sandwiches, Will," Mama said. She'd gone back to rolling out dough for more bread. "We put the calf on Millie during the storm, so we have no milk for oatmeal either. I went over early to separate them, so we'll have milk tonight. What we do have is plenty of fresh bread and butter. Viola, cut him a fresh end piece."

"I'll do it," Ruby said. She came up close and touched him on the cheek. "It's nice to see you," she said, and he could tell she meant it.

"It's nice to see you too," Will said. Ruby was wearing a powerful perfume and dressed up as though ready to go someplace. Will was surprised at how much older she looked than even a year ago, when he'd last seen her.

"I'm sorry you've come home to a house without many provisions, son." Papa Swan said from the rocking chair. "We had roast chicken two days ago and chicken soup and my famous dumplings yesterday with the left-overs. I was intending to go out and see if I couldn't hunt up a couple of rabbits."

"Well, there's plenty of rabbits out there," Will said. Papa Swan went back to reading.

Will looked at the wrapped presents under the decorated tree with a sinking feeling, wondering if he should ask Mama for some of his wages so he could buy presents at George's store. Ruby handed him a piece of buttered bread, then sat down at her game of solitaire. Will sat down with her on an apple-crate chair.

"How have you been, Ruby?"

"Fabulous." Ruby said with a big smile, but her eyes darted away. "I've been fabulous. Couldn't be better."

"That true?"

"No," Ruby said. She made a funny face. "Actually the place where I was living burned down with all my stuff in it." She blew a long stream of smoke. "I mean ALL my stuff!"

It had been hard for Will to see Ruby leave. The house in Cottonwood felt empty without her. After Eddie was sent to reform school, she'd always been the leader on adventures. When they scared up a bird, Ruby was the first to find the nest. She always found the most arrowheads. But Ruby could be as sharp and hard as an arrowhead herself when she was in one of her moods, especially after Eddie was gone and she'd been the one in charge. She could be mean.

"I can't wait to hear about what happened to you in the blizzard," Viola said, still stroking the brush through Papa Swan's hair.

"We were so worried," Mama said.

Will ate the slice of bread and then a second as he told the story of chopping up the sideboards, of sawing down the wheel spokes, of Chopper getting lost, of their finding the Bohunk's barn.

"You get to have all the fun," Viola said. Will put his shoes next to the range to dry and removed his socks to have a good look at his feet. The aching toes on his right foot were bright red and slightly swollen and shiny. He knew he'd be expected to walk over to the Sullivan place to do the milking, and he wondered how he was going to do it. He wondered if he could ask Papa Swan. Mama was going to be so busy getting ready for the dance.

The warmth in the room made him tired. He ate another slice of bread and then went to lie down on Mama's bed. He covered himself with all the blankets in the house.

19

How good the warmer air felt as Adelia walked down High Grade Road, how clean its fragrance after the smothering tobacco and coal smoke and wet wool of her little house. Though she squinted against it and had a bonnet pulled low for shade, the sun's brilliance on the crisp snow made her eyes water. She walked slowly, in her loose galoshes, trying not to think about the two unpleasant tasks she had in front of her. First, she had to break a promise to Will, and a tacit one to herself. She had to take most of what remained of his summer wages and pay down her bill at George's store so she could get more groceries. She would have talked to him about it, but there was no way to do so in the crowded house. Even if it had been only Will and Viola, she would have had to find some way to get more provisions to tide them all over until her next paycheck: flour and now sugar and oatmeal and a ham bone, if George had one. Two large fresh onions and mustard for the egg sandwiches. More potatoes. They were nearly out of everything. And then she had to meet the Goose.

She did not like to acknowledge her fear of seeing Edward again. His letters, always full of interesting observations, well-turned phrases, and sometimes wicked humor, had lately revealed a new side of him. More thoughtful. He was reading Emerson, he said. He had always been a good writer, had grasped Latin more quickly than any of the others, and had been a voracious reader from very early. It had been easy to just let him read on his own in classrooms where he was always so far ahead of others. Things which didn't come easily, he did not do. Would not do. Of all her children, he was the most stubborn and willful. And now he would be home with Swan, whom she blamed for his worst traits and whom he resembled the most in character. Though she resented Swan for not being there to father Will and Viola, with one part of herself she also believed that his absence had saved them from being exposed to the arrogant attitudes and selfish behaviors that Edward and Rubyann had absorbed.

Would Edward have plans? Would he stay long? He would not have any money to help with provisions, of course. And where would he sleep?

She fingered Will's money in her pocket. After the Montgomery Wards order for his coat and gloves, twenty-six dollars were left. How much would George require to open the credit again? She'd started off in arrears, since she had only cook's wages for Cecil's threshing crew in the fall, and now, only four and a half months into the teaching year, she was in arrears at George's store for almost forty-five dollars, since she needed to send her first two months' pay to the Cottonwood Mercantile to settle the debt she left there.

The windows of George's general store were frosted over,

and a thin wisp of blue smoke rose from his chimney into the endless sky. Outside she saw a vehicle she did not recognize, a Packard sedan. She had hoped the store would have no other customers so that her discussions would not be overheard. Anything overheard by anyone was quickly repeated and repeated again and again in Sage Prairie, and exaggerated, she knew, at each telling.

Adelia stamped the snow from her limp, leaky galoshes and entered the store. George saw her and held her eyes for a moment, and Adelia recognized in them his belief that he was in for a new begging. Adelia put her mind from this and inhaled the fragrances of millinery and meat, apples and ointment.

George was a tall, stooped man with a bulbous nose and squinty eyes behind his glasses, always wearing what Adelia considered a filthy apron. He was extremely clever with sums. She had seen him calculate long rows of numbers in his head much more quickly than she could, and she knew herself to be quick with numbers. He was adding sums now for a woman Adelia could not identify who chattered about the blizzard. They had lost a steer and her husband was looking for it with his tractor. Even the vinegar in their larder had frozen. Since Adelia had never seen her in church, she assumed the woman was a Catholic. She wanted to ask her about Father Piletti and the Tuma twins, but she knew George would already have this information.

George helped the Catholic lady to the Packard with the groceries and then came back inside, the grim expression on his face of someone who has a difficult prospect ahead of him.

"Merry Christmas, George," Adelia sang. "I have a payment for you on my account."

If he was surprised, he didn't show it. He took his place behind the counter. "Merry Christmas, Mrs. Anderson. I'm glad to hear that Cecil and the others didn't get caught in the storm."

"Oh they got caught all right," Adelia said. "Will had some stories when he returned. It was touch and go for a while. How about Father Pilletti?"

George was a Lutheran, and his eyes took on a sparkle. "I hear he might lose his nose."

"Lose his nose?" Father Pilletti was known widely for his beaked proboscis.

"Turning black, they say. Tuma Twins have frostbit feet. But they brought back good trees again. All the Catholics have trees." He smiled as if this pleased him.

"Well, I have twenty dollars for you today," Adelia said. "And I trust that you will open up my credit. My son Edward is expected on the afternoon Goose, my daughter Rubyann and my husband, Swan, arrived yesterday. The whole family is here, and there is precious little in the cupboard. I am depending upon your Christmas spirit." Adelia forced a little laugh and smiled.

George took the four five-dollar bills. "Must be crowded," he observed. He opened his cash drawer and lifted the change holder and slipped the bills under it.

"We're just happy to be together and have a roof over our heads and a little coal for the stove. But as you can imagine, I must have extra provisions."

"We have to come to an agreement about your credit, Mrs. Anderson," George said, looking at her over the top of his glasses and wiping his large hands on the apron. "This brings you down to ten dollars and twenty eight cents, which is nearly half a month's wages for you, I believe. I can't let you go more than a month's wages again, so I can let you have only eight dollars—"

"And seventy two cents. I understand," Adelia said. "And I appreciate your generosity of spirit." She smiled again to show she meant no sarcasm. It was not all she had hoped for, but if sales at the dance were good, they could survive until her next month's wages are paid.

But how could she repay Will?

Adelia kept a careful tally of the costs of the items she selected. For the sandwiches she needed three onions and six pickles. She needed cornmeal for the dance floor. She needed flour and salt and sugar and oatmeal and bulgar. She needed potatoes. George had some withered carrots and beets, and she took two of each.

"So I guess there'll be a dance tonight after all," George said.

"Oh, I hope so, George. I truly do." Adelia said. "I think everybody could use a little festivity after the blizzard."

"And I guess we'll be seeing your whole family there."

"You will if Edward is on the Goose."

George glanced at the clock on the wall. "Won't be long," he said.

George tallied her purchase. She came within a nickel of her limit. Pleased with her accounting, she gathered the groceries.

"Merry Christmas, George. Hope to see you at the dance," she said, and left the store.

Adelia considered going to the post office, but she knew there would be no mail for her since Edward was on his way home, so she carried the two sacks of groceries to the station and sat in the tiny waiting room. She tried to generate the kind of excitement she would be feeling if it were Will coming home, or Viola, remembering how intensely she'd loved Edward as an infant, how he represented what she had longed for all her life, a family. She remembered his first steps, which had been toward her, his first word, which had been Mama.

She heard the Goose blow its whistle from far away, signaling those wanting to get on or get off to be ready. From the station platform she saw its cow-catcher plowing through drifts on the track, exploding clouds of dazzling white into the afternoon sunlight. The Goose slowed, then stopped, just briefly, and her Edward got off carrying a suitcase but no bedroll.

They looked at each other for a long moment. He was wearing a fashionable overcoat with creased trousers disappearing into the tops of new galoshes. His ears were bright red, and one cheek looked burned as well. Had he been out in the blizzard?

"Hello, Mama," Edward said, as the Goose lurched and lumbered away.

"Edward. I'm so happy to see you," she said.

He had a fresh haircut and was newly shaven. He'd broadened in the shoulders, and she wondered if she had made the yoke wide enough on his shirt. She was struck by how much he and William looked alike with the same flashing green eyes and thick hair.

"You're looking good, Mama," he said, and she knew this was not true. She was heavier by thirty pounds, or more, than when he had last seen her, and her hair turned half gray.

"You haven't changed," she said, realizing that after all this time they had greeted each other with lies. "Well, you couldn't have picked a better time," she continued. "You'll never believe it. Everybody's here."

"Everybody? You mean Papa?"

"Ruby got here day before yesterday in the middle of the blizzard. And yes, your father is here, too," she said.

Edward didn't respond for a moment. He seemed to be thinking over this information.

"I don't have enough presents," he said.

"I'm sure Rubyann and Swan won't expect you to have presents for them."

"How long has he been here?"

"Since day before yesterday."

"How long's he staying?"

"He hasn't said. Not long, I hope. I have these groceries," she said, indicating the sacks on the floor of the waiting room.

"The suitcase isn't so heavy. Why don't you carry that and I'll carry the groceries," Eddie said.

"Did the storm catch you?" Adelia asked.

"No. I was snug as a bug in a rug. Stayed one night in Great Falls. One night in Havre. Waiting it out."

"Why didn't you just come right through?"

"I...I had some shopping to do. At Buttrey's."

They walked across from each other, each in one of the snow tracks in the road, together but separated. This was going to be hard, Adelia realized. Harder than she thought. She wanted to ask him if he'd heard about Meyer Stallcop, but decided against it. Her mind searched for the right thing to say, but nothing was there. Their steps squeaked in the snow.

"I'm going to be an officer. In the Army," Eddie said at last.

"I thought..." she began.

"The felony will be expunged. You remember my writing about playing chess with the warden and with Chaplain Pierson? They arranged it."

"Oh. How wonderful for you, Edward. You'll make a fine officer," she said. Another lie. Edward had never been one to follow orders. Had prison changed that?

"I'll be getting good wages as an officer. I'll be able to send you money every month."

She looked again at his anxious smile. He wants to please me, she realized, and it gave her a thrill of pleasure to see that in him again. "You don't need to do that, Edward," she said.

"I want to. I want you to have an easier life, Mama."

"My life is pretty easy. I have a satisfying job here in Sage Prairie, which I hope to keep. I have Will and Viola. They're such a help."

"I'll come and visit in my uniform."

"I would like that. I would like that very much."

She wanted to ask him how long he was planning to stay, but decided against that too. Eddie turned to her and smiled as if he could read her mind.

"I'm expected at the induction center right away, so I won't be able to stay long."

"Oh, no," Adelia said. "I had hoped for a good long visit."

"I'll leave tomorrow."

"Tomorrow! Edward, that's not fair."

"Have to," he said.

They walked in silence. Finally Adelia had to set down the suitcase in the snow. "I thought you said it were light," she laughed.

"It's mostly your letters, Mama."

"You saved them?"

"Every one. I can't tell you how important those letters were to me. They kind of saved me, really."

"It was the least I could do. And I enjoyed yours."

"I should have written more often."

Adelia picked up the suitcases and they set off again.

"How's Will?" Eddie said after a few quiet steps.

"The move here to Sage Prairie wasn't easy for him," she said. "As I think I mentioned in my letters."

"And Viola?"

"Turning into a young lady. You'll be surprised at how tall she is. All of you are bigger than me now."

"How's Papa Swan?"

"He doesn't change," Adelia said, thinking nobody does, like the galloping Goose, around and around in the same tracks, making the same stops, utterly predictable. Even herself.

They walked along, each in a track on the road.

"Your ears look frostbit. When did that happen?"

"Took a walk around Havre in the storm. Stayed out too long."

"You should keep them covered." What kind of a mother am I? Adelia wondered. Why don't I know how to talk to my own grown son?

"I met a woman on the Goose down from Great Falls who owns the newspaper in Havre," Eddie said.

"You met a newspaper woman?"

"She offered me a job."

"Really?"

"As a reporter."

"Are you going to take it?"

"I'm obligated to go into the army. But she offered me a job."

"You always were a good writer," Adelia said. Something true at last. She could picture Edward as a reporter easier than she could see him in a military uniform.

"The sun sure is bright," Edward said, shifting the groceries.

"Yes. It is very bright. It feels like a chinook is on its way."

"Is that it?" Eddie said. "Is that home?" The converted grain bin with a lean-to was just ahead, sitting alone not far off the road.

"Yes," Adelia said. "That's it. That's home."

20

Eddie saw the teacherage was small and isolated, stark on the endless, flat, snow-smothered plain and without a single tree or bush around it. Behind the leaning outhouse was a low-roofed chicken coop, a drift to its eve, with some rusted machinery sticking out of the snow. Someone had dug a cave in the drift. Another drift, oddly studded with icicles, climbed up the south side of the house. In front of the house was Papa Swan's Baskin's truck.

The two bags of groceries had grown heavy, and he could detect a damp vegetable smell coming up. Was it onion? His sore left arm could hold the bag against his body, but he could not lift it up. He heard himself clear his throat, again and again. It was raw from all the cigarettes. His left ear continued to ring.

"Will's sleeping and Swan is out hunting rabbits for stew," Mama said.

There was something about Mama he had not expected, a

withholding, a reserve, a distancing politeness, and he found himself mirror that back to her, a survival reflex learned in prison. All of the exuberance he had felt during the Goose ride from Havre had dissolved almost immediately after he saw the anxious look on her face on the station platform.

The kitchen side of the tiny house was covered with at least a dozen loaves of baked bread, and a laundry line had been strung across the room. The windows were completely frozen over, which explained why Ruby and Viola hadn't seen Mama and him coming.

Ruby was playing solitaire when Mama and Eddie opened the door. Her hair was dyed, he saw right away, cut short and done up in the same waves he'd seen on models in magazines at the library. She wore a red beret, angled to the side, and a white purse at her waist, the narrow strap strung over her opposite shoulder like a bandoleer. She got up and stood by the table with her hands on her hips. She was wearing a long wool skirt that showed her figure and a heavy sweater that did not.

"The prodigal son," she said, as if she was not sure whether she were glad to see him or not.

"The black sheep. Baaa!" Eddie said, and they both laughed. He took off his new overcoat and hung it on a nail next to the door. He was glad to see that Ruby was here. She could be stubborn and abrasive, but she was funny and quick-witted, and they had been best friends growing up.

"Billy Boy's sleeping in the lean-to," she said and nodded to a closed door. "He got caught out in the blizzard."

"Is he ok?"

"Frost bit feet is all. Looks like your ears got nipped. Nice suit. Where's your tie?" Ruby asked.

"In my pocket," Eddie said.

"Forgot how to tie it?"

"Never knew."

"I'll help you with that," Ruby said. Her eyes said: *we know something about the world the rest of them don't.*

"Hi Eddie," Viola stepped forward awkwardly and held out her hand to be shaken. She was as tall as Ruby, if not taller, with glossy hair and luminous eyes under heavy lashes. "Nice to see you," she said.

He had imagined this moment many times—arriving home in his new suit, wearing his new shoes. Here it finally was, and he felt conspicuous and awkward. He almost wished he had his old release clothes on.

"You sure look pretty," he said to Viola, and she blushed.

The tree, strung with popcorn and hung with paper ornaments, took up an entire corner of the house, and under it were brightly wrapped presents. He opened his suitcase and Viola watched as he took out his presents and put them under the tree. She immediately picked hers up and shook it, grinning.

"Something pretty," Eddie said. He could not remember a Christmas with so many presents under their tree. He was surprised to see the radio. It looked brand new.

"Can I make you a cup of tea?" Mama asked. "Let's make a whole pot of tea for Edward. I've got some black tea set aside for a special occasion. This is as special an occasion as happens at my house. I propose to make a pot."

Ruby and Viola both said, "I'll take a cup" at the same time, and then had a good laugh.

"And if we're going to get the supper sandwiches done we'd better get started. I need some help. Would you mind chopping eggs, Edward? Here. I have them all boiled up. Rubyann, you were always the best mayonnaise maker. Can you whip some up now? I saved out some fresh eggs, and we have fresh oil. Viola, here are the onions to grate. Busy hands—"

"—are happy hands. We know, Mama. And idle hands are the devil's workshop," Ruby said. Just like when she was younger, she didn't seem to realize how sharp an edge her words sometimes carried, even though she laughed.

"Well, I'm off to visit a friend," Mama said, and took her coat from its hook by the door and went to the outhouse. Eddie wondered if her feelings were hurt.

"Jesus, Eddie. You're out of prison two days and you come home dressed up like a North Dakota bootlegger." Ruby said.

"What the hell did you do to ruin your hair?"

"This is the height of fashion. But what would you know about that?"

"Is that what all the nurses are wearing? Heard you were a nurse."

"Regular Florence Nightingale. Heard you were in college."

"Magna Cum Laude."

"Same to you, buster," Ruby said and gave him her great laugh and Eddie laughed too.

The loaves were cooled enough so they could be stacked, so Ruby and Eddie cleared a section of the kitchen counter and went to work on the large pan containing several dozen hard-boiled eggs, cracking off the shells and mashing the yokes and whites. Eddie dropped the egg shells into the garbage at his feet.

"How've you been, Ruby?" Eddie said.

"Top of the world. And you?"

"Can't complain," Eddie said. "Well, I can, but I won't." They laughed again.

"Is there a dance, then?" Eddie said. "Tonight?"

"Fulps," Viola said.

"They're still playing?"

"And Mama's still selling suppers."

Viola had been chopping pickles and when she was done she handed him Mama's kitchen knife. He remembered it well. It was dull. After Papa taught him how, he'd always kept Mama's knives sharp, but a poor blade won't hold an edge very long. He was thinking of giving Mama her gift of the knife set now, when she got back from the outhouse, when Ruby spoke.

"It's good to see you, Eddie. You look like a damn movie star, actually," she said, as if reluctantly admitting something.

Ruby had her own method of making mayonnaise. She warmed a bowl and then heated the oil to just the right temperature. Mama had a whisk, and it made Eddie feel good to see Ruby whipping up the eggs and oil into her mayonnaise again.

"You look like a chorus girl," Eddie said.

"I am one. Or I was. In Shorty Young's Honky Tonk."

"I heard the Honky Tonk burned down," Eddie said. He chopped the eggs, wishing he could use one of Mama's new knives.

"I know. I know. I was there."

"When it burned?"

"I had a room of my own in the Havre Hotel and it burned down too. All my stuff burned up. Almost."

"Where's your kid?"

"Adopted." Ruby shrugged. "How was Deer Lodge?"

"Worse than you might guess in some ways. There are some really mean people there. Mostly the guards. In other ways it wasn't so bad. I was left alone. I had a lot of time to read. I played a lot of chess." For a moment he considered mentioning his games with Shorty Young, but decided against it.

"I've learned a few games myself," Ruby said under her breath, then caught his eyes with that conspiratorial look. "I'm going to start my own little business in Great Falls. I am. You watch."

"Ruby the businesswoman?" Eddie said.

"You wait and see."

"I will." Eddie chopped the last of the eggs

"How long you staying, Eddie?"

"Tomorrow. Next day. Then I'm off to Officers Training School."

"I don't know where you'll sleep," Ruby said. "Or if there's even an extra blanket. They let the fire go out here at night. Gets cold as a well-digger's...belt buckle."

Eddie saw Viola paying attention to every word. "I'll manage," he said.

"I've got more blankets than I need," Viola said. "Ruby and I can sleep with our coats on."

"Or you can sleep with Papa Swan in the big bed," Ruby said, grinning. "Mama won't."

Mama returned from the outhouse. "Here comes Swan," she said. "Looks like he has some rabbits."

The windows were melting clear, and Eddie rubbed a space on one of them to look out. There was Papa in his long black coat. Eddie was eager to see Papa Swan in one way, but in another he was still feeling angry with him for never writing. Not even a card. His infrequent visits to the family had always been unannounced, and Eddie had half expected an unannounced visit from Papa Swan at Miles City, then at Deer Lodge. Every birthday especially.

"Eddie. My son," Papa cried when he came in the door. He took off his gloves and put both his hands on Eddie's hand as they shook, holding it a long time. "You look like a million bucks," he said. "Look at you," he boomed.

"Shhhh," Ruby said, pointing to the closed bedroom door.

Papa Swan looked exactly as he had the last time Eddie saw him, the last Christmas they'd both been home. Papa had brought presents for everyone that time, too. A compass for Will. A bone-handled jackknife for himself, which he'd kept sharp and carried always until they took it from him when he went into the state industrial school. Papa'd brought a porcelain doll for Viola and a box of watercolor paints for Ruby. He'd brought popcorn and oranges and apples and nuts and candy. It had been their best Christmas. The last one when they were all together.

The bedroom door opened and Will came out. He looked haggard and exhausted. He had his whiskers now and needed a shave. He shook Eddie's hand a single shake, and said hello, glad to see you. There was something wary in his tired eyes as he looked over Eddie's suit and new shoes.

"How you been?" Eddie asked. "You got caught in the blizzard, huh?"

"Yeah. Your ears tell me you did too," Will said.

"Are you okay?"

"I'll be fine. I'm just tired and hungry."

Papa began to issue orders in his booming voice. "Viola, you get the meat off these skinny rabbits. Do it carefully now. Take the scissors and cut off all the white. That's gristle. Then slice it into thin strips. Ruby, you—"

"I've already got my hands full, with the mayonnaise."

"I'll manage the stew," Mama said, looking at the mayonnaise Ruby was beating up. "I love the way you do that,

Rubyann. You have the touch. I could never make it come out like that."

"Where'd you get the radio?" Eddie asked. It was all he could do to keep from turning it on and searching for the news. He wanted to hear it again and again. Stanley had been found. The manhunt was over. He wanted Mama to hear it. It made him want to rejoice even thinking about it.

"Papa brought it for us," Viola said. Eddie saw that she looked toward Mama for a response, but Mama made none. She was ladling hot water into the stew pot.

Viola mixed the onion gratings into the chopped eggs along with the diced pickles, then Ruby poured the mayonnaise on and Eddie stirred it all together with a large wooden spoon. Papa Swan warmed himself by the fire.

"Mama, I'd like to give you my gift now," Eddie said, and he went to the tree and picked it up and handed it to her. He had written "To Mama," on the front with Pickett's pen, and "From Edward."

"Well, I'll give you your present now, too," Mama said and bent heavily to take a shirt-sized package from under the tree. He carefully unwrapped his package and held it in front of himself. It was a dark heavy flannel. A warm shirt. The cuffs weren't finished. He remembered other Christmases, getting a new shirt from Mama when he had hoped for something else. This year he was happy for the shirt.

"I'll measure your arms right now and finish it up," Mama said. "I just hope it's not too tight across the shoulders."

She unwrapped his gift carefully, saving the Buttrey's Christmas wrapping.

"Oh, Edward, this is the most thoughtful gift," she said.

"How long we've made do with those old knives." She folded the paper and set it aside. "Oh. I know you spent too much on these. Too much."

Eddie took the smaller of the knives and handed it to Viola. "This will make your job easier," he said. "I have to show you how to sharpen knives," he said to Will, who nodded.

"And who taught you?" Papa Swan asked.

"You did, Papa," Eddie said. "I'm sorry I don't have anything for you. If I'd known...."

"Don't mention it, since I have nothing for you, either. However, we have the unexpected pleasure of each other's company."

"I really liked that jackknife you brought last time," Eddie said. "I had it for a long time, till..." He stood there and Mama measured out his arm length. He didn't finish the sentence.

Papa Swan sat back in Mama's rocker near the stove, smoking his pipe and reading his book as though alone in the room. Will cut slices of bread with the new bread knife and Viola and Ruby made up the egg salad sandwiches, putting each finished sandwich in the milk bucket.

"Did you hear about Meyer Stallcop?" Swan asked.

"Saw it in the paper this morning," Eddie said, amazed at how calm he sounded. "Did you hear they caught the guy?"

"I don't like having a radio on all the time," Mama said.

"She made rules about the radio the minute it came in the door," Swan informed Eddie, and raised his eyebrows.

"We get Firestone Theater and Amos and Andy," Viola said. She had entirely stripped the meat from the first jackrabbit and was working on the second. The mound of red meat was smaller than her fist.

Will hid himself behind the line of drying clothes, but Eddie peeked and saw that Will had taken off his shoes and was looking at one of his feet.

"Got some frostbite?" Eddie asked. He ducked under the clothesline and saw that the two small toes of Will's right foot were bright red, along with an inch up the side of his foot.

"Looks like it."

"What's that?" Swan said, getting up from the rocker and joining them. "Damn, son, you do. Let's see the other foot." Everybody gathered around Will while he took his other foot out of his stocking. It was still pale with cold, but there were no red spots.

"I'll get some snow. Always rub snow on frostbite," Swan said.

"Absolutely not," Mama said, coming close. "Warm water is what he needs."

"Woman, I know about these things."

"Swan, your children have had frostbite before," she said. "Ruby, when you're done with that bowl, please ladle some warm water in it. Baby-water warm. For Will's feet."

"You're going to lose some skin, son," Swan said. "I've got some salve to keep the infection out. You aren't going to be cutting any fancy dance moves tonight," he said, and laughed as if that were funny.

Eddie didn't think frostbite was funny. He knew that his stinging ears had to be bright red, too. He wanted to see what they looked like, but there were no mirrors sitting out, and he didn't want to draw attention to his ears by asking for one.

"Maybe Will and I'll stay home and play cribbage," Eddie said to no one in particular. "I'm not much of a dancer."

Ruby and Viola and Mama all protested at once, Mama

especially, reminding him that he was leaving tomorrow. She wanted to show off her family, she said, him in his new suit, and Viola said she wanted her friends to see her other brother, and Ruby said she would teach him how to dance all the new dances.

This is the way Eddie had thought it would be, the way it always was, with everybody busy or reading, dodging around each other in the small space. Bread smell in the air. Drawings on the walls. Mama always had lots of drawings on the walls. She herself could sketch and had taught all the kids perspective at an early age. There was the tree house picture he had drawn, what, eight years ago or more? He didn't want to go up and study it, but from across the room it was a pretty accurate representation of the tree house he'd made that summer in the big willow tree near the teacherage at Whitewater. Back when he was still a good, obedient boy, before Cottonwood, and before his sixteenth summer with Papa Swan and the Scaramouch gang.

There were several paintings on the wall that Ruby had done with the paint set Papa Swan had given her those years ago. A fawn they'd found and brought home, curled up with its feet tucked under itself like a cat. A meadowlark on a fence post. A crowing rooster. Mama had glued them to cardboard backing and put string across the back and hung them on nails. There were some drawings of horses, probably by Viola. There was nothing he could see that might have been made by Will.

Will seemed preoccupied. He had always been reserved and watchful, but never as withdrawn as he seemed now.

"I think I'll give you your present now, too, Will. Get it over with. Okay?" Eddie went to the tree and returned with the small box.

"Just like the one I gave you, Eddie," Papa said delightedly after Will had unwrapped the pocket knife.

"Thanks," Will said. He opened both blades. "I've wanted one for a long time, Eddie. One just like this. I've seen them in the stores."

"Watch out," Eddie said. "It's sharp. I'll show you how to keep it that way."

"This is expensive. How could you spend so much on presents?"

"I developed a little business in Deer Lodge that made some cash, and I saved it all."

"Just make sure you take care of it," Papa Swan said. "See this?" He took a folding knife out of one of his many pockets. "Do you know how long I've had this knife?"

"Since before you met Mama," Ruby and Eddie said as one.

Papa Swan got to his feet. "While I was out at the truck I thought of some appropriate gifts for you, Rubyann, and you, Eddie," he said.

Eddie saw Ruby send him a look.

"I hear your smoker's hack, Eddie." He removed a box of Baskin's cough drops from one of his coat pockets. "I remember that you used to go through a case of cough drops and take two or three out of every box, thinking I wouldn't notice. I noticed." He laughed his hearty laugh, and Viola laughed with him. "....and for you, Ruby. You used to want my face cream. Here is a whole jar of my best. Just for you."

"Thanks," Ruby said, but didn't look at him. She took a gift from under the tree and held it out to Mama. "I can't wait to give this to you," she said, and Mama unwrapped a large Bible with a heavy leather cover, embossed with a cross.

"Oh, Rubyann. This is just beautiful. Thank you."

"Now you can get rid of that old Gideon."

"Yes I can. This is a treasure, Ruby."

"Here," Ruby said. She took the book and opened it to its first pages. "This has a whole genealogy chart. I want you to sit right down and fill in the Kinkells."

"What about the Andersons? Is there a chart in there for my side, too?" Papa Swan asked, hurt.

"Yeah. There's a section for the Andersons," Ruby said to everybody else in the room. "It'll be interesting to see who's in that woodpile."

"We'll do it later," Mama said. "Since we're exchanging gifts early, here is mine for you, Rubyann." It was also clearly a book. Eddie hoped it wasn't the manners book, but there was something hopeful and innocent in Mama's eyes that made him realize that it was.

Mama handed Rubyann the gift. "I worried if this was a good gift or not. It's been such an important book for me."

Now Ruby had the book out of its wrappings. For a split second Eddie thought she was going to burst into belly laughs, but she didn't.

"How well I remember this book," Ruby said. "This is the one you got from Mr. Durris as a wedding present. I really can't take it, Mama."

"Please do, Rubyann."

"I see you've got a chapter with a bookmark in it," Ruby said, and glanced at Eddie. She opened the book and read the chapter title. "'The Beauty and Blessedness of Female Piety. Whew!"

"I just hoped...," Mama began.

"Thank you, Mama. I...I know what this book has meant to you, and I'll...I'll treasure it."

Eddie smiled. Ruby knew how to hurt people, but not this

time. He picked up Mama's new leather-covered Bible from under the tree. He'd often thought about owning a Bible, just having one around to thump when he needed to thump one. If he ever needed a Bible to thump, this was the kind of Bible he would have.

Viola hefted and shook his gift for her.

"Oh, all right," Eddie said, and told her to go ahead, and she had it open in a moment, tearing the paper."

"Viola, be careful to save the paper," Mama said, too late. Viola held the necklace in front of her. Eddie had taken his time picking it out. It was delicate, but with a sturdy clasp, the small lavender stones in gold settings.

"Amethyst," Eddie said, basking in Viola's delight. Yes. This was what he'd thought of when he thought of being home for Christmas.

"Oh, Eddie, this is beautiful!"

"Amethyst is your birthstone, isn't it?"

"I just love them."

"One more gift for Viola," Mama said, and held out a package which Viola opened carefully, saving the paper. It contained two dresses. There was a blue and white one with a lacy neck, but Viola seemed very surprised and delighted with the second dress. It had a flared skirt. It was yellow with white buttercups on it and a blue border at the neck and arms. Viola flew into the bedroom with it and was out in a moment wearing it and the amethyst necklace.

"Ruby. Pleeeeeese! Pleeeeeese! Pleeeeeese let me try on the silk stockings."

"Oh, Christ," Ruby said.

"Ruby!" Mama said. "Please."

Ruby went into the bedroom and Viola followed her, up on her toes with anticipation. It wasn't long before Viola came out wearing the white buttercup dress, the amethyst necklace, the silk stockings, and the high-heeled shoes. Ruby had tied a bright sash at Viola's waist and tilted the red beret on her head.

"I give you, tonight, Viola Anderson, who is going to do a torch song," Ruby said, and laughed her hard deep laugh.

"Rubyyyyy!" Viola said, but then she struck a pose.

Everybody just stared at Viola for a moment. Eddie realized for the first time that Viola was going to be a very beautiful woman, almost was one already.

"You're not going to the dance like that, are you?" Papa asked. He looked at Mama.

"Not wearing the beret, she's not. That's mine," Ruby said and snatched it off Viola's head. "And she's not wearing the silk stockings either. I am."

Viola held out a leg. "Silk stockings," she said. "Someday I'm going to have a pair for every day of the week."

21

Mama could have squeezed into the truck with Papa if she'd wanted to, but she said she preferred to ride in the back with Will. Eddie and Ruby said they would walk in later, after the dance got going. Viola rode in front with Papa, more excited than she could ever remember being about a dance, and she had always been excited about dances. She was wearing her new dress and Eddie's necklace, and she was going to dance the Charleston.

The chinook had blown steadily from the south since mid-afternoon, softening the hard surface of the snow, puddling up water up in the low places and making mud in the ruts. A nearly full moon had come up over the Bear Paws.

"Are you meeting a boyfriend at the dance, Petunia?" Papa asked. He had been drinking whiskey. Viola smelled it as soon as she got in the truck, even over the tobacco and all the other smells in there.

"I don't have a boyfriend," Viola said.

"You will. You will," Papa said, as though this did not please him. "And if you don't watch out, you'll wind up like Ruby."

"I like Ruby," Viola said.

"Well, of course you do. She's a regular firecracker. But you're not like her."

"What do you mean, Papa?"

"I mean that you are soft and sweet. You are meant for a different life, a life as a mother and a wife."

"Well, actually not, Papa. I really am going to be a singer."

"You have always had a fine voice with true pitch. I've heard it. But I think that you should have your sights set on more realistic goals."

"I know I'm going to be a singer, Papa," Viola said. "I know it."

"I hope you have a chance to sing, Petunia. I do. But promise me that you will stay with your mother and finish high school."

"Ruby said that she was going to open her own business in Great Falls. She said she'd make me a singer."

Viola could tell that Papa Swan was looking at her in the dark truck, but she didn't look back at him.

"It would be a very great mistake to let Ruby be your teacher in life," he said. "A very great mistake. You must promise me you will not do that."

"I can't promise you that, Papa."

"At least wait till after you graduate. Please promise me that."

Viola thought about it for a little while, and then she promised.

The Fulp brothers were at the Odd Fellows Hall with two carloads from Locklea who had shoveled snow from the road all the way down. A kerosene lantern threw a circle of light by the front door where the crippled brother had set up a cash box and a roll of raffle tickets on a small folding table. He had a stamp and inkpad to mark the backs of people's hands. The Fulps always held a raffle at midnight when everybody was eating supper, and gave away half the door receipts to the winner. Viola knew that many people came to the dances as much for the excitement of the raffle as for the dance. There were dances when the winning ticket was worth a month's teacher's wages.

The inside of the hall was cold, lit by two more kerosene lanterns at the edges of the stage. There was a full tinder box by the barrel stove, and Viola saw Will making a coal fire in it. Viola knew her job. She pumped a pail of water at the Sage Prairie store and poured the wash pan and the large coffee pot full, and put them on the barrel stove. She and Will had done this with Mama many times, and before her Eddie and Ruby had done the same thing.

The Fulps always set up the same. The crippled maintained his station at the door and the tall one made several trips to the car and returned with instruments in their cases. Viola went up on the stage to watch the tall one tune the violin and guitar and mandolin. It didn't matter that the hall was barely illuminated with only the two lanterns. He tuned with his eyes closed.

The saxophone didn't sound right to the tall Fulp, and Viola watched as he put in a new reed, which required much testing so he played a section of the Charleston. Viola absolutely could not stop herself from making a few moves, and the tall Fulp brother looked at her as he played.

"You a flapper?" he asked when he stopped playing.

Viola wanted to say something clever, but instead she heard

an embarrassed, little-girl giggle come out of herself. She suddenly decided to go outside and wait for Ruby and Eddie.

A tractor arrived, pulling a wagon of hay bales and people, all shouting and singing Christmas songs, and seeing that, Viola knew that in spite of the blizzard, everybody would be here, and it would be the best dance ever.

She saw that Papa Swan had parked his truck sideways next to the sidewalk. She thought that was rude and selfish to take up so many parking spaces, and she would have told him, but he was not there.

All the buildings and vehicles and buggies parked along the sidewalk cast long moon shadows on the snow. She saw that down the street the doors of the lumberyard were open, and when she walked down to see what was happening, she saw it was men, drinking whiskey. Just then a noisy three-car convoy, a Ford Roadster and two A Models, arrived, and Viola saw it was the young set from Simpson, including Bart Garsky, the star basketball player for Simpson High and who was thought to be attractive by Clara and the other girls. Several people who were standing around outside and many from the hay wagon went over to meet the Simpson crowd, and Viola joined them.

Viola saw that the Simpson bunch were all drunk. She heard them say they'd shoveled drifts off the road all the way over, starting early in the day with two quarts of blackleg.

Bart Garsky was talking the loudest.

"I tell you what," he said. "I'd have shoveled all the way to Havre just to dance with that pretty girl right there." To Viola's amazement, he pointed at her. The other boys hooted and Viola flushed, though no one could see it in the moonlight, and she turned away and went back into the hall. She was breathing quickly.

Some young men had taken a truck to the Lutheran Church to bring back the church piano, and they lifted it onto the stage, grunting the way men do when they are lifting things. They had muddy feet and tracked right across the dance floor as they rolled in the piano. Mama and Will were setting up the supper table at the very back of the stage. Viola got the mop and cleaned up the muddy prints.

A steady stream of people came to the door to buy tickets and have the backs of their hands stamped. Many brought their lanterns and hung them on the walls, and the Odd Fellows' Hall became brightly lit.

Mama gave Viola corn meal to spread on the dance floor, and the young boys ran at top speed and skidded on it, crashing into one another and into the stage at the end of the hall. Many times Viola had done that, but she was, as Mama often reminded her lately, a young lady now, so she restrained herself. Old ladies positioned themselves in the middle of the benches where they could watch the dancers, their hands folded across their stomachs, all in dark flowered dresses. Mama wore those dresses. She had let herself get fat and was already old. She wore old-lady eyeglasses and moved in a slow waddle and was always short of breath.

Dances always started slowly. The Fulps would face their chairs toward each other, unless one of them was playing the piano, and they would tap their feet and then start playing. During the first few tunes, only the youngest girls danced with each other out on the floor. People generally were talking and going in and out of the building and laughing. Little girls shrieked as little boys chased them, and everybody acted as though the Fulps were not there, as if they didn't notice the music.

Finally some of the older couples began dancing to a slow

song, and the next song more people danced. Often the wives would not go back when the song ended and would grab their husband's hand and stand there, waiting for the next song, which the Fulps would provide without much delay, unless they were changing instruments. Sometimes people found they could not dance to one of the tunes and would just stop trying and go back to the sides of the hall, but the Fulps would finish the song anyway, looking into each other's eyes and tapping their feet. Even when you couldn't dance, it was fun to listen to them play. What they really needed, Viola knew, was a singer.

The Fulps never did sing, but Viola knew every single word to several of the songs, and she sang them to herself under her breath, imagining herself up there on the stage, singing the songs in a way that made everybody dance. She reminded herself that when they finally played the Charleston she was going to go out and do it.

Chopper Martinson's father and uncle carried Chopper into the building on a chair. Viola was surprised he would come to the dance at all, awful as he looked. Both his ears were black and swollen and starting to crack in places, and the ends of all his fingers were black too, black as coal, even under the nails. He had some kind of shiny salve on all his frostbitten places. Viola couldn't help but stare. There was something different about Chopper. The look he used to have in his eyes wasn't there anymore. He had always looked tough, but now he looked as if he might cry at any minute.

Across the dance floor Clara and Margaret and Leona came in, their heads together as if sharing something special secret, and Viola walked toward them, opening her coat so they could see her new dress. Clara Linfield was the true queen bee of the group, but Margaret Dement was the prettiest, and Leona was the most popular because she was so nice to everybody, and they were all best friends with one another. They were stuck up and had not made Viola feel welcome when she came to town. Clara was the one Viola wanted to be best friends with, and sometimes Clara was friendly but sometimes she was not. When Viola got up to them they were talking about Bart Garsky and pretended not to notice she was there.

"I got a necklace for Christmas," Viola said when it seemed like the time for her to say something.

"You already opened your presents?" Clara said, as if this shocked her. "Before Christmas?" And she turned to talk to Leona.

"Did your mother make the dress?" Margaret said. "It's very...colorful." Margaret give Clara a look.

Viola turned and walked away. She began to feel sorry for these Sage Prairie girls. After all, none of them had a new dress or new necklace. It was natural they should be jealous, but it was too bad they had to be petty. When the dance started she would get more dances than any of them, because for sure, she was the best dancer. And that would probably make them even more jealous, because she knew she was going to look great dancing tonight. The dress was made full in the skirt so that it flew up a little, just like she wanted. If only she had been able to wear the silk stockings and high heels, just to dance the Charleston. She hoped Papa would come so he could see her.

Viola was not jealous, but she was annoyed when Bart Garsky asked Margaret to dance first. As Viola danced with other boys, she could tell that Bart was a good dancer. He danced fast ones as though he really liked to, which none of the other boys did. After Margaret, he danced with Clara and then he held out his hand to Viola. It was a slow one, the crippled Fulp playing the saxophone and the tall one playing a violin.

"How've ya been?" Bart said. "Did you know yer the cutest girl in Sage Prairie?"

"No I'm not. Margaret is," Viola said.

"You look like yer hot to trot. Are ya?" Bart asked. It was a really slow dance, and he put his hand in the small of her back and pressed her close.

Viola said nothing. Something was happening to her which had never happened in her life. She could feel Bart's erection under his pants as he held her close. She could smell the whiskey and tobacco on his breath and it didn't smell good, but somehow it made her excited. She had danced slow dances with lots of boys, even cheek to cheek, and she never lost the beat, but now she couldn't feel the music like she usually did, and several times she bumped feet with Bart. She tried to concentrate and make her feet dance, and she just knew that she was flaming red in the face and that everybody in the Odd Fellow's Hall was looking at her.

"Howd'ja like to come on out to the car and have a little blackleg?" Bart whispered in her ear.

"No thanks," Viola said promptly.

"Jist some hanky-panky, then?"

"You're rude," Viola said and pulled away. She left Bart Garsky standing on the floor alone. She didn't really run, but she walked fast to get her coat and go outside.

At the door she saw Ruby standing in her tight red dress and beret over her finger-waved hair, smoking a cigarette in a bored way while two young men were talking to her, one in each ear. One wore his hat at a rakish angle, and the other had full mutton chop sideburns.

"Who's the fella?" Ruby asked Viola, paying no attention to the two young men.

"Jerk," Viola said. "Can I have a cigarette?"

Ruby looked around, and Viola could tell she was looking to see where Mama was. "Here," she said. "Have a drag. I'm getting short or I'd give you one. Hell, Viola. You shouldn't start to smoke." Then she laughed.

Viola inhaled deeply and almost immediately felt light-headed and giddy. It was nice to give herself that little forbidden pleasure. She liked smoking.

The man with the rakish hat pulled Mutton Chops rough-ly aside and said something close to his face. Mutton Chops shoved him in the chest, and for a moment it looked like there would be a fight, but each man was grabbed by a friend and restrained, and Mutton Chops was taken outside. Imme-diately a tall man wearing a bright tie on a blue work shirt slid up next to Ruby and asked her to dance. Ruby handed Viola the remains of the cigarette and went on the dance floor.

It got to be midnight, and the Fulps had still not played the Charleston. Viola was disappointed to hear them start playing the supper waltz, the crippled one sitting at the pi-ano and the tall one blowing into the saxophone. Norbert Langland and several other boys made a beeline to Viola when the waltz started, but she told him them all that she had to help her mother. Sorry. Norbert was Margaret's big brother, and Viola was careful not to give him encour-agement. He'd already graduated from Sage Prairie High School and had started that fall at Northern Montana Col-lege in Havre. Viola knew from Margaret that Norbert had a crush on her. Already tonight he had come up twice to ask her to dance and had tried to start several conversations, but Viola didn't want to be seen talking to him in a friendly way or the girls would begin teasing about it. And worse, Norbert would be encouraged. Viola got the big coffee pot off the stove and set out the cups while Mama uncovered the egg-salad sandwiches.

Nobody wanted to stand out by eating supper alone, so everybody danced the supper waltz with a partner. Viola noticed that all the sweethearts danced together except for married people who didn't have to, so long as they danced with another family member—a child or an elderly person. Catholics danced with Lutherans; feuding in-laws danced; grandpas danced with granddaughters; mothers danced with sons; students danced with teachers: everybody smiling their politest smiles as they shuffled quietly around the Odd Fellows Hall, their shoes sliding on the pulverized corn meal. Even Pastor Bakke was dancing with his wife. He was having a hard time with the waltz, and his wife wore a humiliated expression and stared over his shoulder. The only people not dancing were a few people who walked with canes, and Chopper who sat watching everything with that new expression on his face. Viola saw Bart Garsky dancing with Leona, who had her head against his chest, and Viola knew she was feeling his erection. Not that she cared. She didn't even care. She didn't really like Bart Garsky anyway. Then she did something she'd never done before. She poured herself a little bit of coffee in a cup, watching Mama to see if she was going to object, but she didn't seem to notice.

When the Fulps finished playing the supper waltz, all the couples got in a long line up the stairs and across the stage to the pile of egg-salad sandwiches. The couples shuffled through the line, talking quietly with one another or loudly with other couples, ready to drop their coins into the one-pound Hills Brothers coffee can. At the end of the line Viola poured coffee and punch for people who dropped a nickel into an oatmeal box, if they wanted a drink with their supper.

Over the years Mama had collected cups and glasses and there were nearly thirty of each for the coffee and punch. Will's job was to pick up the cups and glasses as soon as they were empty and give them a rinsing and get them back on the table so that Viola could sell more coffee and punch. He limped as he went back and forth with this job.

The Fulps made a last call for raffle tickets and then counted out all the money. The tall one stood up and announced there was twenty-seven dollars and fifty cents in ticket sales, so the winning ticket would be worth thirteen dollars and change. Some of the drunk men whooped to hear this.

The lame one had put the torn half-tickets into a paper bag. He held it shut, shook it hard, and held the bag above his head. The tall one reached in and pulled out a number. Everybody was watching and the room became very quiet. Even those people standing at the plank table stopped picking up their sandwiches and coffee and watched.

"The first number is six..."

Everybody had six for their first number, Viola knew. She had looked.

"Four."

No one in the hall changed expression.

"Seven." There was a murmur in the hall, and a number of people threw down their tickets or put them back into their pockets or turned to resume conversations.

There was one only one more number, and Viola looked down the line to see who was still holding their tickets. She knew there were ten people holding tickets that might win, and yet no one let on. There was one thing that everybody in Sage Prairie was better at than she was: keeping their inner feelings to themselves.

"One," the tall Fulp called out.

Everybody looked around, but nobody shouted or raised a ticket in the air.

The tall Fulp repeated the numbers. "Six. Four. Seven. One."

"Oh. Well. Look here," someone said, and Viola saw that it was Carl Linfield, Clara's father. There was a groan from the crowd. Everybody knew Carl to be the richest man in town. Here and there people laughed at someone's joke, and then the food line started to move again and talk resumed.

Then Viola heard the violin, and there was Papa Swan standing on the stage, playing, his hat upturned on the stage at his feet. He was playing a beautiful classical song with all the fancy fingering. For a moment people stopped eating and watched in astonishment, but then they started talking again, continuing in the supper line.

Suddenly a commotion broke out, and Viola saw two men rolling around on the dance floor punching each other and getting covered with corn meal. One of them was a man who had been in the supper line with Ruby, and the other was Mutton Chops. Ruby was standing not far from the two men writhing on the floor, watching. Viola was astonished to see a smile on Ruby's face. Papa Swan continued his classical music, but all the attention was on the fight. The two men clambered to their feet and then took each other in a bear hug and galloped in a circle, each trying to throw the other down. They both seemed to slip on the corn meal at the same time and landed together with an awful thud and began to roll again before they both let go, got up, and started haymakering each other from a distance. They did this for a time, and the grunting and smacking fist sounds disgusted Viola. Finally Papa Swan just stopped playing and picked up his empty hat. He stepped off the stage and walked out the door with his fiddle case under his arm just as Mutton Chops was knocked down. He whacked his head so hard on the floor that he didn't get up. Some of the men cheered and whooped while his friends dragged him off, and everybody else went back into the supper line.

When the Fulps started playing again, they played polkas to get people going. The tall one played an accordion and the crippled one a trombone, and soon they had the whole floor full of swirling smiling people.

When would they play the Charleston?

Viola was helping Mama clean and pack up the supper things when she saw Norbert hanging around the stage stairs. She knew he was waiting for her to come down so he could ask her to dance. Norbert was very red in the face and pretending that he wasn't waiting for her. Viola delayed as long as she could, at least until the polka was through. The next song was a not a fast one, so she came down and they went out to dance.

Once they were dancing Norbert seemed to relax a little. "Is that your sister? In the red dress?" he asked.

"Umhum," Viola said, but she didn't look at him.

"And your brother in the suit and tie?"

"Umhum."

"That's a beautiful necklace."

"It's amethyst," Viola said. "My birthstone. My brother gave it to me for Christmas."

"It sure looks nice...," Norbert gulped, "...around your neck."

"At our house we always open our gifts the day before Christmas."

"I really like the sunflowers on your dress."

"Thank you."

Norbert's feet made all the right steps, but he was off the beat. Viola had to concentrate to stay with him. She wondered if he had an erection, too.

"Do you know that you're the most beautiful girl on the Hi-Line?"

"No I'm not. Your own sister is."

Everyone agreed that Margaret was truly beautiful. Her face looked nice from every angle you could look from. Viola knew her own features were not like that.

"But you've got the eyes," Norbert said. "They sparkle. Just like your necklace."

Viola glanced at him. Norbert's face was beet red.

"Thank you," Viola said, and for the rest of the dance she didn't say anything that would encourage Norbert.

"Thank you so much," he said, his forehead and cheeks looking damp and flushed as he led her off the floor. "I enjoyed dancing with you. You dance beautifully."

Viola said nothing. She could tell that he'd rehearsed this, and she felt sorry for him.

Viola decided she'd find Eddie and teach him to dance and make sure he was inside the hall to watch her dance the Charleston. They'd be playing it soon, she hoped. She put on her coat and went outside. He was standing alone, looking up at the moon, smoking a cigarette, and had to be coaxed to come inside.

Eddie didn't seem ready to have fun and was too nervous and self-conscious to dance very well, standing out in his new suit and tie. Finally Mama came out and rescued Viola by dancing with Eddie herself.

Clara came up to Viola, followed by Leona and Margaret, as usual. "Who were you dancing with," she asked.

"My brother, Eddie."

"How old is he?"

"Twenty-one. He's been in college. He's a chess champion."

"Oh," Clara said, putting her hand on her heart and rolling her eyes to the ceiling.

"I can get him to dance with you," Viola said, and then wondered if she really could.

"I'll marry your brother, and then I'll be your sister-in-law," Clara said.

"Then you'll marry Norbert and you and Margaret will be sister-in-laws," Leona said to Viola.

"And then you'll marry Will, and we'll all be sisters-in-laws," Viola said. She knew Leona had a crush on Will.

"And all our kids will be cousins," Margaret said.

"And we'll take picnics in the Bear Paws," Leona said. Leona wasn't very bright and had copper colored hair and no eyebrows. Will wouldn't marry her in a thousand years.

"When they play the Charleston, let's all dance in a line." Viola said. She had seen them practice it at school and knew they could do the Charleston, though not as well as she could.

"Let's," Clara said, as if it were the best idea she ever heard. "We'll be the Sage Prairie Charleston Girls."

All three giggled and tipped their heads together, and this time Viola giggled and tipped her head with them.

That was when the Fulps started playing the Charleston.

Suddenly Leona and Margaret and Clara all appeared to have someplace they needed to go.

"Wait," Viola said. "You promised."

Leona just shook her head. "My folks won't let me," she said.

"Mine too," Margaret said.

"Your parents tell you how you can dance? It's just the Charleston. It'll be fun."

Leona and Margaret gave each other a look.

"C'mon, Clara. Please," Viola said. "I'll do it alone if I have to."

"Okay," Clara said. "Let's do it."

But then Viola saw Ruby out on the empty floor dancing the Charleston all by herself, Ruby in her red beret and high heels and silk stockings, her thick little purse on the long strap flying. Every person in the room stopped what they were doing and watched, the room completely still except for Ruby and the Fulps. Someone started clapping to the beat, and pretty soon almost everyone was clapping as Ruby kicked up her heels and swung her shoulders. The longer the Fulps played, the more new moves Ruby put into the Charleston. It was the best dancing Viola had ever seen, or imagined seeing. That was *dancing*. Ruby danced the Charleston so much better than Viola had ever even dreamed of dancing it that it made her feel embarrassed, and glad she hadn't gone out there to make a fool of herself. When the music stopped, everybody grinned and clapped and nodded to one another, and lots of people threw dimes and nickels onto the dance floor. Ruby walked away and didn't pick up a single coin.

Clara and Leona and Margaret raced out and began picking up the coins, and so Viola did too. Without even talking to each other, they went up to Ruby and offered her all the dimes and nickels. Ruby didn't even acknowledge them. Everybody was trying to talk to her at once, telling her how great she danced and begging her to show some of the moves.

The man in the rakish hat offered to pay the Fulps extra to play it again. Ruby didn't seem to be listening to anybody. She flipped her silver cigarette case open and took one out. Then she took a second one out and handed it to Viola. "You want to share this with your friends? It's Turkish. The best."

All four girls looked to see where their mothers were as Viola took the cigarette.

"Not in here," Clara said, and she and Leona and Margaret followed Viola outside. They went below Magnusson's lumberyard and stood in the shadows.

"She's a professional dancer," Viola said. "For Shorty Young."

"Light it," Clara said.

"Turkish!" Leona said, and they all giggled.

"I'm not gonna," Margaret said. She was always the goody goody one. "I promised," she said.

"You promised who?" Clara asked in a disdainful voice.

"My mom. And my dad. That I wouldn't start."

"Well you're not *starting*. You're just *trying* it," Leona said.

"We're all gonna do it," Viola said. "We'll be the Sage Prairie Ladies Smokers League. C'mon, Margaret. Or you won't be in our club."

Viola lit the cigarette and knew to take in only a small amount of smoke.

"Ah, Turkish," she said, and handed it to Clara, who smoked and handed it to Margaret. Margaret started coughing immediately when she put it to her mouth, and Viola knew that she didn't really smoke any of it before she handed it to Leona.

They heard a commotion and looked around the corner to see the Simpson bunch coming down the boardwalk. Ruby was in the middle of them. Their cars were in front of Magnusson's, and when they got in and turned on their lights, they lit up the four girls.

One of the vehicles honked, and the caravan pulled away. Where in the world could they be going, Viola wondered.

22

The money for the sandwiches and drinks sat in their cans on the plank table. Much as Adelia wanted to count the money the minute the last sandwich was sold, she knew not to do so in front of everyone. But she knew roughly how much was there. By her mental tally Viola had sold twenty-two cups of coffee and twenty-four glasses of juice, so there was two dollars there. Fifty sandwiches at a quarter each yielded twelve-fifty, so there should be nearly fifteen dollars altogether. She knew, though, that some people probably dropped a nickel through the slot in the can, knowing it should be a quarter. However much there was, it wouldn't be sufficient to replace Will's wages. She would need another dance in the spring to get enough for that.

Greedy. It was greedy and unthankful to be concerned about her profits, she knew. She asked the Lord only to provide the dance, not the money. And He had provided.

She saw Eddie on the dance floor in his shiny suit, dancing

with Viola who was trying to teach him a complicated step. On an impulse Adelia walked onto the floor and cut in. Edward seemed relieved.

"We haven't had much of a chance to talk," she said.

"It's pretty crowded. At home."

"One person too many," Adelia said. "And I don't mean you, Edward."

"I know."

"How do you feel about going into the military?"

"Feel?" This appeared to stump him. He lost his step and had to start again. "I...I guess it's...I...."

Adelia watched his face, trying to read it, but he just flashed his charming smile. "I feel it's an opportunity for advancement," he said.

"Advancement toward what?"

"Well...doing what I want. With my future."

"Which is...?"

"Travel. See the world."

"Over the sight of a gun?" When it was out, Adelia worried that it was too harsh. Eddie was silent for a moment and didn't smile.

"I don't really have any choice, Mama. "It's Deer Lodge or the military."

"Weren't you close to the end of your sentence?"

"Six months."

"And how long will you be obligated in the service?"

"Three years. I'll probably re-enlist after I finish Officer Training School. Make a career of it."

He swirled her in long sweeps with a waltz.

Adelia said nothing. A uniform would not suit him, she felt certain. In her mind it was clear what the right choice should be.

"Before this opportunity for Officer Training School, what career were you considering after you were released?"

Eddie lost the step again. She had taught him that when this happened, you simply stopped and started over.

"Find some way to go to college?"

"And what would you study?"

"I don't know. Engineering?"

"Engineers need math. Lots of math. It was never your strong suit."

The waltz ended and most of the dancers began to shuffle toward the sides of the hall, but Adelia stayed, wanting another dance with Edward, a chance to have a real conversation, to start over without all the questions.

The Fulps decided to change instruments. The tall one strapped on an accordion and the small one sat down at the piano, so Adelia knew it would be a polka. She hadn't danced a polka in many years. It was so fast, and she was so heavy, but just as she decided to lead Edward to the side of the hall and sit this one out, the music began, and so she danced the polka with Edward.

Surprisingly, she found herself light on her feet as Edward swung her around and around. The two of them began to laugh with the pleasure of it, and all of her old feelings for him came back in a rush, and she loved him again with all her heart.

She was glad the next song was the Charleston, and Edward led her to a chair, out of breath with the polka and the laughter. She watched with a mixture of pride and humiliation as Ruby stepped to the center of the floor and began to dance. There was the chairman of the school board, August Fenner, watching intently, unsmiling.

Adelia had to admit that Rubyann danced very, very well,

but this was no surprise. She had been dance-crazy from the time she was fifteen and would walk five miles in cold weather to attend a dance. That was when the disagreements had started, when Ruby simply would not obey any longer, and no entreaty, no threat could stop her from doing just what she wanted to do, which was go to every dance within thirty miles. She never failed to get a ride home. She always came back very late, and sometimes the vehicle would sit in the driveway an interminable time before Ruby got out and came into the house, smelling of liquor, walking past Adelia, still awake in her rocker, as if she were not there.

She watched as Rubyann turned her back on the dimes and nickels people threw on the floor, and then the young crowd enveloped her. Ruby had been here two days and was already the star. Poor Viola had been here half a year and had not begun to make a friend until tonight.

Lord, your world is a mystery to me.

After the Charleston the Fulps began to play waltzes again, and Adelia knew the evening was close to being over. Thank God Swan had not asked her to dance, because she had decided she would refuse him.

She still couldn't catch her breath from the dancing. She felt the edge of the sinking coming on, like sensing something in the air, a change of weather even before the color of the sky changed. The only seat available had been next to Nadine, who was crocheting. Adelia had been in Sage Prairie long enough to know that the chair was vacant for a reason. Nadine loved to pry for gossip, and once she had it she would pass it to everyone who came into the post office.

"So I see your son made it home," Nadine chirped. She could talk and crochet and not drop a stitch. "All new clothes," she observed.

"I'm just too short of breath to talk, Nadine," Adelia said, fanning herself with a piece of stiff cardboard she kept for that purpose in her purse.

"That your daughter? The dancer?"

"She came down from Havre."

"She work there, then?"

Adelia noticed someone walking toward her and turned to see that it was Swan. Oh, no, she thought. It would be unwise to refuse him in front of Nadine.

"Nadine, this is my husband, Swan," she said, and Swan bowed and smiled his charming smile. Nadine just stared at Swan, her crochet hook silent for a moment, as her face formed a smile. Adelia often had seen that response to Swan's magnetism, from women of all ages.

The Fulps were playing "On Moonlight Bay," a song Adelia loved, the tall one playing the drums, and the other the trumpet. Swan was, of course, a very good dancer, though she remembered now that his flamboyance had embarrassed her in the past. Thank God he did not want to talk. Adelia smiled at her neighbors, holding up the corner of her dress with one hand so she could make the long glides Swan employed in his waltz.

As she danced she noticed Viola talking and laughing with Clara and the other girls, and for the first time it appeared that she was one of them. They were gathered around Rubyann, who was smoking a cigarette, her beret perched on the side of her head. She knew August Fenner had watched the men fight over Rubyann with his cold eyes, judging, as he had judged Swan with his hat turned up on the stage, and Eddie in his shiny suit and bright tie.

Just let me have two more years here in Sage Prairie, Adelia prayed. Till Viola is finished with school. William she was not worried about. She knew he would find a way to go to college.

There he was, her sweet William, sitting with Chopper, being kind. Adelia felt warm watching them, knowing she had been right to insist that he go on the Christmas tree trip, even though it had turned out to be dangerous and harrowing. William was slow to accept and slow to forgive, but Adelia knew he had a good and steady heart. He would be a good man and someday a good husband.

"You have broken my hearrrrrt," Swan sang.

"Sent me awayyyyyyy.

As we sang love's old sweet song at Sage Prairayyyy."

Adelia smiled at her neighbors and did not speak until she said her "thank you" at the end of the song to Swan's elaborate bow. Then, rather than sit again with Nadine, she started up the stairs to the stage, ready to put the coins into her coal bag and get one of the children to help her disassemble the table and throw out the dishwater, still hot on the stove. Fanning herself, she looked around for Viola, but did not see her or Rubyann. She didn't want to ask Will to climb the stairs again. Clearly it was painful for him to walk.

On the third stair Adelia felt the sinking, the darkness beginning. She tried to take a deep breath, but her chest was suddenly bound as if with a girdle, and would not expand. Her vision dimmed, like turning down the wick on a kerosene lamp.

She looked half blindly for something to hold on to, but there was no railing. Try as she might, she could not continue up the stairs, even to get to the top step and sit down, nor could she turn around and go back down. She felt her legs weaken. She knew she was falling, but instead of panic, a sense of well-being spread through her, a sense of peace and wonderful calm and exquisite clarity that was not part of the falling. She was at Ombrie on the Rhy, the girls in white bonnets by the blue water framed by the green fields, rounded brown hills behind them. She could hear their laughter. She could hear their laughter clearly. She was one of them. She was one of them again. Her family.

CHRISTMAS DAY

23

Will woke at first light and vaguely heard someone, it had to be Eddie, get up and move about in the dark and leave with the milk pail. His feet ached and he'd gone in and out of sleep in the rocker. It was his first night home and his third night of poor sleep. He'd been having dreams of flying, flying high above another part of the world, watching for something below. Waiting for something to call him down. He heard Papa Swan making a fire in the range. He was hungry but knew they'd soon have oatmeal.

He heard Viola begin to cry in the bedroom, as she had cried inconsolably last night, low moans rising to a wail. It had always been his job to calm her when she was distraught over something, but he felt without energy to make the effort now, and strangely without feelings. He knew he should be feeling grief, as Viola did, anger, as Eddie did, self-pity, as Papa Swan did, but there was nothing there. Last night, late, after Cecil and the other men who brought Mama's body home had left, their hats in their hands, he sat in Mama's rocker wrapped in a blanket trying to think, while Papa Swan snored on the cot, but nothing was in his mind but a frozen silence. Everything had changed. Again. Everything, and he did not know what to do about it.

"Will. Oh Will," Papa Swan said when he saw Will was awake. "We've lost it all now, son. After all I've been through, and now this. Now this." He paced a circle around the slowly warming range, wearing his long coat, his hands raking through his hair.

Like Viola's wails, Papa Swan's whining entered Will like words whispered down a well, echoing distantly back and then falling silent. Inside his own mind, Will was quiet and cold and dark.

"What will happen to you, my son? What will happen to my sweet Petunia? I must leave today. I have promises to keep, and I can't take you with me." Again and again his hands raked through his dark wavy hair.

Just go, then, Will thought. Just go so I can look for my money. He remained in Mama's rocking chair, knowing that if he got up his father would quickly take it.

"I can do no more than I can do," his father said. "I hope that you will understand that, Will. Sometimes life calls for hard choices."

Will heard a vehicle and rose to look out the window. Papa quickly settled himself in the rocker. It was Cecil's grain truck, the one Will had been allowed to drive during the threshing. It stopped behind Papa's Baskin's truck and Cecil slowly got out. When he reached the door, Will opened it.

Cecil kicked the snow off his boots and entered, looking grave.

Papa Swan rose from the chair. In the bedroom, Viola's voice of sorrow rose again.

"My father, Swan Anderson," Will said to Cecil. "Father. This is Cecil Halstead. I worked for him last harvest. We went to the Sweetgrass together for the trees."

"Most pleased to meet a friend of my family," Swan said. He gestured toward the rocker. "Won't you sit, sir?"

"No. Don't think so," Cecil said, finding one word at a time. "Don't think so. But I thank you." He turned to Will. "Were you planning bury your mother here in Sage Prairie, or...?"

Will hadn't considered this, and he realized that it would be his decision to make, that from now on everything would be his decision to make. This information made a small ripple in the smooth pool at the bottom of the well.

"Yes," Will said. "Here in Sage Prairie."

"Today, or...?"

"Today. Yes."

"We'll git ready then. Dig you a grave."

"Thanks, Mr. Halstead."

"It'll be ready. At the Lutheran Cemetery."

"We are so grateful for your generosity, sir," Swan said. "So very grateful."

"So," Cecil said to Will. "Do you know when you'll be wanting to do the service?"

"When will the grave be ready?"

"Won't take that long. Pastor Bakke'll be ready when you are. He's on his way. Be here soon, I guess. Lester's making you up a coffin. He took the measurements last night and has been at it pretty much since then."

"Thanks. Do you know...did he tell you what he charges?" It occurred to Will that except for the quarters and dimes and nickels from the supper, they had nothing. Unless he could find the twenty-six dollars Mama had kept of his summer wages. Surely he would be able to find it.

Cecil waved his hand at the question. "Don't think about it," he said. "Lester, he does a good job." He turned to go. "Nice to meet you, Mr. Anderson. Sorry for the circumstances."

"The pleasure's mine," Papa Swan said heartily.

Will shut the door, and from the bedroom another keening rose from Viola, as if she had discovered Mama's death all over again.

"Your mother was well loved," Papa said, "Well-loved wherever she went. She was a good woman."

Will turned his back on his father and looked out the window. *Why don't you just leave*, he wanted to say. *Why don't you just take your radio and get in your truck and just leave us alone.*

"I've decided that I will provide a marker," Papa Swan said. "I will make sure that she has something appropriate, something to let the world know that Adelia Anderson was loved."

Silence.

Adelia Kinkell, Will thought. He knew Papa Swan would never make good on his promise. It would be up to him to provide the marker, and since it was his choice to make, it would read *Adelia Kinkell*.

"Well. Why don't you say something, son?" Papa Swan said irritably. Will knew he wanted to be thanked for offering the marker.

"There's not much to say, Papa."

Will was embarrassed at what he was thinking about over and over, wondering where Mama had secreted away his wages. There weren't that many places she could have hidden it, but he knew she was good at concealing things when she didn't want them to be found.

"Where's Eddie?" Papa asked, as though just remembering there should be one more person there.

"He's gone over to milk Sullivan's cow," Will said. "He should be back soon. I'll start some oatmeal."

Even at the end of the tree trip, Will had never been as hungry as he felt now. Yesterday there had been the Bohunk's potato and Mama's bread. Mama's bread. A pebble echoing down the well. Another distant echo of new understanding. There would never again be Mama's bread to eat.

Will heard another vehicle on the road and went to the window. A roadster slowly approached. Ruby, Will thought, finally coming home from the dance. He watched the roadster pull in behind Papa's truck. He saw the man with the rakish hat lean over and give Ruby a peck on the cheek before she got out. Will could tell by Ruby's pleased smile that she didn't know what had happened.

"Who is it?" Papa said. "Another neighbor?"

"Ruby. It's Ruby."

Papa Swan got up and met her at the door. "Oh, Ruby," he said, when she came in.

"What," Ruby said quickly, looking around the room. "Where's Mama?"

"Oh, Ruby," Papa Swan lamented. "It's your mother! She's gone!"

Ruby stood as if struck. She looked pale in the ragged early light, her lipstick a bright slash on her face.

"Gone?"

"Her heart. Her heart." Papa pointed to the bedroom door just as Viola sent up another wail. He held out his arms to Ruby, but she brushed by him and opened the bedroom door.

"Oh, my God. Mama," she said in a whisper, just loud

enough for Will to hear. "Oh, my God. When?" she asked Will.

"Last night. At the end of the dance."

"Oh no," Ruby said, and tears began to roll down her face. "Oh, my God."

"We're going to bury her today," Will said.

"But...but I have a ride to Great Falls. I'm...I have to go to Great Falls. I was...."

"Go ahead," Will couldn't stop himself. "Do just what you want to do. You always did."

Ruby turned a look on Will so full of hurt that he regretted saying it, but he didn't say he was sorry. "There'll be some oatmeal soon. And fresh milk," he said.

Ruby went into the bedroom, leaving the door open, and Will could hear her saying something low to Viola. Then, a moment later she came out, brushing at her face, and went outside. Will saw her get in the roadster and sit there with her face in her hands. The man in the car looked toward the house and saw Will looking out the window.

The door opened and it was Eddie, his face pink with the cold, wearing his fancy overcoat and suit, carrying a pail of milk. On his face was an expression Will did not remember seeing before. There was something new in his eyes. They seemed more open than before.

"Thanks for milking," Will said.

"You never forget how to milk," Eddie said. "But my milking muscles are gone. You want to strain this? I'll pump some water."

Will strained the milk through a clean dish towel into two of their gallon jars. He could tell by the amount of milk that Eddie hadn't milked her dry.

Will heard the roadster door slam and back away.

Ruby came back inside, all business. "She's going to have to be washed," Ruby said to no one in particular. "Somebody heat a pot of water."

"I'll do it," Eddie said.

"And why don't you make a pot of coffee," Ruby said, looking briefly in Papa Swan's direction but not at him.

"I don't appreciate being—"

"Make some coffee, goddammit," Ruby said. "Be useful or be gone." She went into the bedroom and slammed the door behind her.

"So this is what I get for a family," Swan said. "So this—"

Ruby came boiling out of the bedroom, but before she could say a word Eddie clapped his hands together with a loud smack, just the way Mama used to do when she wanted to stop a dispute. "We've got plenty of trouble enough. Hold your tongue and hold your temper," he said to Ruby. Then he turned to Swan. "If you've got coffee for God's sake make a pot. You shouldn't have to be asked."

From the bedroom another wail rose from Viola.

"I was going to," Swan said softly, "In my own time. Your demand has prevented an act of generosity."

There was a gentle knock on the door and Will knew it was Pastor Bakke.

He wore the same cocoa-colored wool trousers and yellow muffler he wore on the Christmas tree trip. He had walked out from Sage Prairie and now unwrapped his muffler to reveal a face almost as pale as Ruby's. He withdrew a sack from his pocket. Will was sure that it contained some of Mrs. Bakke's raisin-less, nut-less oatmeal cookies, and he was surprised that he could hardly wait to get one in his stomach.

Will introduced the pastor to Eddie and Papa Swan. They shook hands gravely.

"Pastor Bakke," Eddie said. "Thanks for coming out. We are just putting on some coffee. Will you stay for a cup?"

"I thank you, but no," Pastor Bakke said. He held out the sack to Will. "My wife sends you these cookies," he said.

"We are humbly grateful," Papa Swan said, "for any sweetness on this bitter day." He went to the door. "You'll excuse me. There is something I must obtain from my truck."

"You all have my sympathy," Pastor Bakke said, and after Swan left he dropped to one knee. "Let us pray together."

Will was ready to refuse, and to do so in hard terms, but he caught Eddie's eyes so he gripped his hands together in front of himself and bowed his head, but he did not kneel. Pastor Bakke rambled with his prayer, talking about God's unknowable will and the blessings of heaven. He was still rambling when Papa Swan came back with his coffee. Papa Swan didn't stop and close his eyes when he heard Bakke praying, as any other person surely would have done, but went right to the pot and noisily ladled water into it and clanked it on the stovetop.

There was a silence at the end of the prayer punctuated by Viola's new wailing. Will could hear Ruby comforting her.

Pastor Bake finally said "Amen" and rose to his feet. "Are you intending to take the body to the funeral home in Havre for an internment?"

Again, it took Will a moment to realize that he was the person being asked. "No," Will said. "We intend to bury Mama today. Cecil said the grave would be ready this morning. My father has to leave today, and the rest of us will be on the afternoon Goose. I hope it isn't inconvenient."

"Not at all. Not at all. I fully understand. Whatever you and your family wish, "Pastor Bakke said. "I will perform a graveside memorial service for Mrs. Anderson whenever you are ready." Then he added, "Um, do you know when that will be?"

Will considered. The Goose came through at three-thirty.

"Two-thirty," Will said.

"And will I see you all this morning at Christmas Day service?"

Will thought before he answered, understanding what would be required of him now. "I'll be there," he said. "I can't speak for the others."

24

Viola didn't want to stay with Mama in the bedroom, but she couldn't leave her. It wasn't Mama anymore, there on the narrow bed. She knew that. She knew about Mama's heart, had known for years that someday she would die, but now that it had happened it didn't seem possible. It didn't seem fair.

"You've got to eat something, Petunia," Ruby said. She carried the tin mixing bowl half full of warm water and a wash cloth into the room. "Do you want oatmeal?"

Oatmeal was the last thing Viola wanted, and the thought of eating made her almost sick to her stomach.

"What's going to happen to me?"

"You're going to come with me to Great Falls," Ruby said.

"I don't want to go to Great Falls."

"I suppose you could stay here in Sage Prairie," Ruby said. "There is probably someone who would take you in. Do you want to do that?" She dipped the washrag into the hot water and then squeezed the water out of it and held it in front of Viola's face. Viola closed her eyes and let Ruby wash her face as she had done so many times years ago. When she finished she began to brush Viola's hair.

"We have to go to church this morning," Ruby said. "I know you don't want to go, and I don't either, but we have too, so let's not hear a word about it." Viola realized that this was what Mama used to say when she would brook no argument.

"I don't want to stay here and I don't want to go to Great Falls. I want to go with Papa."

"You don't want to go with Papa."

"Yes, I do!"

"No. You want to come with me. Remember? My new business? After you finish school I'm going to make you into a famous singer. Make sure you have a fresh pair of nylons for every day of the week."

Viola thought about this a while as Ruby brushed her hair in long strokes. "I'm not going to finish school," Viola said, finally.

"Yes you are, Petunia. Yes you are. You're not going to do what I did," Ruby said. "There. Out of the bedroom now. Eat something. I need to get Mama washed and dressed. Unless you want to help."

The house was chaos. Papa and Eddie were hauling boxes out of the back of Papa's truck and into the house, making room for Mama's coffin, when it came. Will was in the kitchen, opening every container and emptying every shelf. He was not putting things back, and the kitchen counter and the floor in front of it was a mess of cans and containers.

"What are you doing?" Viola asked.

"My summer wages. Mama hid them someplace. Do you know where she hid it?"

Viola shook her head.

"Would you help me look? I've got to find it. It's twenty-six dollars. It's all the money we have."

"Maybe Mama had to spend it."

"No, she wouldn't have done that," Will said. "Not without telling me."

"Even if she ran out of money and needed it?"

Will said nothing. "Would you help me look?"

"What are we going to do with everything?"

"Everything what?" Will exclaimed. "A little flour and baking soda? Some bulgur? Some lard? A couple cups of oatmeal?"

"We can't just leave it all, can we? That wouldn't be right." All of it had been important to Mama, Viola knew. All of it. Every little bit was precious to her. In all of their moves, they had never left anything that had any use left in it.

"We can't take it with us, can we?" Will said, continuing to look into and behind things, feeling into the backs of the little drawers on Mama's Singer. Viola saw that Will had emptied Mama's purse on the kitchen counter. The canvas sack that Mama used to bring home coal was there, heavy with quarters, nickels, dimes, and pennies from the dance, along with Mama's good linen handkerchief, her hair brush, and the key to the school. There was the little packet of lavender Viola had sewn for her that Mama carried everywhere. Viola brought it to her nose, then put it in the pocket of her dress. She would never in her life smell lavender, she knew, without thinking of Mama.

"The things you want to take, you should get together," Will said. "After the burial we won't be coming back here at all. Not if we're going to be on the afternoon Goose."

"At all?" This hadn't occurred to Viola somehow. "Why do we have to leave today?"

"I don't want to spend another night in Sage Prairie. I don't want to sleep another night in this dump of a house. Do you?"

"No," Viola admitted.

"When Ruby finishes washing and dressing Mama, you should empty your tick. Turn it inside out. Get all your clothes and put them in there. All your stuff. You know how to move. It's time to move again."

"Are we leaving Mama's books?"

"We're leaving everything we don't take," Will said impatiently. "And we don't have long. Go through her library, will you? Maybe my money is in one of the books."

Will had built Mama a shelf on one of the walls, and that's where her books were kept, all but *Dr. Gillvaray's Medical Advisor*, which was always hidden. Viola took them down and leafed through them one by one, setting aside the complete plays of William Shakespeare with the tiny print. She would take that with her. And the ragged copy of *Grimms' Fairy Tales*, which Mama had read and read and read to them when they were little. She set aside other books, too, the *Iliad* and the *Odyssey* and *The Tale of Two Cities. Oliver Twist.* She wanted to take all the books, all of them, but knew there was no way she could do that. Over and over she brought out the lavender packet and held it to her nose, and every time it brought fresh tears to her eyes.

"She must have hidden it in the bedroom someplace," Will said, and he went in there. Viola could tell he didn't want to go into the bedroom with Mama's body, but he took a deep breath and opened the door.

"Stay out," Ruby commanded.

"No," he said, and went in and shut the door behind him. Viola didn't go in.

Papa Swan and Eddie continued to bring boxes of Baskin's products into the house, and every time they opened the door the cold swept in with them. Even though the chinook was melting the snow outside, the room seemed freezing cold, even near the stove.

"Are you ready in there?" Papa shouted toward the bedroom door.

"No," Ruby shouted back in a furious voice. "Don't hurry me, goddammit, unless you want to come in here and do it yourself."

Viola knew Mama would never have allowed Ruby to swear in the house. But now there was the feeling all around of things being different, wrong, the world she had just come to know sliding away and changing so fast it made her dizzy.

Eddie came over and stood in front of her. "How are you doing?" he asked. She saw his eyes were red too, and it made her less frightened. There was something gentle in Eddie's eyes she hadn't noticed before, something that made her think of Mama.

"I want to go with Will," Viola said in a little girl's voice. "Back to Cottonwood."

Eddie said nothing. Viola saw he didn't know what to say.

Papa turned on the radio, and it began playing happy music, but he turned the dial until he heard the news, which told about the funeral for Meyer Stallcop, It was attended by hundreds of people.

"Why don't you turn that damn thing off," Eddie said sharply. "This isn't the time for listening to the news."

"I'm not used to being told what to do with my radio," Papa said, but he switched it off. He sat in Mama's rocker. "I think I'll just take this old rocker with me," Papa Swan said to no one. "I've always liked this chair."

"Can't I come with you, Papa?"

"Oh, Petunia, how I wish with all my heart that you could. How that would please me. But I have no home, no home but my truck. I depend upon the generosity of my friends and my customers. Where would you go to school?"

"I don't need to go to school."

"Yes you do. You do need to go to school, Petunia, until you find a man to take care of you, and that will happen sooner than you think."

Will came out of the bedroom with a brown envelope in his hand. Viola could tell by the look on his face that he had not found his money. "Well, at least I found our birth certificates," Will said, throwing the envelope on the table.

"What were you looking for?" Eddie asked. He went to the table and looked at the envelope and put it in his breast pocket. Viola made a note to herself to ask him for hers later.

"Mama had my harvest wages from last summer. I can't find it," Will said irritably.

"How much was it?"

"Twenty-six dollars. I've looked every place it could possibly be. There aren't that many places."

"She probably spent it, son," Papa said. "Your mother was never very good managing money."

Ruby came out of the bedroom and stood in the center of the room for a moment, very pale. "All right," she said. "Mama's ready."

25

They walked single file on the road, dodging the pools of melt. No one said anything, and Eddie heard no sound except the sink of galoshes into the wet snow and the ringing in his ear, swelling a little with each heartbeat. By the time they got to the edge of town, Will was limping badly on his right foot, though Eddie could tell he was trying not to.

Many trucks and cars were parked in front of the Lutheran Church when they arrived, and the vestibule was full of hung coats and galoshes and the smell of wet wool. Eddie had taken nickels from the sack of Mama's supper money, and outside the church he gave one each to Ruby and Will and Viola, just as Mama used to do, and they took them without comment. Then they walked into the church, nearly full of Sage Prairie Lutherans in their Sunday best.

Pastor Bakke, or someone, had put a black ribbon across the front pew so it remained empty. Eddie knew it was for them, and he took the lead and removed the ribbon and stood aside while the rest of the family entered the pew, and then he joined them. Swan sat in the middle.

It had been a long time since Eddie had been in a church—since Cottonwood and Pastor Griggs. This one was plain and small, as that one had been plain and a little larger. On the altar were two heavy brass candleholders with unlit candles below an unadorned wooden cross. A thin lady wearing a high-necked dark dress was playing a mournful hymn on the piano. Pastor Bakke sat on a chair behind the lectern with his hands folded in front of himself, looking out over his congregation. He wore a white gown with a purple border around the neck and the ends of the wide sleeves. A moment or two after Eddie and his family were seated, Pastor Bakke rose, stood at the lectern, and began the service.

Pastor Bakke's thin reedy voice barely filled the small church. He explained there would not be the traditional Christmas Day sermon, considering the sad circumstances in the Anderson Family, of which everyone was aware. Instead, he wanted to talk about how all events in life, even the most tragic, can be seen as God demonstrating compassion and grace and mercy through his son Jesus Christ.

"Precious in the sight of the Lord is the death of his faithful ones," he read from Proverbs, making this the text of his sermon.

Eddie didn't listen. He was thinking about Emerson, remembering Emerson's quote that death was like a bottle of water broken into the sea, and he was thinking about Mama's glowing presence, not dissolved into the sea at all, but still there in the church with him. Didn't the others feel her there too? If they did, they didn't show it. Will had slipped his right foot out of his shoe. Stony faced, he was staring at his hands, twisting his fingers slowly together. Viola's shoulders shook, but she made no sound. Ruby had an arm around her, whispered something in her ear, and patted her arm.

"...In the name of the Father, the Son, and the Holy Ghost, Amen," Pastor Bakke concluded his convocation prayer.

"Amen," the Lutherans muttered.

Though Eddie understood the Father and the Son he had never understood the Holy Ghost, but now, suddenly, he saw it was Emerson's Over-soul. And Mama was part of that now, a part, but still somehow separate, still Mama. She was part of the Holy Ghost, and she was here with him now, hovering just over his shoulder. Eddie felt his chin crinkle and his chest constrict and this time he could not hold back the tears. He covered his eyes and tried to make no sound as his chest heaved. He knew that every eye in the room was on him, but he couldn't stop. He always had Mama now. She would always be with him. She would be there for all of them, Will and Ruby and Viola, if they could just see her. Feel her. How could he explain to them that she was still here, that her spirit would always be with them? How can you make something real for someone if they can't see it, can't feel it, or smell it or hear it?

Eddie looked at Pastor Bakke gripping the lectern with both hands and reading words about God's grace.

"...through Grace gave us eternal comfort...."

"...Grace and Mercy are upon his Holy Ones...."

"...truly comprehend the Grace of God..."

"...not by earthly wisdom, but by Grace..."

"...Grace to you and Peace from God our Father, Amen."

There in a room of tearless Lutherans Eddie again felt his throat constrict and his chin tremble, and again he did his

best to stifle his sobs, but he could not. He had been granted Grace, somehow, through Mama. He had been granted
Grace.

The congregation stood and began a final hymn.

What a pri-vi-lege to caaaaaryyyyy
Eeeeeevrything to God in Prayerrrrrrrr.

Papa Swan's voice swelled on the chorus, and Eddie remembered this about him, and also remembered that when
the collection plate came around, his father would put his
hand into the plate and flick a finger into the coins to make a
sound, but put nothing in.

After the last song and the last prayer, Pastor Bakke walked
solemnly up the aisle and stood by the back door while the
lady with the high-necked dress played another mournful
piece on the piano. People rose and shuffled into the aisles
and shook hands with the pastor one by one as they filed into
the vestibule to get their coats and galoshes. Viola had cried
the whole service and continued to do so, her palms covering
her eyes, Ruby's arm still around her shoulder. The Anderson
family was the last to shake hands with Pastor Bakke.

Outside, Papa Swan held his hat in both hands in front
of his long black coat. His glossy hair shown in the sun as he
shook hands with a number of uncomfortable-looking men
who came up to him, offering condolences. Papa Swan accepted their consolations graciously, with a small bow at the
waist.

"Excuse me, Mr. Anderson," Eddie heard one fellow say,
the last in line waiting to shake Papa Swan's hand. He was
a lanky stooped man with a very red nose. He seemed more
uncomfortable than the others. "I am sorry to hear of this...
circumstance," he said, reddening even more. "I found your
wife to be an...a...very...remarkable woman. Ya."

"Thank you," Papa said with his small bow. "She will be sorely missed by her family."

"I...I'm...I have the store here in town." He paused as if to let this sink in. Eddie knew exactly what he meant but saw that Papa pretended not to.

"So...so...ya. Mrs. Anderson, she did all her shopping in my store."

"I see. I see," Papa said, nodding his head.

"And there is the matter, unfortunately, of an...ah...of an outstanding balance. I hate to bring it up, but I understand...I heard...I wonder...?"

"I see," Papa said. "I understand. But I must regretfully tell you, Mr...Mr...?"

"Lingard. George Lingard."

"...Mr. Lingard. I must regretfully tell you that I cannot be responsible for my poor wife's mismanagement of her money. This is not the first time I have been confronted by this situation. It grieves me, but I am a businessman myself. This is one of the risks of doing business and offering credit. I, myself, do not offer credit."

Mr. Lingard's nose was now even a darker red.

"You...ah...you are refusing me?"

"I am. It is a matter of principle. I wish you a good day," Papa said. He stepped back, put on his hat, and turned around as if to see who else might want to offer him their sympathy.

Mr. Lingard just stood there, stooped, fingering his hat and moving his lips without saying anything.

Eddie stepped forward. "Excuse me, Mr. Lingard," he said. "May I ask how much money my mother is in arrears?"

Lingard's lips were a grim white line. "Eleven dollars and thirty-two cents," he said in a soft voice, as if admitting something he was ashamed of having to admit.

"Will you take ten dollars to settle the account?" Eddie said just loudly enough to be heard by Swan.

Now the man's full gaze came on Eddie, and his tongue came out to flick over his pursed dry lips. He nodded. Eddie took a ten-dollar bill from his new wallet.

"I thank you for the courtesy you extended to my mother," Eddie said. He shook Mr. Lingard's hand. "You'll excuse me," he said.

Viola and Ruby were walking down the street toward the miserable teacherage. Two men had drawn Will aside and were leaning earnestly toward him. The man doing the most talking was a short man in a blue suit and an overcoat that did not match. The other man was old and worn and peered through wire-rimmed glasses with wintry eyes. Will listened to them with his hands in his pocket, looking at his feet. Eddie saw him straighten up. He said something, shaking his head no. He shook both their hands, then turned and walked away. The two men looked at each other, and Eddie could tell that they were not happy.

"What was that about?" Eddie asked when he had caught up with Will.

"That was August Fenner, chairman of the school board, and Mr. Albertson, the principal. They asked me to take over Mama's classroom till the end of the year. They said they could get me an emergency certificate and continue to pay me Mama's wages." Will had a small, satisfied smile on his face. He started down the rutted muddy road, limping, and Eddie joined him.

"So?"

"Not if they begged me," Will said. "Actually, they did beg me." He laughed.

"But if you did took the job, Viola could stay with you in the teacherage. Then you both could move back to Cottonwood next year."

"I don't want to spend another day in this town. I'll finish school in Cottonwood. Stay with the Hendersons."

"Then?"

"Join the Marines. Or the Navy. See the world."

"Hendersons know you're coming?"

"No."

"It wouldn't be good to turn up broke and unannounced." Eddie said. He opened his new wallet. "I found your money." He held out two tens, a five and a one, then closed the wallet. "Now all you'll be is unannounced."

"What? Where?" Will stopped short.

"Under the sewing machine."

"Can't be, Eddie. I looked there."

"Didn't look well enough. She had it rolled up tight."

Will took the money, folded it carefully, and put it in his pocket. "Thanks," he said. "I really needed this."

"Boys!" Papa Swan shouted from behind. "Wait for me."

"Oh, Christ!" Will said. "I can't take another minute of him."

"Go on ahead. I'll wait," Eddie said, and Will limped on ahead.

"Eddie. I'm glad we have this opportunity to talk," Papa said, patting him on the back with a gloved hand. "I've been concerned about you. How have you been?"

"I've never been better, Papa. I've got a second chance, and I intend to make the most of it." Eddie had never been more serious.

"An officer and a gentleman. Ahh, Eddie, your mother would

have been proud of you in your uniform. She would have taken you to church to show you off. Slipped you a nickel to put in the collection. She loved to show off her family."

"We haven't all exactly made her proud," Eddie said, and for a moment, until he got control of himself, he thought his chin might pucker again.

"Her pride. Her pride," Papa Swan said, shaking his head and looking at the ground.

They walked a few steps in silence. Eddie wanted to argue this point, but knew his father would have the last word.

"All I ever wanted, my end goal for all I did, was Adelia's happiness," Swan said. "...for my family's happiness. I raised an eighth of a million, son, and lost it in the crash."

"To be so disappointed. After all you did for your family. I'm sorry for you, Papa," Eddie said, and he was.

"Well, I want to wish you the very best, Eddie." Papa stopped in the road and took his glove off and held out his hand. Eddie took off Stanley's glove and shook hands with his father solemnly. "I wish you the best as an officer and a gentleman. I really do." Then they put their gloves back on and walked silently the rest of the way, leaving all the rest unsaid.

26

Viola was still far from the house when she saw something on the snow next to the doorstep, and she was quite close before she realized it was a short, wide coffin, and again Viola felt the icy truth go through her. Mama was gone. Soon she would soon be in that wooden box and put in the ground, and covered with dirt. She would never see Mama again. Not ever. Viola was able to stop sobbing, but she was not able to stop trembling. She had always wondered how Ophelia could feel so hopeless as to throw herself into the water and drown herself, or why Juliet would take poison, and she believed William Shakespeare was being overly dramatic, but now she knew. When there was nothing to look forward to, and all the good times were behind and the world was cold and lifeless and empty, that's when people did those things. She wondered if she would ever want to sing again. She wondered if she would ever be happy again.

When Papa Swan and Eddie arrived, they carried the casket into the bedroom, and Viola knew that they were putting Mama into it.

The teacherage, normally so tidy, was cluttered and chaotic with the piles of boxes from Papa's truck and Will's mess from looking for his money. Viola knew she had tasks that needed to be done. She needed to pack though she didn't know where she was going. She took her tick outside and emptied out the straw on the rotting snow and then turned it inside out and hung it on the clothesline and beat off the remaining straw with the side of the broom. Then she took the tick inside and put all of her clothes in it, including her two new Christmas dresses. It wasn't much. She added the books that she had selected to take, books that she had heard Mama read from so many times: *Leatherstocking Tales, Roughing It, Robinson Crusoe, Huckleberry Finn*. Then she went and got *Swiss Family Robinson*. She didn't care so much about Mama's religious books.

Ruby was making a fire in the range with the last of the coal. "We need to make up some sandwiches to take along. Help me here, Viola. Let's make up some more egg salad."

"Do you have some money to get us started in Great Falls?" Viola asked.

Ruby glanced at her and patted her little white purse on its shoulder strap. "Don't you worry," she said.

"I don't want to go to school in Great Falls," Viola said.

"We talked about this, Petunia," Ruby said firmly. "If you come with me you're going to do what I say. Got it?"

Ruby had always been a bossy, and Viola didn't like to be bossed.

"Got it?" Ruby insisted in a louder voice.

Viola started sniffling again and was unable to stop her tears all the way through the sandwich-making process.

When the sandwiches were done, Ruby, moving fast like she always did, set fire to the pile of tick straw that Viola had left outside. Then she came out of the bedroom with Mama's mattress tick and emptied its straw onto the fire. Will began to help, and then Eddie, and Viola watched in a kind of stunned horror as they emptied the house, throwing blanket, sheets, towels, and all Mama's clothes on the fire, then the wooden crates that had been used for end tables and storage, the cardboard boxes, and food containers. The books that Viola had not taken. As the fire grew, she had to back away from it. As she numbly watched the flames, Viola was horrified to see Ruby throw the shoe boxes of Eddie's letters into the fire. She tried to get them out with a stick but it was too late.

"What were those?" Eddie said, coming up.

"Your letters to Mama."

"She saved them?"

"Mama saved every letter she ever got from anybody," Viola said helplessly. "And now they're all burning up! They're all burning up! Everything is burning up."

"I've still got the ones she wrote to me. Those are the most important anyway."

"You still have them?" Viola had never considered that this was possible.

"I kept every one. One fat one each week for seventy-three weeks. They're in my suitcase."

"Can I have them?" Viola blurted. It just came out of her unexpectedly.

Eddie smiled and turned away and went into the house and came back with a heavy shoebox, bound with string.

Viola began to sob, all that was left of her. She put Mama's letters into her tick with her clothes and books. She Saw Papa Swan take Mama's sewing machine and irons, and he tied her rocking chair on top of his truck. It looked strange up there.

The last thing that went into the fire was the Christmas tree with all of its decorations, Viola's angel on top. Then Papa Swan, Eddie, Will, and Ruby carried Mama's coffin to Papa's truck, slid it into the back, and closed the door.

27

Will didn't want to walk to the graveyard, he'd already done too much walking, so he rode in the truck with Papa Swan while Eddie and Viola and Ruby walked behind in the muddy tracks. There wasn't room to ride in the back of the truck with the casket.

"I'm happy to have this chance to speak to you alone, son. I've been meaning to ask you what your plans are," Papa Swan said as soon as they were underway. The truck cab smelled of tobacco and Papa's hair oil. The chains on the back tires began to clang against the under-carriage. Other vehicles had been on the road and the ruts were slushy.

"Finish school, I guess. At Cottonwood."

"Your mother told me you have hopes of college."

Will considered how to answer this, and finally just told the truth. "No, I don't. I don't see how I could do it."

"But if you could, what would you study? Would you be a teacher like your mother?"

Will looked at his father to see if he was serious and saw by his expression that he was not. "Not hardly," he said.

"What then? Say there were no financial obstacles. Say that a generous benefactor paid your way."

Will listened to the clanking chains and looked out the window. "I don't see the point," he said.

"To satisfy my curiosity is all. For a long time I nourished dreams of giving you that opportunity. I was that close, son." He held out a gloved hand and showed a distance between thumb and forefinger. "I imagined that you would become an engineer. Build bridges and dams. Lay out new roads. Make real things."

Will was surprised to hear Papa Swan mention engineering since it was exactly what he'd imagined himself. At Cottonwood he'd created elaborate dams in the creeks and built paths through the woods.

"Would have been nice," Will said.

Papa Swan turned a knob on the dashboard and a clattering heater fan came on. "If wishes were horses," he said.

"...beggars would ride." Will finished.

"So. What next? What's follows on the heels of matriculation at Cottonwood High School?"

"Well, I...I thought about joining the Navy."

"I'm glad to hear that you're considering the military," Papa said. "That's very practical considering the circumstances. But I wonder at your choice of the Navy."

"Well, I want to see the world," Will said, as if that would be obvious.

"There is romance in the idea of visiting foreign ports, I'm sure," Papa Swan said, "but as a career, it would mean a lifetime of living in close quarters on boats. I know I wouldn't be suited to that, growing up in open country as I did. As you have."

Will hadn't thought of that but at once saw it was true. "... or the Army," he said.

"You know, that might be the ticket. Join the Army Corps of Engineers, and they'll give you an education you can use when you get out after a few years."

"I could join in the Corps of Engineers?"

"Once inducted you'll be tested, Will, and when they discover that you are a very bright young fellow, they will do everything they can to make you happy enough to make a career in the service. If only you could find a way to get into Officers Training School. That would be ideal. You would, I believe, make a fine officer."

While the heater clattered and the chains rattled and the transmission ground along in second gear, a picture formed in Will's mind of himself not just in a uniform, but in one with bars on the shoulders. A hat with a shiny bill. Could he make it happen, he wondered, with just a little luck? If he worked hard?

"I'm going to tell you something now, Will, and I want you to listen to me carefully. I've been out in the world as your mother never has, and I know things about how it works that are not in her books. When you get in the military you will be starting off on equal footing with all those around you, and you will want to rise to the upper ranks as quickly as possible. The military is all about attaining leadership positions."

"Yes, I know that," Will said, and then he wondered, did he really know that?

"But do you know how to rise to be a leader? What it takes?"

Will thought for an answer, but Papa Swan talked on.

"Confidence and style. The man with the most confidence

and style, even if he has less ability and industry, will rise through his fellows. I've seen it again and again, read examples of it again and again."

Will wondered if he had ever seen this for himself, and he searched his experience for an example but couldn't find one.

"You mother did not appreciate that I came home wearing a fine shirt and nice shoes and a good coat. She scorned my carrying an expensive pocket watch. But that gold watch, displayed at the right moment and in the right way, has sealed many a sale and convinced many a customer and gained many a confidence. Those who glimpse it conclude that its owner is a man of substance."

They came to the place near the grain elevators where they needed to turn off the high-grade road to cross the railroad tracks, and Papa shifted down into the lowest gear. After they turned, they could look back and see Eddie and Viola and Ruby walking in the ruts not far behind them.

"Ruby and Eddie will survive," Papa Swan said. "I know. They may even thrive. They have grit. It's sweet Petunia who concerns me. For now, Ruby will have to care for her. It is not an ideal situation, but...," Papa Swan shook his head. "I can do no more than I can do."

"Maybe she could come with me?" Will hadn't considered that before.

"No, William. That's even a worse idea. You, yourself, need the help of others. You're in no position to care for Viola."

They rode in silence for a few moments.

"I predict that you will go far, son. Very far indeed."

Then they turned into the Lutheran Cemetery.

Someone had shoveled passages through what was left of the bigger drifts on the cemetery road, and Will was surprised to see a number of cars there, including the Linfield's new Packard. Why would they be here? And was that the Martinson's Ford? A mound of fresh dirt, dark as a pile of coffee grounds against all the snow, was piled on one side of the grave, a well-worn shovel sticking out of it. All of the people, bundled up, stood together on the other side. Will took it all in, knowing that he needed to remember this final moment when what was left of the family was together.

After Papa parked the truck as close as he could to the mound, Will got out and opened the back. Then he and Eddie and Papa and Cecil slid out the coffin and set it on the wet ground beside the open grave. It seemed lighter to Will now, somehow, than it had been when they carried it to the truck, as if not all of Mama was in there anymore.

Eddie seemed to be in charge and Will was grateful. Next to the mound of dirt were two pieces of heavy rope, and Will and Eddie lifted first one end of the wooden coffin and then the other while Papa slipped the ropes beneath it. Eddie glanced at Will to take up his end of the rope. Papa and Cecil took the other rope ends and, very carefully, the four of them, without a word, lifted the wooden box a bit, swung it over, and then very slowly lowered it into the grave a few inches at a time, keeping it nearly level. When the coffin settled on the bottom, the two ropes were pulled out, and then Will and Eddie and Papa Swan went to stand with Viola and Ruby at the front of the grave.

Eddie gave Pastor Bakke a folded piece of paper and whispered something, and Pastor Bakke nodded. Ruby wore no lipstick, and her face was pale. Her unwashed, bleached hair clung close to her head, her curls uneven. Eddie had his head down and his hands folded together in front of his dark new overcoat, holding his new hat. All the men, solemnly dressed, were holding their hats. All the women wore black. The earth seemed utterly empty of color in all directions.

Pastor Bakke began reading from the paper that Eddie had given him. "Dearly beloved. We are gathered here to mark the end of the life of a loving mother and a magnificent teacher. As a loving mother she opened the eyes of her children to the magic power of language, and to literature to fire the mind and lift the spirit. She inspired them to believe in their own powers to lift their own lives. She encouraged their imaginations to see beyond the horizons. She cheered their accomplishments, forgave their failures..."

Will was jarred by a strange choking sound and turned to see Eddie's chest heaving. The sobs broke out with an awful groan as they had in church, and Eddie covered his eyes with his hands. Pastor Bakke continued to read.

"...who has been a steady beacon in the lives of so many children, giving them the enduring tools of education, the steady model of discipline, and the example of compassion and understanding."

Now Viola began to bawl, and Ruby wrapped both arms around her. For the first time Will noticed that Viola was almost as tall as Ruby. How had he missed that, he wondered.

"There are dark times and there are bright times, and through all of them this remarkable woman, this remarkable human being, was steady, calm, cheerful, and optimistic...." Will looked at Papa Swan who was standing with his eyes closed and his head slightly back, no expression on his face at all. Will looked away. Am I like him, he wondered? Am I like him after all, and not Mama? It was this thought that brought his first tears, and in his grief and fear he did not hear any more of Eddie's eulogy. He felt himself swelled, his heart stretched tight with all that was inside that did not know where to go.

When the words were finished, Pastor Bakke gave a short prayer, followed by a long silence as everyone composed themselves, and then Papa Swan, in a show of physical energy that Will could not remember seeing before, seized the shovel and began to fill the grave.

Pastor Bakke came over and shook Eddie's hand and led Will a few steps to the side.

"Will," Pastor Bakke said. "Are you going back to Cottonwood then?"

"Yes."

"I want you to remember my offer. There will be a place waiting for you at Concordia College if you change your mind. Even if it's a year from now. Even if it's two years. All you have to do is write to me and I will write to my Uncle Magnus and tell him you are coming. You are a fine young man, and you could find joy and spiritual fulfillment, I know, in doing God's work."

Will realized that Eddie had come to stand next to them and was overhearing the words.

"I won't forget," Will said.

"Will?"

It was Cecil.

"If you were thinking you might be needing a place to stay here in Sage Prairie...."

"I'm going back to Cottonwood," Will said. "I'll finish school there."

Cecil spoke in his careful cadence. "Well, could I talk you into maybe thinking about coming back to help me with harvest next summer? I could give you a loan against the wages. If you want."

"Thanks, Mr. Halstead. But no. After I graduate I'm probably going to join the Army."

"Yer a good lad," Cecil said. "Good luck to ya. Whatever ya do." He gripped Will's hand hard and clamped his other hand on Will's shoulder, standing arm's length for just a moment, then he turned and walked away. Will could feel the place where Cecil's hand had gripped his shoulder for some time.

Chopper's father, Elmer Martinson, drove their Model A over close to where Will was standing. Chopper rolled down the back window.

"I'd shake with you, but I can't," Chopper said.

"That's all right, Chopper."

Chopper smiled an embarrassed smile. "You can call me Rolph if you want."

"You can call me Cottonwood, Chopper." Now Will smiled back.

"I just want to tell you. I wish you were staying."

"Thanks. But I'm not."

"Well. Anyway. Thanks for the apple."

"You're welcome."

"Okay then."

"Okay."

"See ya."

"Yeah."

Chopper rolled up the window as Elmer Martinson drove the Ford away. Chopper waved through the back window, and Will waved back.

Will was ready to take his turn with the shovel when he noticed that the Linfields had taken Viola aside and were talking to her. Clara held Viola's hand. Will wondered if what he thought was going on, really was, and he walked over to them. Carl Linfield removed a glove and held out his hand. Will took it. He looked at Viola, damp-cheeked and red-nosed, and saw in her eyes something hopeful.

"William," Carl said, "Clara here suggested that since we have an extra bedroom, Viola might stay with us. At least to finish out the school year."

Will looked at Viola's eyes, and there was no doubt what she wanted.

"Mama would have been very grateful," Will said.

"So it's all right with you, then?" Mrs. Linfield said. She taught Lutheran Sunday School, and everyone knew her to be stern and severe.

"What do you want, Petunia?" Will asked, and Viola just nodded her head.

"She's going to have to learn to milk, though," Carl Linfield said, and reached out to tousle Viola's hair. Carl Linfield was a man without sons. Will knew Clara had been driving tractor and truck for a couple of years now. Viola would have to earn her keep, but she would be in good hands.

Will and Viola left the Linfields and walked to Papa's truck. Will removed Viola's tick with the clothes and books and Mama's letters. In his own suitcase he had Mama's coal sack with all the supper money. He took it out and put it in Viola's tick with the books.

"Are you sure this is what you want, Petunia?"

"I don't want to go to Great Falls with Ruby," Viola said, shrugging.

Papa Swan came up.

"I'm going to stay with the Linfield's," Viola told him. Will could see that, like Mama, she was going to make the best of it.

Viola briefly held onto Papa Swan, crying again. Then she shook hands with Ruby and Eddie and gave them short hugs. Then she came to Will and hugged him.

"You've got to write to me," she said, tears leaking down

her pretty cheeks. Will said that he would, vowed to himself that he would.

He saw that Cecil and Dort, the school janitor, had shovels and were busy filling the grave with the dark earth. Then Viola left with the Linfields in their new Packard. When the grave was filled, the rest of the family silently stood around it.

"Ah, my children," Papa Swan said finally. "If I'm going to be where I need to be, I must be leaving now. As Macbeth observed, 'if twer done twer best twer done at once.' I'll leave your luggage at the station before I go back to the shack for my boxes. I've only got room for one in the cab. Come ride with me, Rubyann. We need to talk."

"I prefer to walk," Ruby said.

Papa turned to Will, and Will was surprised to see that Papa's eyes were misty. "Ride with me," he said.

"It's not far, Papa. I'll walk with Ruby," he said.

"Edward. Please?"

"No, Papa. We'll all walk together."

"Best of luck, then, all of you. In whatever you do. You can write me in care of Baskins. Let me know how you are. All of you."

"When I'm rich and famous, come look me up," Ruby said. "I'll buy you a cup of coffee."

"I hope you will make us all proud," Papa Swan said, and tipped his hat to her. Then he got into his truck and drove away, Mama's rocking chair tied on top.

I hope I never see you again, Will thought.

28

Eddie heard the Goose coming from a long way off. When it stopped at the station, the conductor opened the door to the single coach. He set down a step and the three of them boarded the warm, nearly empty car. Ruby went first, carrying her yellow leather suitcase, followed by Will holding a collapsing cardboard suitcase with twine wrapped around it and his folded army cot. The Goose jerked and began to edge away from the station even before they found their seats.

Eddie slid into a window seat by himself at the back of the car, the same seat he'd sold to Lynn Strawn. In a few hours he would be in Great Falls, and tomorrow or the day after, or the day after that, he would go to the induction center and start his new life. For the first time since it had been proposed, he began to feel misgivings. He wondered what kind of an officer he would make and what that life might be like. An officer is always over some and under others. Would he have to be under fools, as he was at the state industrial school and then at Deer Lodge?

Eddie rubbed out a clear space on the steamed window with Viola's gift handkerchief. The late afternoon sun was almost too bright on the last of the melting snow that covered everything as far as he could see. In the distance the low profile of the Bear Paws edged over the horizon, the wide sky above it a thin bleached blue, the color, almost, of Mama's eyes.

The coach was less than a quarter full, and most of the passengers sat toward the front near the grimy stove. The dirty windows were clear near the stove and progressively steamed up toward the back. The air was acrid with coal smoke and stale cigarettes, which made Eddie want to smoke. He knew Ruby had only one or two left and was hoarding them until she had a chance to buy more. Eddie surveyed the other passengers, wondering who he could bum a cigarette from, then put that thought out of his head, remembering how quickly his throat began to hurt when he'd started again, and how soon a package of Luckys got empty with him smoking one after the next.

Eddie saw that Ruby was reading *Titcomb's Letters*. He walked forward and slid into the seat next to Will, who sat with his forehead on the sweating window, his eyes closed. Will didn't move or open his eyes even after Eddie cleared his throat.

The conductor, in his wrinkled blue suit and shiny brimmed cap, walked toward them, steadying himself on the seats, a look on his face as though he were having a bad day.

"Merry Christmas," Eddie said, and smiled.

"Destination?"

"I'm bound for Great Falls," Eddie said. "And my brother here is going through to Cottonwood."

"Buck and a quarter for you and a buck six bits for him," the conductor said.

Both Will and Eddie produced five-dollar bills. The conductor made change and punched two tickets.

"What was that I heard the pastor talking to you about?" Eddie asked, when the conductor had gone on his way. "What was that about Concordia College?"

"It's a college for preachers and missionaries. In Minnesota." Will turned back to the window.

"And...?"

"And he said he'd write a letter for me to get in there if I wanted."

"So there's your chance, if you want to travel the world."

"As a missionary?" Will's tone left no doubt how he felt about it.

"Mama always wanted you to be a pastor, though, didn't she?"

Will shrugged. "She joked about it. Yeah, I suppose it's what she wanted," he said gloomily. "What did she want you to be?"

"A writer. She wanted me to go to college to be a writer."

"I liked your eulogy for Mama."

"Thanks."

"I'm glad to see you, Eddie, if I didn't say so before. I'm sorry I'm so...." He shrugged. "It's been hard."

"Still going to the Henderson's in Cottonwood?"

"Aw, hell, Eddie, I don't know. Mama wanted me to finish school. Mama was the one who kept talking about college. Mama wants me to do this. Mama wants me to do that. I don't really know what I want for myself."

"Mama was right about college."

"Mama went to college," Will said bitterly. "Look where it

got her." He scratched absently at a pitch stain on his canvas coat, a drawn expression on his face. He hadn't shaved since before the dance. Eddie saw that Will's beard grew exactly as his own, thick on the chin and sideburns, thin on the upper lip.

"You're smart. You should go to college."

"Smart? Mama was smart. So what? Papa Swan is very smart. Look at him."

Eddie sensed that Will almost said he was smart too, and look where it got him, but instead Will turned his gaze back to the window. He used his sleeve to clear a spot through the steam.

"So you aren't going back to school?"

"Who's to make me? Who cares anyway?"

Eddie thought about telling Will he cared but decided Will already knew he did and didn't need to be told.

"What I really want is to join the Army," Will said. "That's how I'll see the world."

Eddie looked away. He thought that Will would make a fine officer, probably a better one than himself. He reached in his suitcase for his letter from Chaplain Pierson and found the envelope with the birth certificates. He realized he had not given Viola hers. He'd have to send it care of the Linfields.

Eddie walked down the swaying aisle and sat next to Rubyann.

"Listen to this," she said, and began to real aloud from *Titcomb's Letters:*

"*Young Women. It is my opinion that God meant you to be dependent upon men, and that in this dependence should exist some of your profoundest and sweetest attractions and your noblest characteristics. You were not made to wrestle with the rough forces of nature. You were not made for war, or commerce, or agriculture. In these departments the iron wills and the iron muscles of men are alone at home."*

"Amen," Eddie said with a smile.

"What crap," Ruby said. "Listen to this. This is the chapter called 'The Blessings of Poverty.'"

"If there is anything in the world that a young man should be more grateful for than another, it is the poverty which necessitates starting life under very great disadvantages. Poverty is one of the best tests of human quality in existence."

"Mama believed all that stuff," Ruby said. "She wanted us to believe it too."

"Viola does. So does Will, more or less," Eddie said.

"When did you wise up? Hey, you want to share a smoke? Last one."

Eddie knew this was not a time to refuse. Okay then. This would be his last one. Ruby struck a farmer match under the window sill and lit her cigarette. "Merry Christmas," she said, and handed it to him.

He drew in a deep lungful of the smoke and then let it out. Almost immediately he felt the ringing in his ear change pitch and felt his heart speed up. "I thought I was pretty wised-up in the Cottonwood years," Eddie said, "but I wasn't as wised-up as I thought." He handed the cigarette back to Ruby. "Gonna start your own business, you say. Pretty bold."

"I know enough to start small. But I know what to start *with*," she said, giving him that look again. "I kept my eyes open around Shorty Young. There's money to be made."

"You'll be needing this," Eddie said. He removed the brown envelope from his suitcase and pulled out Ruby's birth certificate. Ruby glanced at it, then turned so that he could not see her put it in her little white purse. "So you're really going into the Army. This isn't just a story?"

"Officer Candidate School."

"You just don't look like a soldier boy to me," Ruby said.

"Looks are deceiving."

"No, they're not," Ruby said.

If encouraged, Eddie knew Ruby would argue the point to a frazzle. Were things as they appeared or not? Eddie wondered if she were right, and he wondered if the Army might be another kind of prison, something not at all like he had hoped or expected.

"I'm probably going to hang around Great Falls for a few days," Eddie said. "Can I help you find a place? Get settled?"

"I'd like that," Ruby said. He could see that she meant it, and it made him feel good.

Eddie went back and gave Will his birth certificate. Will folded it into an inner pocket of his coat. Will had taken off both his shoes and was massaging his frostbitten foot. On impulse, Eddie opened his suitcase and took out the Bible that Ruby had given Mama for Christmas. Mama would want Will to have it, he knew. He felt he had her permission. He smelled the leather and opened it up and saw that Mama had somehow found time to make a few entries in the family tree. There they all were through Mama and to Hugh and Helen Kinkell. Below them Mama had written, "Clan at Ombrie on the Rhy." Mama had a flowing hand, and it soothed him to see it, as the flowing handwriting of her letters had soothed him so many times. His chin began to pucker, but he got control of himself.

The Goose began to slow with a sound like a long spike being pulled out of a plank, and Eddie saw by the sign on the station that they were already at Simpson. A man in a filthy milking coat stood on the platform smiling a three-whiskey smile. The Goose jerked to a start as soon as the man got on. He swayed down the aisle, grinning big, looking around as if expecting to see an old friend. He saw Eddie and sat in the seat across the aisle from him.

"Jesus Christ," the man said, studying them. "Don't take a lawyer to see you boys is brothers." He pulled a Durham sack from his coat and began to fumble together a cigarette.

"So how's yer Christmas going for ya, there, boys? On yer way back from a Christmas visit to yer mom, are ya?"

"Our mother is sadly passed. Just recently," Eddie said.

"Damn shame," the drunk man said. His pale eyes had a red rim, and his cheeks had a high color that wasn't from the cold. "Sorry as hell." He drew the cigarette across his tongue and rolled it tight. "Life's a bitch," he observed sadly.

"Sir," Eddie said. "My brother, here, is a missionary. We would appreciate it if you would be cautious of your language."

"Sorry as hell," the drunk man said.

"Friend, are you saved?" Eddie asked. He put Mama's new Bible on his lap. "Have you accepted Jesus?"

"Scuze me," the drunk said, and shuffled to another seat.

For the first time since he'd been home, Eddie saw Will wearing a small smile. They rode for a time, saying nothing. Out the window farmsteads flashed past, farms with many out-buildings and mature wind breaks. Machinery parked beside the barns.

"Did you ever wonder what would have happened if Papa and Mama hadn't lost the homestead?" he asked. It was something that he'd considered many times.

"And we all grew up on a farm?"

"Maybe the gods smiled on us after all."

"We are to the gods as flies...."

"...to wanton boys. I know. Thank you, Swan."

Will smiled again. "You got me," he said.

The Goose was not far from Midway now, rattling through the melting countryside on its endless round. The farther east they went, the more the chinook winds had created melt-water ponds, all reflecting the blue sky with its few puffy clouds, some large enough to be rippled by the wind. Golden stubble stuck through the remaining drifts. Distant homesteads looked stark in the white. Eddie was aware that Mama was looking out the window with him. It almost seemed that if he turned quickly enough, he would see her, smiling.

Eddie began to think about what he would do if he didn't join the Army. He'd have to leave the country. Could he just go up to Canada? Start again with a new identity? Could his birth certificate be changed?

Eddie looked at his birth certificate. It showed his birth weight and length. His father's name. His mothers. The date of birth. *The date of birth was wrong.* It took him a moment to realize he was holding Will's birth certificate: *William Swan Anderson.*

Eddie held Will's birth certificate a long time, then he opened his suitcase and took out his letter from the warden in its formal envelope. He tapped it on Will's shoulder. "Read this," he said.

Will read the letter and put it back in the envelope. "Well, there's your ticket," he said, handing it back to Eddie. Eddie didn't take it.

"Now read your birth certificate."

Will took it out of his pocket and saw immediately. "This is yours," he said. "You gave me the wrong one."

"I've got an idea," Eddie said. "How about if it's *your* ticket?"

"What?" Will said. "I don't understand."

"Who can challenge what you're holding in your hands there? Nobody."

"But you can't be *me*," Will said.

"No?" Eddie said. He opened Will's birth certificate. "Says here I was born in the year of our lord nineteen hundred and fifteen. On August fifteenth. Says here my middle name is Swan. First name William."

Eddie and Will stared into each other's eyes for a long moment.

"You can't go to high school in Cottonwood," Will said.

"Don't intend to."

"What'll you do?"

"Maybe find a little newspaper someplace and try to get a job as a reporter. Maybe send Bakke a letter when the time is right. Maybe go to Concordia College and become a missionary."

Will's laugh had never come often, but when it erupted it was infectious, and Eddie began to laugh, too.

Ruby heard their laughter and turned around to see them. Then she came down the aisle, grinning.

"What's so funny?" she asked.

THE END

ABOUT THE AUTHOR

Richard Sterry was raised on a wheat farm on the Hi-Line of Montana. He took a B.A. at Northern Montana College, where he had a baseball scholarship and wrote satirical articles for the student newspaper, the NoMoCo. Following graduation, he taught high school English at Chester, a small town on the Hi-Line, and then enrolled at the University of Montana where he took a master's degree. While studying there, he spent two summers manning a fire tower overlooking the Bob Marshal Wilderness. He was awarded a Woodrow Wilson Fellowship and enrolled in the American Studies PhD program at Michigan State. He has taught at Monmouth College in New Jersey and at Idaho State University, and he was a visiting professor at Otaru University in Hokkaido, Japan. He is a doting grandfather and an avid gardener. He's been married to the same tolerant woman for almost fifty years.

CPSIA information can be obtained
at www.ICGtesting.com
Printed in the USA
BVHW030013240719
554209BV00001B/1/P